To Martyn

# Of Light and
# Shadow

Thanks for the help
with the 'Lily' radio
adaption.
    Best wishes
        Steve
        Westcott

I was delighted at the author's versatility with this taut, eerie fast–paced chiller. *Of Light and Shadow* is an exciting page turner from the off, the plot hits the floor running and doesn't stop. I thoroughly recommend this enjoyable, gripping read for anyone who likes a skilful touch of the occult blended into their thrillers.

Raven Dane, Dark Fantasy and Steampunk author

# Of Light and Shadow

S.R. Westcott

Priory Press

Published by Priory Press Ltd
The Priory, Abbots Way, Abbotswood,
Ballasalla, Isle of Man IM9 3EQ
www.priory-press.co.uk

First published 2011

ISBN 978 0 9551510 8 8

Edited and typeset by
Frances Hackeson Freelance Publishing Services,
Brinscall, Lancs
Printed in Great Britain by
Bell and Bain Ltd, Glasgow

*And the word became flesh, and dwelt among us.*

John 1:14

# 1

Trees, set stark against fields silvered by a full moon loomed over the devastation, their skeletal limbs sinister and unmoving as a staccato rain of stone and debris clattered to the tyre-streaked asphalt. As suddenly as it started the deluge subsided and silence settled, only to be broken by the heavy, assured tread of booted feet.

Night sounds rushed back at the intrusion, but the man walking toward the car embedded in the stone wall remained oblivious. He only had eyes for the occupant, whose blood-splattered head rested against the steering wheel. Eyes glazed over in death stared into the star-bedecked night without seeing, and the man's lips quirked into a crooked smile.

Its job done, he slipped the remote detonator into a pocket of his overcoat and then reached into an inside pocket for the mobile he had been left when given the contract, to thumb the only number stored in its memory. His call was answered almost immediately, and he said, "It's sorted."

"Witnesses?"

"No."

He arrived at the car and reached inside the shattered driver's side window to grab the wooden cross that dangled from the rear-view mirror, snapping the thin cord with ease.

"Good. Make sure you leave no evidence."

He pondered the origin of his employer, as he had done ever since they'd first spoken many years ago, but, as with previous contact, the voice synthesiser made positive identification impossible. Even so, there was an accent to the words, possibly European, but he had long given up on trying to identify the man behind the voice. He paid well, and promptly, which was the primary concern. "You worry too much. Have I ever let you down before?"

There was a moment of silence before the voice said, "Just make sure. We cannot afford mistakes."

A light breeze brought the scent of petrol and the man looked down. A rapidly expanding puddle of fuel pooled at his feet, and he smiled.

"Are you listening to me?"

"Who's next?"

"Let me worry about that. I will contact you in due course, in the usual manner."

The line went dead and the man snorted in wry amusement. Knowing what must be done, he tossed the mobile into the petrol, closely followed by the cross, before walking away. After ten paces he stopped and turned, pulled a pack of cigarettes out of his pocket, took one out and lit it. The tip glowed brightly as he inhaled. He took another drag and then, with a flick of a finger, sent it arcing through the air. He did not hang around to see the end result, but turned and walked away. By the time he reached his car the glow from the cigarette had mushroomed into a flame that incinerated everything within its embrace.

∗∗∗

Despite the lateness of the hour he knew he had to make the call, and punched in the private number for Monsignor Louvière. Unexpectedly, given the time difference, the call was answered after three rings, and he raised a brow in surprise.

"Allo."

"Monsignor Louvière?"

"Qui?"

"It has begun."

There was a momentary pause before the Monsignor spoke again, this time in English, his French origins obvious. "You are certain?"

"I am certain. The time is upon us. They made their move earlier this evening."

He heard the sharp intake of breath, and guessed what the Monsignor's next question was likely to be . "The Missio is safe. For now."

"Good. Make sure it stays that way, for all our sakes."

The line went dead and he sighed. After pressing the 'end call' key he tossed the telephone onto his desk and then leaned back in his chair. Fingers steepled, his gaze unfocused, he tapped at pursed lips, and murmured, "And so it begins."

# 2

The narrow, cobbled lane leading down from the shop was deserted as Louisa made her way to Bar Street, from where it was a short walk to the shopping centre and the supermarket. She knew the lack of people was not only due to the early hour. Turkey's main tourist season wouldn't start for another month, after which the streets, roads and marinas of Marmaris would become saturated with humanity and the locals would be out in force to lure unsuspecting tourists to eat at their restaurants, cruise on boats they called gullets, or buy genuine fake Gucci, Armani, Diesel or other copied designer gear from their stores. But for now she could enjoy the relative peace and quiet, before madness descended.

A warm breeze tugged at her light skirt as she made her way past the restaurant at the bottom of the hill to turn right into Bar Street. She loved this time of year, when the temperature was a balmy twenty-two degrees, the rains had ceased and everything smelled of newness, before the summer's sun had chance to parch everything, and everyone.

Behind her, the Old Fort stood guard atop its hill, its grey-white stones gleaming under the morning sun, watching over the bay and the surrounding sprawl of buildings as it had done for centuries.

Mehmet had texted her two days ago to say he was due back that evening, which was the reason for her trip to the supermarket. She wanted to cook his favourite meal; lamb casserole, or *kuzu güvec* in Turkish. Cubed lamb, green beans, tomatoes, aubergine, peppers and the like – just the smell of it cooking would be enough to welcome him home from wherever he had disappeared to this time. It had been two months since he'd left and she was eager to see what he had acquired on his travels.

A smile quirked her lips as she recalled their first meeting, soon after her arrival in Turkey. She had called into his shop after a visit to the Old Fort, and, at the time, it seemed as though fate had drawn her to that spot. As soon as their eyes made contact she felt as though she knew him. Deep within the core of her being she felt as though she had always known him. His olive skin seemed to burn with an inner fire that glowed through the flesh, setting the dim interior of his small shop aglow. In Mehmet she found a kindred spirit, and talked to him about life, her aspirations, her journeys, her ex and the reasons for her sabbatical. Before she knew it dusk had fallen, she had bought nothing and the street outside was deserted, the tourists having drifted to the main town for the evening. Mehmet had taken her to dinner and, after eating, offered her the job. For the second time in her life, she did something impulsive and accepted. And Turkey was not a bad place to start afresh. The people were friendly, the weather wonderful and the food outstanding. What more could she have asked for?

It did not take long for her to purchase the items she needed and start the short walk home. Although neither she nor Mehmet drank very much, with this trip having been his longest yet, she felt some sort of celebration was in order and had picked up a bottle of red wine. It was locally produced, and she hoped it was okay.

On making her way up the hill towards the small shop with its apartment above, she paused in her stride as she neared the front door. It was open, and she was sure she had closed it when leaving. Frowning, she walked slowly on until she came level with the dark opening, then halted and poked her head through.

The interior was gloomy, the single window shadowed by the building opposite, and it took a moment for her eyes to adjust. Even so, she could make out the racks half-stacked with curios for the coming season, the glass displays that held the more expensive items and the bead curtain in the rear wall that covered the doorway leading through to the apartment stairway. Everything appeared to be just as she had left it.

"Hello? Is anybody there?"

Her voice came out tremulous and fearful, and she mentally chastised herself for sounding weak. She cleared her throat and tried again.

"Hello? Is anybody there?"

There was no reply. Sighing, she stepped through, deciding that she mustn't have latched the door fully when she'd left. Arms laden, she heeled the door closed behind her and made her way across the floor and through the bead curtain to climb the stairs. On reaching the small, timbered landing she shouldered open the door to the apartment – and screamed. The bags of shopping crashed to the floor. The wine bottle smashed on contact, and a burgundy tide blossomed on the boards.

# 3

The hurried shuffle of soft soles intruded on the quietness of the library. Duncan looked up, as did the scattering of students around the reading area who were using their lunch break for revision, and he scowled as he spotted the portly figure of Peter Forbes heading straight for him. Duncan sighed. Studying the work of Aquinas was mind-numbing enough without the added complication of another of Peter's dilemmas. He grimaced, and closed the book he had been reading.

Peter stopped beside the reading desk, face white, thumbs fidgeting in clasped hands. There was a watery glimmer in his eyes and he radiated uncertainty. Duncan gestured for him to take the seat opposite with a wave of a hand. Aware that all heads were turned their way, he wanted to minimise the distraction. However, the harsh, discordant scrape of the chair on parquet flooring ensured they remained under close scrutiny.

Duncan closed his eyes and sighed again. To add to his frustration, Peter said nothing once seated, and stared at his hands, clasped on the desk-top.

The silence between them grew until, eventually, Duncan's patience snapped. "Come on. Out with it." He knew his words sounded harsh, and regretted them as soon as he spoke. Reaching across, he grasped Peter's hands, gave a squeeze of encouragement, and smiled a tight-lipped smile. "Sorry. But I've got loads to do and there's not long until the exams."

Looking up, Peter briefly met his gaze, then looked away. "It's bad news, Duncan."

Duncan frowned, and nodded for him to continue.

"It's ... it's ... Father Mason." The effort of speaking proved too much and he raised a hand to rub at his eyes.

"What about him?" Duncan asked.

"He's dead."

Although whispered, the words roared through the silence, and Duncan slumped back under their onslaught.

"How?" he heard himself murmur, not believing what he had just been told. Steff Mason had been his mentor and friend for the past two and a half years; he had been a sounding board for all his uncertainties, helped him through his doubts and instilled self-belief and self-worth in him, taken over from where his parents and the army had left off. He couldn't be dead. There must be some mistake.

Peter's voice cracked as he said, "Car crash. Last night." He paused for a moment before looking up to meet Duncan's gaze. "He stood no chance. I ... I'm sorry. I know how close you two were."

In a daze, Duncan rose and pushed back his chair, oblivious to the scrape of wood against wood, and gathered his books by reflex before striding from the library with them cradled in his arms.

Emerging onto the main thoroughfare of Saint Giles, he pushed through the crowds of students ambling along the roadway. Wrapped snug against the chill spring breeze in their heavy coats, brightly coloured scarves and assorted hats, their chatter and laughter was in stark contrast to the gloomy confines of the library he'd just left. He jostled and barged his way through the throng without apology, ignoring the glares and curses cast his way. He had to get to Father Mason's office, to see for himself he was not there. Although Duncan had no reason to doubt Peter's story, he had to be sure. People like Steff Mason couldn't just die in a car crash.

Still dazed, he turned off the road at the gates to Blackfriars and made his way through the arched stone entrance and up to Father Mason's second-floor office. The door was ajar when he arrived and he paused at the threshold, reluctant to enter. Staring at the brass name plaque, he read the inscription, still not able to believe he was gone.

*Steff Mason OP Phd*
*Dogmatic and Sacramental Theology*

The words glared at him, as though daring him to enter. After a moment's study, he plucked up the courage to reach out and push the door fully open. The familiar scent of beeswax and books reached out to welcome him, and he found himself smiling despite the solemnity of his visit. The small room, every wall lined with shelves that reached from floor to ceiling, each packed with tomes and papers on Catholicism and theology, always felt warm and friendly, as though Steff Mason had imbued it with his aura, which settled the most troubled of souls. But today Duncan felt uneasy as he stepped inside. He had an uncomfortable feeling that the room had been violated, and a cold shiver worked its way down his spine.

A shaft of sunlight from the tall, slim, stone-mullioned window in the far wall slashed across Father Mason's desk to pool on the bare, waxed boards of the floor. It did little to lift the gloom, and Duncan found himself glancing around in an attempt to discover the reason for his unease. All seemed as it had the previous afternoon when he had called to discuss the upcoming exams. Stepping forward, he placed his books on the desk, and it struck him. Father Mason's computer was missing. He remembered seeing it only yesterday.

When he had entered, Father Mason was busy on the telephone and gestured for him to sit while he finished the call. Duncan browsed the shelves and the multitude of books, his eyes finally coming to rest on the small pile beside the now missing computer. The titles that had caught his attention. Texts such as *The Nag Hammadi Library in English, Beyond Belief: The Secret Gospel of Thomas* and *The Fifth Gospel: The Gospel of Thomas Comes of Age*, could only be teachings of

Gnosticism, a teaching that flirted with blasphemy, and not something he could ever envisage the priest advocating.

"Quite interesting reading, I can assure you."

Duncan had jerked upright at the words, feeling his face redden, and Father Mason had smiled, the expression not lighting his clear blue eyes.

"But not for someone who is having doubts."

There was a tight edge to his voice that had puzzled Duncan at the time, but before he could ponder the matter further, Father Mason had grasped the books and removed them from view, to place them on the floor behind the desk. With a small smile of apology, he then said, "I'm sorry, but you have to go. Something has cropped up." He gestured towards the door. "I'm sure you understand."

Too disturbed by his uncharacteristic brusqueness, Duncan had left wordlessly, not thinking that that would be the last time he would ever see him.

The room darkened as a cloud obscured the sun, and Duncan leaned forward, hands splayed on the desk top as, head bowed, he stared into nothingness. A small pile of books caught his attention, stacked against the wall behind the desk, and he realised it was the books that Father Mason had removed from view the previous day. Intrigued, he made his way around the desk to pick them and place them next to his own, intent on flicking through their pages, but a clipped, cultured voice from the doorway intruded.

"What do you think you are doing here?"

Duncan flinched and looked up, hands paused in the process of opening the topmost book.

It was Regent Kearson. Although Duncan had only met the man a couple of times, he had taken an instant dislike to him. Tall and wand-thin, a thick head of grey hair that looked permanently dishevelled, he peered at everyone as though they were not worthy to walk the same ground as he, and his impossibly dark eyes seemed to bore into anyone unlucky enough to cross him. And at this moment they were fixed on Duncan.

A flicker of recognition crossed the Regent's angular features. "Connors, isn't it?"

Duncan nodded, and licked at dry lips.

For an instant the dark eyes appeared to swell and darken further, before the Regent smiled, tight-lipped in commiseration. "I should have expected you to come here once you heard the news. You and Father Mason were close, I believe."

The Regent's manner unnerved him, and Duncan was unsure whether it was all to do with his position as Regent or his own feelings of guilt at being caught in a dead man's office.

"So it's true, then? About the crash?" Duncan's words were hesitant and subdued.

The Regent nodded. He clasped his hands in front of him, and said, "His passing will leave a vast hole at Blackfriars, as I'm sure you will agree. Men like Father Mason are rare."

The Regent's confirmation unleashed the gloom that had been hovering over Duncan since Peter Forbes had relayed the news. It settled heavily on his shoulders. He lowered his gaze to stare in abstraction at the two piles of books on the desk.

"Arrangements for the funeral have been made for the end of the week. I will understand should you require a couple of days' leave to offer prayers to the deceased." Stepping to one side, he gestured towards the door. "Now, I must ask you to leave. Members of my staff wish to prepare the office for the next incumbent."

Duncan frowned and looked up. "So soon?"

"Life, as they say, goes on. And I'm sure Father Mason would not want his students to suffer through lack of guidance. I've selected a stand-in from the pool of supply lecturers, until something more permanent can be arranged. Father Tumbletee will take over as of tomorrow morning." The Regent smiled. Again, the expression did not reach his eyes. "So, if you have any last minute questions before your examinations, I'm sure he will be more than pleased to help."

The concept of Father Mason's replacement coming so soon after his death was a difficult one to grasp, made all the more so due to the Regent's apparent indifference. Snatching up his books, Duncan placed them on the three he had picked up from the floor and clasped the pile to his chest before making his way to the door.

As he was leaving, the Regent reached out and grabbed an arm, his long bony fingers grinding into flesh. In annoyance, Duncan pulled free of the grip and held the books more tightly. He had no idea why he had added them to his own, acting more out of impulse than design, but now he had them he was not going to let them go.

"One moment of your time before you leave."

The Regent's dark eyes pinned Duncan with their gaze.

"Did Father Mason ever discuss his current research project with you?"

The question threw him, and Duncan blinked, breaking the connection, his earlier annoyance dissipating. Even so, his answer was short and sharp. "We never discussed his work."

After a moment spent studying him, the Regent nodded, a frown creasing his brow. "That's a pity. I understand it was something quite revolutionary, and that his investigations could have proved most beneficial to the Church. But never mind. I'm sure his findings will turn up – sooner or later."

The Regent grasped the door handle to signal the conversation was over, and Duncan moved out into the corridor to begin the short walk to the stairwell. Behind him, the door closed and he heard the click of a lock. He stopped to look back, and met the intense gaze of Kearson. It felt as though he were being assessed and found lacking.

With a slight curl of a lip and a curt nod, the Regent turned to walk in the opposite direction, bouncing the key to Father Mason's office in the palm of a hand.

For a moment, Duncan watched him stride along the corridor before he made his way down the stairs. There was an arrogance in the Regent's stride that reminded him of his platoon's commanding officer, an arrogance that did not sit right with a man of God, and he found it disquieting.

Duncan was halfway across the quadrant when an uncomfortable feeling between his shoulder blades warned him he was being watched. It was a sixth sense he had heeded many times when in the army, and he turned to peer back at the building. His eyes latched onto a lone figure standing in an upper window. Although he could not make out the features he knew who it was, and briefly returned the Regent's stare before turning and walking away. He had an unquenchable urge to escape, and had no idea why.

# 4

It was quiet and peaceful now the other mourners had left. The hectic pace of Oxford felt miles away, and Duncan found himself staring into the dark maw of the grave remembering the man whose body lay within. As the priest had said during the eulogy, Father Mason would be sorely missed.

Stooping, Duncan grasped a handful of dirt from beside the opening and threw it in.

"Rest in peace, Father."

The words were clichéd, but he could think of nothing better to say. After a moment of silent prayer for the deceased, he turned to make his way back into the city and his bedsit. The last place he felt like going was the university and although his third-floor room was cramped, and damp from the leaking roof, it was the one place he could relax.

Head bowed, hands thrust deeply into the pockets of his battered trench coat, bought from a local army surplus store, Duncan picked his way through the neatly tended graves and onto the tarmac of the road bisecting the graveyard. A light breeze ruffled his shoulder-length hair as he walked, and the sun threatened to break through its blanket of grey cloud, but the morning remained gloomy and dull, much like his humour.

The past four days had been spent attempting to figure out where he was heading with his life, and he'd come to realise that entering the Church was a decision made from grief more than belief. In a belated attempt to offset perceived guilt over the death of his parents he had plunged head-long into the one thing he knew would have pleased them, much like he had joined the army to do the one thing he knew would displease them – his stab at teenage rebellion. On reaching that conclusion, he realised there was only one option to take: Jack it all in. For once in his life he would make a decision based on what *he* wanted to do. He was twenty-nine, for heaven's sake, not some wet-behind-the-ears kid seeking approval for his actions.

He shook his head, scowled, and kicked out at a pebble.

He had told no one of his conclusion yet, not even the spirit of his friend and mentor, but knew he would have to formally hand his resignation into Blackfriars soon, before questions were asked as to his commitment. Having made up his mind he felt a sense of relief, but also a little saddened. Inside, he knew Father Mason would have empathised and, perhaps, accepted his choice, but his parents would never have understood.

He snorted in wry amusement. Even though they had been gone for over a decade, he still sought their blessing.

"Can I offer you a lift?"

Startled at the sound of the voice, Duncan stopped to look up. He had reached the wrought-iron gates of the cemetery without realising.

Standing in the half-moon turning area was the Regent, tall and imposing in his burgundy robes. Hands clasped before him, hidden inside voluminous sleeves, he smiled his condescending smile. "My car is a little way along the road."

Although he did not like the man overly much, Duncan realised he would only put off the inevitable if he refused, and nodded in begrudged acceptance.

The Regent's car proved to be a BMW 5 series, silver-grey, sleek, and upholstered in beige leather. It was more a wealthy businessman's car than personal transport for a servant of God, and the image of Father Mason's battered Fiesta sprang sharply into Duncan's mind. It would appear that rank within the Church had its privileges, much like in business.

The Regent thumbed the remote and the indicators blinked as the door locks sprang. "Get in," he said, walking into the road to open the driver's door.

Inside, the car was immaculate, and Duncan winced as mud from his boots scraped onto the carpet.

"Not to worry," said the Regent, fastening his seat belt and eyeing the mess with distaste, "the car is due a valet at the weekend." Turning the ignition key, the engine purred into life. "Now, where is it I'm taking you?"

"You can drop me in George Street. I can walk the rest of the way from there."

The Regent shrugged. "As you wish."

It was when they pulled up at traffic lights, some ten minutes later, that the Regent finally asked the question Duncan knew was coming.

"Did Father Mason ever mention the Gnostic Society during your discussions?"

Duncan didn't answer. A young mother negotiating the pelican crossing had caught his attention. She was pushing a buggy containing a sleeping baby with one hand while dragging a reluctant toddler with her other.

Unaware of Duncan's distraction, Regent Kearson continued: "Specifically, the Apocalypse of Thomas?"

The youngster stopped, hauling his mother to a halt in the middle of the road, and turned to peer into the car. As he stared in, his pupils expanded until blackness claimed his eyes. He fixed Duncan with a gaze so malevolent that he felt the blood drain from his face. Without warning, his throat closed and he began to struggle for breath. Gasping, he tore away his tie and dragged the collar of his shirt clear. The top button popped at the rough treatment, but the exposing of his neck did little to ease the constriction. He could not break free of that gaze, and was suffocating in the dark, bleak depths of the youngster's eyes.

"Duncan? *DUNCAN!*"

A hand grabbed his shoulders and shook him, and the constriction eased. Air rushed into his lungs in ragged, raspy breaths and he sagged in the seat, feeling drained and confused. Beads of sweat formed beneath his eyes.

"Duncan, are you all right?"

The Regent's voice was filled with concern, and Duncan became aware of the man's hand still resting on his shoulder. Opening his eyes, he lurched upright to stare at the crossing, but it was deserted.

"Duncan! What *is* the matter with you?"

Looking to his left, Duncan's feverish gaze fixed on the mother and her two children. The buggy stood to one side, the infant within screaming as the mother stooped beside the toddler, gripping both of his shoulders while shaking him and shouting at the same time. Head bowed, the youngster sullenly accepted his scolding, looking every inch the young boy he was.

Duncan rubbed at his eyes and sagged back into the seat. Had he imagined it all?

The blare of a horn indicated the lights had changed, and the Regent sped off, flicking a glance of annoyance at the rear-view mirror.

"What happened? Are you ill?"

Duncan glanced sideways at the Regent, and rubbed at his throat. "I – I don't know. Maybe." His voice was hoarse despite his ministrations, and he swallowed to produce saliva in an attempt to ease the rawness.

"You should see a doctor."

Duncan glanced to the Regent, who nodded, as if the matter were settled.

"And since I am in control of where we are going, you can come back to Blackfriars with me."

Duncan made to protest, but the Regent fixed him with his dark eyes before switching his gaze back to the road, stifling all protestations before they could gain voice.

"No argument. I have some Macallan single malt that will help your recuperation from whatever it was that afflicted you."

To Duncan's relief the rest of the journey was made in

silence, but try as he might he could not shake the image of those dark eyes staring out from the boy. It felt as though they had belonged to another, darker, more malign presence. He shook the thought from his mind, convinced his hallucination was nothing more than fatigue and the stress of the past few days, but decided that despite his aversion to doctors, he would make an appointment as the Regent suggested, just to make sure.

Regent Kearson's office proved to be large, bright and airy, with two wide, arched windows admitting a generous supply of daylight that spilled over the gold carpet, enriching the colour with its touch. The Regent's teak desk sat between them, and large, matching bookshelves stood in opposite corners. They faced into the room, but their shelves were remarkably devoid of books. Instead, they held photographs, awards and framed certificates, and were used to showcase achievement rather than knowledge.

"Here we are."

The Regent handed Duncan a tumbler with a finger's width of whisky in the bottom before gesturing for him to sit in the high-backed, padded chair in front of his desk. Not meeting his gaze, Duncan sat, and swirled the drink in the bottom of the glass before taking a sip. The golden liquid burned his gullet before it slid down to warm his stomach.

The Regent moved around the desk and sat, waiting a moment before speaking. "I am aware you are probably still suffering after your ... illness, but I have to ask you again. Did Father Mason ever discuss the Gnostic World View with you, or mention the Apocalypse of Thomas?"

Duncan shook his head, pushing back the image of the three books he had picked up from the floor of Father Mason's office, the three books he had not even looked at since taking them to his bed-sit.

"We never discussed anything other than my ..." Duncan faltered, not ready, or willing, to admit his doubts to the Regent "studies."

Leaning back in his chair, nursing his whisky, the Regent's

eyes glowed darkly at Duncan's answer, but Duncan quelled feelings of unease to ask a question of his own.

"Why do you ask? What makes you think Father Mason was involved with the Gnostics?"

The Regent raised an eyebrow at the question. "I don't think Father Mason was involved." He leaned forward, fixing him with his gaze. "But I do think he found something in *their* myths that has a bearing on *our* Church."

Duncan took another sip of his drink to disguise his rising discomfort, and then said, "The Apocalypse of Thomas?"

The Regent leaned back and smiled a rare smile. "Maybe. That is what I'm trying to find out. Are you sure he never mentioned anything to you?"

Duncan shook his head, wondering what could be so important about the works of Gnostics that would interest the Church.

Clearly unhappy with his lack of knowledge, the Regent scowled, and then rose to his feet, placing his now empty glass on the table. "May I offer you a lift to your home?"

Leaving his drink unfinished, Duncan rose and placed his glass next to the Regent's, confused and irked by the abruptness of his obvious dismissal. "No thanks. I can walk from here."

The Regent nodded, face closed and unreadable. "I'm sure you can find your own way out." Turning, he clasped his hands behind his back and stepped to one of the windows to peer out at the world below.

Duncan strode towards the door, but faltered when he spotted a computer base unit tucked under a table next to it. It was Father Mason's; it still had the black sticker on the side, the one with the slogan 'In God we trust' picked out in white lettering.

Duncan reached for the handle and yanked the door open, closing it none too quietly as he made his way into the corridor. His footsteps echoed short, sharp and loud as he walked, to mirror his mood.

On passing Father Mason's office he halted. A new plaque

had taken the place of the old one, a plaque bearing the name of a Father Tumbletee. He shook his head in disgust and made to walk on, but the door to the office opened to reveal a short, balding, portly figure whose deep-set eyes lit up on seeing him. Fleshy jowls dimpled as Father Tumbletee smiled in welcome.

"Duncan Connors! I was wondering when you would pop in to see me." He opened the door further and waved his arms to usher him in. "Come in, man, don't just stand there gawking. Come in. I don't bite."

Not knowing what to say, Duncan paused for a moment before stepping into the office he knew so well. It was much as he had last seen it, Father Tumbletee not having had time to set his own stamp on the room, but it did have a recent addition; a new computer and flat-screen monitor.

Father Tumbletee waltzed past Duncan to pull out the chair in front of the desk before scuttling around to ease his sizeable form into his own. "Take a seat and we'll have a little chat, hey? I'll bet there're a few things you want to ask me." Clasping his hands over an ample paunch, he leaned back and grinned, waiting for Duncan to sit.

"Good man. Now then, what can I do for you?" A shadow crossed the priest's features. "Sorry. How silly of me. I forgot. It was Father Mason's funeral today, wasn't it? Please accept my apologies if I appeared too genial on such a sad occasion."

Duncan snorted in wry amusement. "To be honest, it's good to see a happy face."

With lips pursed, Father Tumbletee nodded. "I didn't know Father Mason at all, but understand he was a good man."

That he was, Duncan silently agreed, which was why he might as well take the opportunity to tell Father Tumbletee of his decision. Out of respect for the departed priest, he owed it to his successor to at least be honest.

Bracing himself for what he had to say, he took a deep breath. "I'm leaving Blackfriars."

"Hmmm?" Father Tumbletee frowned. "Say again?"

Meeting the priest's querying gaze, Duncan said, "Father Mason was aware of my doubts, of my uncertainty in continuing with my studies, and with his death ... well, I've reached the decision that the Church is not for me." He raised his hands to forestall what Father Tumbletee was about to say. "There are more ways for me to do God's work, ones that don't involve preaching to the converted."

He leaned forward, hands clasped, forearms resting on his thighs, and said, "I have decided to go where help is needed."

"A missionary?" The thought had Father Tumbletee frowning again. "But what of your exams?"

Duncan smiled, this time with feeling, and settled back in the chair. Now that he had confirmed his decision he felt a glow within that told him he was right. "More like a relief worker, and I won't need exams for that. Only a belief that what I am doing is right."

"But why, man? There are plenty of charity organisations out there providing what you intend to do, whereas the Church is desperately short of priests of your potential. Have you thought this through?"

"Believe me, my mind has been torturing itself over the decision far longer than the five days since Father Mason's death. It's not a decision made from grief, I can assure you."

Duncan's words seemed to surprise Father Tumbletee. Eyes wide, mouth open, he looked at a loss as to what to say.

"Sorry to hit you with this on our first meeting, but my mind is made up. I'm paid up at the bed-sit until the end of the month, and then I'm off." He gave a small shrug. "Where to, I'm not sure, but I've a couple of weeks to sort out where best to go." Rising, he offered the priest a hand.

Father Tumbletee grimaced, and hauled his large frame upright. "And there is nothing I can say to make you change your mind?"

Hand still extended, Duncan shook his head. "There are

21

good students here, Father. Students more worthy of your time than me."

After a moment's pause, the priest gripped Duncan's hand. The grip was firm and strong, not at all what Duncan was expecting, and he found himself liking the man. On first impressions, Father Tumbletee was a worthy replacement for Steff Mason.

"I am sure there are, Duncan. But I somehow doubt there are many that would match you for resolve or determination. If I may be so bold, I think your decision is a rash one, and I hope you do not come to regret it."

"As I said, Father; the decision was made a long time ago, it just took me a while to realise it."

Releasing his grasp, Father Tumbletee signed the cross in the air between them, and said, "May the Lord bless you and guide you on your travels. Amen."

"Amen," repeated Duncan, dipping his head. After a moment's pause he looked up, gave the priest a brief smile of gratitude, then turned and exited the room, feeling light of heart for the first time in an age.

Too immersed in his relief, he never noticed Regent Kearson at the opposite end of the corridor as he made his way to the stairs, or the dark look cast his way as the Regent strode towards the office of Father Tumbletee.

# 5

Duncan stepped into the scruffy entrance vestibule to his apartment block and scowled. The place was a dump. Cracked, dirt-encrusted floor tiles vied with peeling, floral wallpaper for attention, and the fusty smell of damp made his nose wrinkle. His leaving could not come soon enough. But he had things to attend to before then; like what he was going to do with the rest of his life. Looking to his pigeon-hole he spotted an envelope in the slot, and reached in. The letter had been posted locally and was probably junk, like most of the mail he received, so he shoved it into a pocket for later perusal. As he made his way up to his third-floor flat his thoughts turned to the puzzle of what Father Mason had been delving into; something so important that the Regent felt the need to investigate, but he was none the wiser as he shoved the door to his flat closed behind him.

Once inside, he removed his coat and hung it on a peg beside the door. The creased white envelope caught his eye. It stuck out of his pocket like a tombstone.

Surprisingly, the letter proved not to be junk mail, but a missive sent by a firm of local solicitors; David Crabtree and Associates, Notary Public & Commissioner for Oaths. Frowning, Duncan moved across to his moth-eaten couch and sagged into a cushion dipped through years of use, to read on. As he read, his confusion deepened.

Dear Mr Connors,
Re: Client no: BG/DAC1093 – Father Steff Mason

Further to the recent demise of Father Steff Mason, could you please contact the above office to arrange a meeting with our David Crabtree.

Yours sincerely,

Brenda Gelling (Mrs)

The letter wilted in his hands. What on earth had the death of Father Mason got to do with him? He peered at the letterhead again. Their office was just around the corner. Wanting to satisfy his curiosity, he rose and walked over to his coat to fish inside a pocket for his mobile, and punched in the number given under the address.

After three rings his call was answered and a voice dripping with professional indifference said, "David Crabtree and Associates, how may I help you?"

"Mrs Gelling, please."

"Speaking."

"It's Duncan Connors here. I've just received a letter asking me to make contact with Mr Crabtree."

"Reference, please."

Duncan frowned. "Pardon?"

Sounding bored, Brenda Gelling said, "Have you a reference, Mr Connors?"

Duncan glanced to the letter. "BG/DAC1093 – Father Steff Mason."

There was a momentary pause, followed by; "One moment, Mr Connors."

The line clicked and the strains of 'Bridge Over Troubled Water' could be heard. Duncan sighed. From experience this meant either he was in for a very long wait or he was about to be fobbed off and dealt with by a menial.

The song clicked off after a couple of lines, and a male voice said, "Mr Connors? David Crabtree here. When can you come in to see me?"

***

The only time Duncan had been in a solicitor's office previously was for the reading of his parents' will, and it was with some misgiving that he stood outside the half-glazed door bearing the title 'David Crabtree and Associates'. There was something about death and solicitors that gave him the creeps.

The feeling remained as he entered. Seated behind a curved rosewood desk to his left, Brenda Gelling looked as professional as she had sounded on the telephone, as she peered in his direction over a pair of half-moon spectacles. The wrong side of sixty, her short, silver-grey hair was perfectly groomed, and a hint of a smile crossed her face as he closed the door behind him.

"Mr Connors?"

Duncan nodded.

"Please take a seat." She gestured to the row of chairs beside the door, "Mr Crabtree will not keep you long."

Taking the middle of the three low, padded chairs, Duncan eased himself down and leaned back, forearms resting lightly on his thighs, hands clasped. It was all he could do keep them from fidgeting.

Brenda Gelling phoned through to David Crabtree. "Mr Connors is here to see you, Mr Crabtree." Placing the receiver back on its cradle, she said, "Mr Crabtree will see you now."

The room David Crabtree occupied was along a short, ill-lit corridor running back from reception. Brenda Gelling knocked on the wood-panelled door, opened it and indicated for Duncan to enter.

Nodding his thanks, he stepped inside.

The room was not much larger than reception, but whereas that area was sparsely furnished with the occasional potted-plant dotted around, this one was full of books. Hundreds of tomes on law, rulings and the judiciary crammed the floor-to-ceiling shelving that ran down each side of the room and across the far wall, reluctantly leaving a small gap for a window that looked over Oxford from its second-floor vantage point. In some ways the room reminded him of

Father Mason's office. It had that same aura of peace and tranquillity, and he felt some of his tension seep away.

"Mr Connors, so glad you could come at such short notice."

From behind a leather-topped desk, a short, balding, bespectacled man in his late fifties moved out, immaculate in pale-blue shirt, yellow tie and expensive suit, a neatly folded red handkerchief protruding from its breast pocket. Stepping forward, he offered Duncan a hand. His grip was strong and firm, and as his brown eyes met Duncan's they crinkled in welcome.

Waving a hand to two finely crafted chairs that probably cost more than all the furniture in Duncan's bed-sit, David Crabtree said, "Please, take a seat."

Duncan watched as the solicitor moved to the other side of the desk and sat. With fingers laced, he planted elbows on the desktop and leaned forward. "You must be wondering why I asked to see you."

A knock on the door announced Brenda Gelling's arrival and she stepped into the office to place a manilla file on David Crabtree's desk.

"Thank you, Brenda."

Smiling, she nodded and turned to leave, but halted when David Crabtree said, "No calls, please. Not until we're finished."

"As you wish, Mr Crabtree."

He turned his attention back to Duncan, and said "I was sorry to hear of Steff's demise." A shadow crossed his features. "We grew up together, you know?"

Duncan assumed the question was rhetorical, and said nothing.

"A right pair of rascals we were, too. You wouldn't believe the scrapes we got into. And to think he ended up a priest." He shook his head and smiled in memory, then turned his attention back to Duncan. "But that does not explain why I asked you here." Looking down, he opened the file his secretary had placed on the desk and removed two pieces of paper, handing them to Duncan. "He left these for you."

Duncan frowned and reached out. The papers proved to be a letter, written in the priest's neat, flowing script and as he read on, he felt the blood drain from his face. Once he'd read it, he looked up to find David Crabtree studying him intently.

"B-b-but – this makes no sense," Duncan spluttered. "How could he know he was going to die?"

David Crabtree shrugged. "I have no idea, but it seems he did. Although I doubt he suspected it would be in a car crash. If you look at the date when it was written, and witnessed, it was last November, so whatever unnerved him must have been recent. Had he been ill that you know of?"

Duncan shook his head, and then read the letter again.

Dear Duncan,

If you are reading this you already know I am no longer of this world, and that God has a greater purpose for me, which leads me nicely to my point. In taking me into His arms, He has left my work on earth unfinished, for what I can only assume to be a valid reason. And I believe that valid reason to be you, Duncan.

During my research into the past I have come across teachings related to what is commonly known as Gnosticism: teachings that offer an alternate worldview on creation and the creator. Teachings that make me question the role of the church from its inception to the present day. My faith is not shaken, more stirred by the revelation. My faith in our Lord is unquestionable, but I have become aware that the needs of the world lie in us being out there with the people and not in buildings designed for the self-righteous to congregate and atone for their many sins.

I know of your doubts regarding your vocation, and also sense your yearning to be out amongst the unfortunates, spreading light and the word. To this end, I believe you capable of continuing the research I am now unable to complete, free of theological and church constraints. If you choose to continue where I left off, your findings will have a major influence on world matters, and repercussions for the faith. Repercussions that I believe will be for the better.

27

More than this I cannot say, for reasons that will become clear should you undertake my request. I understand how vague I am being, and that I am asking a lot for you to agree to my request on faith alone. But there is no other way.

I know you Duncan, almost as well as you know yourself, and believe in you. Of all the students I have met over the years, you are the only one that has held the flame of our Lord within, a flame that burns brightly and sets you apart from your peers. I believe it is a remnant of your heritage. In you is the true spirit of Light. In a world filled with Shadows, your spirit shines brightly, no matter how flawed you see yourself. It has been my pleasure to know you these past few years, and I hope to meet you again in a better place.

Steff Mason.

Duncan stared at Father Mason's signature, trying to make sense of what he had just read, but could not get his head around it. Although he stated he had not lost his faith, the wording gave a different impression. Reading the letter, Duncan was sure more than ever that Steff Mason had known he was going to die. But he had seemed so healthy. Surely someone diagnosed with a terminal illness would look – well, ill.

Looking up, he said, "Do you know what Father Mason was researching?"

David Crabtree shook his head. "I have no idea, but he seemed genuinely excited by it. After our meeting in November I did not see him again so could not pursue the matter. I never dreamed that the next time I would see him he would be in a casket." He gave a sheepish smile. "I wanted to attend the funeral, but, unfortunately, I had urgent business to take care of."

Duncan got the impression religion did not play a huge part in his life, and dipped his head in understanding. "So you have no idea what it is he wants me to continue with?"

"I'm afraid not. He kept his own counsel on that. I understand the subject of his research was quite sensitive. But he did speak highly of you at our last meeting. I rather got the impression he looked upon you as the son he would never have; a more than competent heir to continue his research.

"Should you decide to accept, I have been instructed to give you this." He pulled a yellowed ticket from the file and held it for Duncan to see before dropping it back on the desk. "It's a receipt for a safety deposit box at Coutts, London, I believe."

Duncan was stunned. It appeared that Father Mason had planned everything prior to his death to ensure his research could be continued. But what was he researching? Immediately he knew the answer: the Apocalypse of Thomas. But how could he hope to follow on from a man more qualified than he? Where would he begin?

His thoughts were interrupted by David Crabtree.

"Steff did say you would have doubts as to your ability to continue with his studies, but that I should tell you to dispel them. He believed in you, Duncan, and from experience, he did not put his faith in those who were not worthy. He also said I should tell you to trust your spark, that it will not lead you astray. He sensed you were drawn to Blackfriars for a reason. That you were of the Light." He gave a small shrug. "Whatever that may mean."

Despite the argument being pretty persuasive, Duncan remained unsure. How could he accept knowing he might well make a complete hash of everything that Father Mason had worked for? But how could he refuse knowing that years of research would be wasted if he did so? Yet again he felt pressured, having just made a decision to run his own life for a change, even if he had not made any arrangements for his travels yet.

So why not agree and see where the research took him? And had he not wanted to be an adventurer when he was a youngster; solve mysteries hidden from mortal understanding? Well, now was his chance.

Not at all sure it was the right thing to do, he met David Crabtree's querying gaze and nodded. "Even though I think Father Mason is wrong about me, I'll do as he asked."

David Crabtree smiled. "Good man. He knew he could

rely on you. As I said earlier, Steff did not put his faith in those not worthy." He pulled a paper from the file and slid it across the table, and then handed him a pen.

Duncan looked down while reaching out to take the ball-point. "What is it?"

"A receipt – for this." He handed the yellowed chit to Duncan. "And may I wish you every success."

∗∗∗

As soon as Duncan opened the door to his apartment block he knew something was amiss. The inner door had been forced; the glass panel next to the latch smashed. The hairs on the back of his neck stood on end and he took the stairs two at a time as he raced up to his bed-sit.

On reaching the third-floor landing he skidded to a halt, his worst fears realised. His door had been kicked in. The bottom panel was splintered and the frame split where the mortice had smashed through the wood.

Adrenaline coursed through his body, setting his nerves to tingling. He padded to the shattered doorway to pause at the threshold and listen for signs of activity within, but all remained quiet and he stepped inside.

The sight that greeted him had him groaning in disbelief. His room had been trashed. Every drawer from his cupboards and dresser had been dumped on the floor amongst his scattered possessions, torn books and broken crockery. His TV and hi-fi had been smashed, his bed ripped apart and the cushions and pillows slit open, the stuffing pulled out and strewn about like fluffy confetti.

Stepping further in, his boot crunched on broken glass. Looking down, he saw it was the photograph of his parents, the one he kept on the mantelpiece, and he stooped to pick up the mangled frame. He stared at the photograph for a moment before tipping out slivers of glass, then removed the picture and slipped it inside his coat pocket. It was then he noticed the one item missing from the room – his laptop. He had put it in the kitchenette, plugged in and on charge, and now it was gone. A low growl formed in his throat and he strode to the area where he had left it, scanning the wreckage in case it had also been dumped on the floor, but it was not there.

For the first time in as long as he could remember, a rage took hold of him and he clamped clenched fists to his side in an attempt to control the urge to lash out. At what, he had no idea, but he needed to hit something, anything to vent his anger. He took deep breaths to suppress the rising tide of emotion, but it was difficult – his home had been violated, and he had a good idea by whom.

A noise, alien and whisper quiet came from somewhere below and his eyes flicked open. Allowing his emotions to gain control, he hurtled out of the door and bounding down the stairs in an attempt to capture the perpetrator. The inner door to the vestibule nearly flew off its hinges as he yanked it open, as did the outer. He skidded to a halt in the street. His breath came in ragged gasps as he scanned the pavement one way and the other, eyes narrowed as he looked for sign of a figure racing away. But he saw no one.

Two students appeared from around a corner and began to walk towards him. Duncan grabbed one of them as they walked past. He needed an answer.

"Has anyone just run past you?" His words were growled, each one punctuated by a tightening of his grip on the student's arm.

The lad, looking fresh out of high-school and with a face full of acne, jerked back at the rough handling. Eyes wide with fear, he spluttered, "E-easy, dude. We ain't seen no one, have we, Ben?"

Ben looked ready to flee before Duncan's wrath, leaving his friend to it, but shook his head at the question. "Not until you come bustin' out."

His voice quivered as he spoke, and Duncan felt his anger begin to dissipate. Easing his grip, he smiled a weak apology. "Sorry, guys. Someone just trashed my flat and I thought I saw him running out of the building. Must have been mistaken."

31

"No one came out but you, dude," muttered the student he had grabbed, backing away.

Duncan rubbed at his forehead and searched the street again, but saw nothing out of the ordinary. He could feel a migraine coming on and decided to go and see if he could find some aspirin amongst the debris, and made his way back to the building.

His thoughts turned to the Regent. It was obvious that, not content with raiding Father Mason's office to search for answers, he had sanctioned the destruction of Duncan's bed-sit in an attempt to discover exactly what the priest was researching, which meant he thought Duncan was implicated.

Deciding that two could play the search and destroy game, he stepped inside to close the door behind him, but a movement at the periphery of vision, a ripple in the air, had him turning to peer out into the street. His eyes narrowed; the roadway was deserted. Lips pursed, he shook his head. As if the day's events were not bad enough, now he was seeing things – again.

# 6

The hinges creaked as Duncan eased the door open. He winced and held his breath, half-expecting to hear rapid footsteps approaching his hiding place, but all remained quiet and he exhaled in relief. He had been holed up in the storage cupboard for hours, waiting for the building to empty, and even though the lights had been turned off twenty minutes ago, had wanted to make certain everyone had left before daring to venture out.

The rapid beating of his heart quieted and he opened the door further, and then slipped out into the corridor, closing it softly behind him. After the total darkness of the window-less cupboard the gloom of the corridor was a relief, and he padded towards the stairwell leading up to the first floor.

The light of a full moon lifted the murkiness still further as he made his way up the stairs, but the additional light only added to his unease. The wraithlike glow that streamed in through arched, stone-mullioned windows cast a ghostly, silvery sheen over everything. Shadows lengthened, and there seemed to be a coldness within the light that ate into the building. Duncan shivered. The sooner he retrieved his laptop and was out of there the better.

He passed the office of Father Tumbletee on the way to the Regent's, and paused at the door. To his disappointment, the pull he used to feel when visiting Steff Mason there had gone, and he felt a twinge of sadness.

Lips pursed, he shrugged away maudlin thoughts and continued to the doorway at the end of the corridor, where he stopped outside to press an ear to the timber panel. He could hear nothing, and reached down to grasp the handle. To his relief – his plan never having got as far as how to get in if the door had been locked – it opened with ease. After closing it softly behind him he padded further into the room.

Moonlight streamed in through the windows and, as with the stairwell, he felt unnerved by its silvery luminescence. He swallowed in an attempt to produce saliva in a mouth gone dry and scanned the room for signs of his laptop, eager to grab it and escape the building, but it was nowhere to be seen. Father Mason's computer was still under the table beside the door, but there was nothing resembling his own.

Into the silence a noise from behind, short and sharp, had him spinning. His heart beat painfully against his ribs, and beat harder again as a crack of orange light, L-shaped and bright, appeared in the corner farthest away from him.

By reflex, he ducked behind the desk and pressed against the wooden side. He held his breath, not daring to breathe in case he was heard. Even so, he was convinced the loud beating of his heart would give him away.

The pool of orange light from the doorway stretched until it sliced across the desk and out onto the carpet. A long, dark shadow appeared at its centre, but disappeared as the light to the concealed room was extinguished. With a barely audible click, the door closed and Duncan heard the soft tread of feet on the carpet. He expected imminent discovery, but was both relieved and surprised when the footsteps passed him by and made their way to the door through which he had entered. He dare not look out to see who it was in case he be discovered, but knew it could only be one person: Regent Kearson.

The door opened and closed, and the sound of footsteps faded as the Regent moved away from the office. Duncan exhaled noisily and sucked air into lungs deprived for too long. Goosebumps sprung up on his arms and he sagged against the desk. Every nerve in his body tingled and it took a while for him to gather the courage needed to rise and investigate where the Regent had appeared from. To his knowledge, there was no other access to the room other than the way he had entered.

Each footstep was slow and deliberate as he made his way towards the bookshelf he felt sure was a doorway to a secret room, his every sense alert for the Regent's return. But all remained quiet and he reached his objective without mishap.

Despite the brightness of the moon it was too dark for him to see much in the way of concealed catches so he ran his fingertips down the side of the bookcase, his fingers probing for a hidden switch. He found it readily enough, a cleverly masked grommet that could easily be mistaken for the cover of a shelf support screw, and pressed it in.

There was a soft click. The bookcase opened a fraction, and his heart recommenced its rapid beating as he eased fingers into the crack and pulled. The skilfully disguised door swung open without a sound, and he stepped inside.

The room he entered was pitch black, there being no window to allow the brilliance of the moon to illuminate the interior. Knowing that any light from within could not be seen from the Regent's office, he closed the door behind him and fumbled on the wall for a switch. At his touch, the room bathed in a pale, orange glow that emanated from a single, uncovered bulb, and he gasped. His jaw dropped and, eyes wide, he struggled to take in what he was seeing. The room was not much bigger than the storage cupboard he had hidden in, being around two metres by three, but it was the paraphernalia of the occult that had him gasping.

A small desk occupied the rear wall, on which a two-foot tall wooden crucifix dominated. A black candle stood either side, and there was an open book before it. Unlike the Regent's study, which contained no books, the shelves that lined both the left and right walls were filled with them.

Only these were to do with exorcism, black mass, witch-craft, devil worship and other literature that no God-fearing churchman would approve of.

A hasty scan of the shelves showed no sign of his missing laptop, and he stepped to the desk to peer at the book that lay open before the cross. To his astonishment, he discovered it was a copy of the Bible, which seemed completely at odds with the tomes that graced the shelving. It had been left open on the teachings of John, and two sections of wording had been highlighted in pink.

Puzzled, Duncan traced the words with a finger and whispered them quietly to himself:

*In the beginning was the Word, and the Word was with God, and the Word was God.*

His frown deepened as he noticed a black line drawn through each 'Word'. Alternative wording had been written in the margin of the page in the Regent's small, neat handwriting: sound, voice, resonance.

Further down the page another passage had also been highlighted; John 1:14

*And the Word became flesh, and dwelt among us.*

Again, 'Word' had been scored out and the previous alternative wordings written in the margin, as was a stick symbol of a bird flying from cupped hands.

Duncan took a step back and wiped his hands on his jeans, suddenly feeling unclean. It was no wonder the Regent was so interested in what Steff Mason was researching, especially as it appeared to touch on the mysteries of the god he worshipped, which would appear to be a totally different god to that which the rest of the Christian world subscribed.

Claustrophobia gripped him. His face flushed and he struggled for breath. He had to get out and away. Turning, he stumbled to the door and flicked the catch to open it. It glided open with ease and he almost fell into the room beyond. Without pausing for breath he pushed the door closed and made good his escape, unmindful he had left a glowing clue to his unlawful entry.

***

Concealed within the shadows, the man watched as Duncan fled the grounds, and waited until he had disappeared out of the gates before making the call. As was the norm, it was answered after three rings.

"It looks like our Mr Connors has been doing some breaking and entering of his own."

"Really? Did he find anything?"

"Hard to say, but whatever he found sure scared the shit out of him. He's run off as if the devil himself chased him."

He heard the soft snuffle of laughter.

"Perhaps he has. You have the merchandise?"

"Aye. I'll be popping it into the safety deposit box tomorrow. You want him eliminated now?"

Again the laughter, before the voice said, "No. I want him kept safe. He has a mission to accomplish, although he may not know it yet, and you are to follow him and ensure he comes to no harm."

The man scowled, not liking the idea at all. "I'm not a bloody nursemaid."

"I know this, but you shall be well rewarded. Will double the usual fee be in order?"

"Plus expenses. As I said, I'm not a bloody nursemaid."

There was a moment's pause before the voice said, "Agreed. But he has to be kept free from harm. Inform me of any further developments."

The line went dead and the man cursed. This was all he needed. The job could go on for months. Not his style at all. He smiled. But at least the pay was good. Pocketing the mobile, he made his way out of the grounds, hands sunk deeply into the pockets of his overcoat to ward off the chill, and headed to his car. On sliding into the driver's seat he glanced at the laptop nestling on the passenger's side, and wondered why his paymaster wanted it so much.

# 7

At Louisa's scream the man in the kitchen spun, dark eyes wide, coffee sloshing from his cup to soak the front of his white T shirt.

"Louisa?"

"Mehmet?" Louisa sagged in relief. "What are you doing back so early?" She stared in dismay at the wreckage on the floor, and sighed. "Now it's ruined." Running a hand to smooth a stray lock of blonde hair that had spilled free of her ponytail, she met Mehmet's querying look. "My surprise!"

Mehmet nodded, his dark eyes flashing in amusement. After placing his cup on the worktop he stepped forward, his highly toned physique using economy of movement as he stooped to help her pick up the mess. Pausing to peer into one of the bags, he grinned, and plucked out a cube of lamb and a pepper. "*Kuzu güvec*?"

Slapping his hand, Louisa met his twinkling gaze and laughed. "Of course, you fool." Standing, she carried one of the bags to the worktop and emptied the contents. "Fortunately, I should be able to salvage enough to make the meal." She turned and stared in dismay at the dark liquid staining the boards of the floor. "Although we may have to drink water to celebrate your return."

Clutching the other bag, Mehmet rose, and, with a small shrug, said, "Water is good."

Louisa smiled and shook her head, watching as he placed the bag on the worktop before grabbing a brush and shovel to clear away the broken bottle.

"Was it a good trip?"

Mehmet looked up. For a moment, a cloud settled behind his brown eyes before his ready smile drove it away. "It was okay." He shrugged, then rose to tip the broken glass and wine mixture into the bin beside the door. "Some good things, some bad." With a knowing grin, he said, "But all will sell, yes?"

Louisa chuckled. All would sell. He had a knack for obtaining junk he could sell on for ten times its worth to unsuspecting tourists who were useless when it came to haggling over price.

"The shipment will arrive soon. Maybe tomorrow. In time for the tourists." Moving past her he made his way to the percolator. "You want coffee?"

The reaction was *so* Mehmet. He had been gone for two months yet treated his return as though he had just been down to the shops for a loaf of bread.

Bread!

She groaned. She knew she had forgotten something.

Mehmet left soon after their coffee to 'do some business' and did not come back until much later, leaving Louisa in peace to fetch fresh bread and prepare the meal. When he did return, he appeared edgy. Not so much that the casual observer would notice, but enough that she could. His smile was not quite so ready, and his attention drifted while they ate, as though his mind was still on his travels even though his physical presence was in the room. Conversation was minimal and eventually she had to ask him what was wrong.

A dark, hooded look appeared in his eyes, similar to that he had given her earlier in the day. But this time it remained as he held her gaze. Even his half-smile was insufficient to disguise it.

"It is nothing. I am merely tired after my journeying." He dabbed at his mouth with a napkin. "But this meal made my return all the more pleasurable."

This time his smile succeeded in driving away the shadows,

but it was not enough to divert Louisa from further questioning. After scraping the remains of her casserole to one side, she placed her cutlery on her plate, and said, "Something's wrong. I've known you too long. You're worried; I can see it in your eyes. Now, are you going to tell me or ..." she arched a brow "do I have to withhold the baklava until you do?"

Mehmet laughed; the first real sign of genuine amusement since he'd got back. The expression lit his face. Holding up his hands, he said, "You are a cruel woman, Louisa Cooke. No Turkish woman would treat a man in such a way. What is it you would have me say?"

"The reason behind your dark mood would do for a start."

Mehmet shook his head, his shoulder-length black hair dancing with the movement. "No dark mood, Louisa Cooke. Merely tiredness, I assure you. I had business to see to here in Marmaris, so caught an earlier plane from Frankfurt. I have little sleep in the last two days and am suffering." He leaned forward and grasped her hands, his brown eyes holding hers. "And now, I fear, I shall have to miss the baklava and take to my bed, before I fall asleep on my plate. I have many things to do in the morning."

Raising Louisa's hands, he pressed lips to her knuckles. "I would thank you for a very fine meal, and apologise if I appear rude. That is not my intention. Tomorrow, I will be fine. Tonight ... "

Rising, he bid Louisa goodnight and retired to his room, leaving her to gaze in disbelief at his back. Something was wrong, she knew it. She had never seen him so out of sorts, but knew that she would get nothing from him until he was ready to talk. If he ever was. When clearing away the dishes she decided to broach the matter again in the morning, but by then it was too late. He had already left.

***

Louisa placed the handwritten note back on the kitchen worktop, and sighed. It read;

'Business to see to. Back Later. Mehmet.'

Filling the percolator, she prepared a coffee, needing a fix of caffeine. Her questioning of Mehmet would have to wait a little longer.

She had no sooner taken a sip of her drink when she heard the drone of a wagon negotiating the hill, and wandered through to the living room to peer out of the window. Further down the lane, a battered Bedford with German plates made its slow but steady progress towards the shop, and Louisa knew it was the goods Mehmet expected. Trust him to have disappeared when everything arrived.

Taking another sip of her coffee, she made her way out through the kitchen and down the stairs to the shop. By the time the wagon pulled up outside she had opened the door and created enough space for boxes to be stored.

The driver, a middle-aged man whose craggy, lived-in face looked at home in a wagon, wound down the window and leaned out. "Mehmet Ozric?"

Louisa nodded. "That's here. But he's not around right now."

The driver scowled, heavy brows meeting as he did so. "Then who help unload?" There was irritation in his voice, his English heavily accented.

Smiling sweetly, Louisa said, "That would be me, then."

The driver snorted in disbelief, then shook his head. "Boxes heavy. Lady no good. Need a man."

Annoyed by the slight, but determined not to show it, Louisa said nothing, folded arms across her chest and arched a brow. "This lady is good, believe you me."

Back home, she had been brought up on a farm and was used to heavy work. Coupled with the fact she had been hefting boxes and goods around the shop for the past three years, she was sure she could handle what the driver thought impossible.

"Want to test me?"

The driver grinned, and eyed her clothing. "Maybe you get changed first."

Louisa looked down, and agreed. Sandals, skirt and blouse were not the best attire to be humping boxes around. "Wait there, I'll only be a minute."

It took over an hour to unload the crates, boxes and bags that were crammed in the back of the wagon, by which time Louisa was shattered, the shop looked like a bomb had gone off and every muscle in her body ached. Mehmet had not made an appearance so it was left to her and the driver to sort it all out.

When finished, Louisa offered him a drink, gave him one hundred Turkish lira for his help and waved him on his way. Too tired to do much else, she sat on one of the boxes and surveyed the disaster area. It would take an age to sort it out. The shop had very little shelf space as it was, and no storage, so she guessed most of it would end up in the apartment until room could be made for it.

Curious as to what Mehmet had bought, she eased open a flap to a cardboard box next to the crate she was sitting on. It contained leather wristbands and bead necklaces. Her eyes fixed on the stand next to the door, the one overflowing with similar cheap trinkets, and she shook her head. As if they did not have enough of those already.

From outside, she heard her name whispered, and peered towards the doorway to see who was there, but saw no one. Puzzled, she rose to investigate, but the street was deserted, aside from the lone guard positioned at the entrance to the fort at the top of the hill. She returned his wave as he looked down and then, cursing her overactive imagination, stepped back inside, but paused at the threshold, mouth agape.

Inside the shop stood a man. Despite the heat of the day he wore a long black trenchcoat, his feet enclosed in black military-style boots. His back was to her as he studied the interior.

The hairs on the back of her neck rose and she stepped back, raising a hand to wave for the guard's help. But before she could complete the summons the man turned and smiled, and for the second time in as many seconds her

42

mouth dropped open.

His ebony features were both flawless and androgynous as he gazed at her with eyes that were dark and almond-shaped. Snow-white hair and goatee beard, tightly curled, stood out in stark contrast to his skin.

Her arm dropped to her side under his scrutiny, and an aura of peace settled on her. His smile deepened and her fears fled.

"C ... c ... can I help you?"

The question sounded lame, but she could think of nothing else to say.

He nodded and beckoned her forward.

After a cursory glance up to the guard, who had his back to her, Louisa stepped hesitantly into the shop, swallowing as she did so. Not that she was frightened; the emotion she felt was far different. It was almost anticipation. The stranger indicated that she should seat herself, so she perched on the crate she had vacated moments earlier.

With a smile, he turned and took a pencil from the glass counter, then moved to the cardboard box and proceeded to sketch a diagram on its lid. When finished, he inclined his head towards the sketch.

Having followed his every fluid movement, Louisa had not studied the drawing, her eyes glued to the man whose presence filled her with awe.

Reluctantly, she broke away from studying him and looked to the drawing. From the angle she inspected it she could not make out what it was, so swivelled on the crate to view it better. A frown tugged at her brow. On the lid of the box was drawn what looked to be a child's stick drawing of a dove flying from cupped hands.

Puzzled, she shook her head and looked up.

He smiled, and then leaned forward to tap the diagram with a long, narrow index finger, and said, "He comes."

A shout sounded from outside the shop; a loud greeting to the guard atop the hill. Louisa looked up to see Mehmet's figure silhouetted in the doorway, arm raised in salutation before he turned and entered. On seeing the mound of boxes inside he halted, hands on hips, to study them. Looking up, he spotted Louisa and shrugged, lips compressed and eyes wide in apology.

"Looks like Bernt arrived early. Sorry, Louisa. If I had known I would have put aside my business to help you unload."

Surprised that Mehmet had not noticed the stranger in their midst, Louisa jerked her head in an attempt to draw his attention away from the boxes.

He frowned. "What is wrong?"

Lips pursed, Louisa sighed and jabbed her head more sharply.

Mehmet shook his head. "Sorry, Louisa. I do not understand. Are you angry with me?"

Frustrated, Louisa gave up, and said, "Have you not noticed we have a customer?"

Mehmet's frown deepened.

A low growl erupted from Louisa's throat and she turned to apologise to the visitor, to discover he had disappeared. Her eyes swept the room as she shot up from the crate, and Mehmet lunged forward to wrap an arm around her shoulder.

"Louisa, what is it? What is the matter?"

"He's gone." Her voice came out as a whisper, her eyes still flicking around the shop in case they deceived her.

Turning her so that her attention was fixed on him, Mehmet said, "Who has gone, Louisa?"

Eyes wide, she met his querying gaze. "The man. The man with the white hair."

Mehmet shook his head. "There is no one here. Come, I think you need to rest. The carrying of boxes has tired you."

She shook free of his grasp and swung round to stare at the sketch on the cardboard box. "He was here, and he drew that!" Her hand shook as she pointed to the strange hieroglyph.

Mehmet peered over her shoulder, and gasped. Stepping past, he stooped and studied the drawing. After a moment he looked up, face pale and eyes wide. Rising, he gripped her shoulders. His gaze was intense, and sent shivers down her spine.

"This man, what did he look like?"

After she had described him, he asked, "A name? Did he give you his name?"

Louisa shook her head, shaken by the urgency in his tone.

"Did he say anything?"

Again, she shook her head, then remembered the only two words the stranger had uttered. Meeting Mehmet's earnest gaze, she said, "He said, 'he comes'."

# 8

**D**uncan rubbed at eyes that felt tired and grit-filled as he stepped off the train. He had slept little the night before, the trashing of his flat and worry of what he'd got himself involved in being at the forefront of his mind. Although he'd tried to snatch some sleep on the journey, the constant rattle and swaying of the carriage ensured he remained awake, and his patience was worn thin through tiredness.

Standing on the platform, he paused to get his bearings, and stumbled forward as a figure barged into him from behind. Cursing, he muttered 'Welcome to London', and glared at the culprit's back before he joined the throng that headed towards the exit.

Once in the open air his poor humour worsened. It had been many years since he was last in the capital and he'd forgotten how busy it was. The walkways were rammed with a heaving mass of humanity, whose ebb and flow depended on the colour of the pedestrian lights, with the roads being equally as bad. Cars vied for position with bright red buses, and black cabs darted in between, horns blaring if another vehicle dared get in the way. The place was chaos, and his vision of a perfect hell.

A shudder ran through him and he sighed. With shoulders hunched, hands thrust in his pockets, he kept his head down and forced his way through the crowd to begin the short walk to Coutts, the ever present roar of the traffic a constant companion.

As he walked, he became aware of the ghastly, foul-smelling pall that hung over the place. Even though London had cleaned up its image since last he had visited, to him it still seemed as though a malicious disease had taken hold and spread from building to building in a cancerous rampage, to seep into stone and brick, and he began to have doubts as to the wisdom of his course of action. Before they could blossom and his nerve fail him he arrived at the entrance to the glass-fronted building that was Coutts, and halted to peer at his reflection in the glass.

With his dark hair now cropped short, wearing a tatty army-surplus trench coat, dark jeans and red Converse boots, he looked anything but a client of the bank and, even though he'd put on the white shirt and dark tie he had worn for the funeral, he knew he looked out of place. But as this was where he would find out what Steff Mason had been up to, he had to enter, and straightened his lapels before walking through the door.

Once inside, the surrounds of the bank caused his flimsy aura of assurance to falter. The whole feel of the place was one of opulence. Having been brought up on a rough council estate in Liverpool, it was not something he was comfortable with.

"Can I help you, Sir?"

Startled, Duncan swivelled to his left, meeting the querying gaze of the girl on reception, and gave a hesitant smile. Fishing inside a coat pocket, he pulled out the receipt given to him by David Crabtree.

"I–I–I have this."

He held it aloft like a ski pass as he stepped towards the desk to hand it to her.

Pinched between forefinger and thumb, she quickly read the receipt number before looking up and giving him a dazzling smile.

"Thank you, Sir."

She returned the yellowed ticket and Duncan nodded his thanks. Was it his imagination or did the *Sir* sound more sincere this time?

"If you would like to take one of the escalators up to the next level someone will attend to you there."

The girl gestured to the rear of the room with a slender, tanned hand made for such a movement.

Duncan's boots squeaked on the marble floor as he turned to walk in the direction she had indicated, and he winced, feeling his face redden as she stifled a laugh. His discomfort did not lessen until he made the sanctuary of the moving stairs, whereupon he stared straight ahead until he reached the top, resisting the urge to turn to see if she still watched him. Once he reached the first floor, however, all thoughts of the girl disappeared, and he navigated the scattering of leather sofas and small tables bearing trays of soft drinks, juices and tumblers, to make his way towards a large reception desk to the left of the escalator.

"Can I help you, Sir?"

Duncan returned the girl's smile and showed her his receipt.

"If you would like to take a seat, Sir, I shall get someone to attend to you. Do you require a private room for your viewing?"

Not knowing what it was he was about to open, Duncan decided that some privacy was probably in order, and nodded.

"Please help yourself to a drink. We shan't keep you waiting for long."

Duncan had barely sipped at his apple juice when a man approached his table. Tall and slim, standing at least six-foot-four, a ledger tucked under an arm, he wore his designer suit with ease as he strode the floor with confidence. On arriving at Duncan's table he dipped his head.

"Mr Mason?"

"Yes ... er, no." Rising, Duncan felt the heat of embarrassment colour his cheeks.

The bank official frowned, then removed the ledger from under his arm, opened it and scanned the entries. "You do have receipt number 67439?"

Duncan nodded, and handed the ticket over, not sure whether he liked the man's condescending manner.

After checking it against the entry the man handed it back, and said, "That number is allocated to one Steff Mason. Are you saying we have made an error?"

Irked by the man's tone, Duncan fought to prevent it showing in his voice. "Fath ... Steff Mason passed away last week. I was left this –" he raised the ticket "in his will."

"And you have proof of this?"

Lips compressed to prevent him uttering an expletive, Duncan fumbled inside his coat and pulled out a crumpled piece of paper, which he handed over. It was the letter David Crabtree had given him, the one Father Mason had signed on headed notepaper granting him authorisation to access the safety deposit box.

"Sorry about the state of it. My place got trashed by burglars and everything's in a bit of a mess."

Ignoring Duncan's explanation, the man read the contents and checked Steff Mason's signature against the one in his ledger. Looking up, he said, "You have identification?"

Duncan bit back an angry retort and delved in a pocket for his driving licence. Even though he no longer owned a car, finding it too expensive to run, it was a constant companion.

After checking the details the man handed both the licence and the letter back and then closed the ledger with a bang. Tucking it under an arm, he smiled and held out a hand. "Chris Broadhead."

Taken aback by the abrupt change in manner, Duncan responded with "Duncan Connors" as he shook it.

"We received a letter from Messrs Crabtree this morning, informing us of your imminent arrival and instructing us to allow you access to Mr Mason's deposit once we were sure you were who you said you were. Now, if you would care to follow me, I will show you to a room where you can peruse the contents of Mr Mason's deposit at your leisure."

The room proved to be on a gallery that overlooked the first floor and, halting outside a door, Duncan's escort reached out to push it open. "Here we are. Make yourself comfortable and I will arrange to have the deposit delivered." Thrusting out a hand, he gripped Duncan's with a firm shake. "My commiserations on your loss."

Once inside, Duncan slumped into a leather chair and leaned forward, hands clasped, elbows resting on thighs as he stared vacantly at the glass-topped table in front of him. Now that the moment had come he was filled with anxiety. What would he find out? Would he be any closer to knowing the secret behind the Regent and what Steff Mason was investigating?

The door opened and a young man entered, a large padded envelope in his hands. Placing it on the table, he backed away. "Just press the buzzer by the door when you're finished and I'll call back to show you out."

The door clicked softly closed on his exit, and Duncan stared at the envelope, eyes drawn to the label showing the number 67439.

A thrill of anticipation ran through him, and his hands shook as he reached out to grasp the buff package. It was surprisingly light, and he stared at it in outstretched arms for a good minute before rousing the courage to open it.

The tearing of paper sounded loud in the small room, and he found himself pausing to look around before upending the envelope. Two documents slipped free, dropping onto the table. Duncan frowned and raised the envelope to peer inside, but it was empty. He had no idea what he had expected it to contain, but two sheets of paper seemed a bit of a letdown.

The first proved to be a banker's draft, made payable to Duncan Connors in the sum of thirty-five thousand pounds. The amount staggered him and, open-mouthed, he had to read the amount three or four times before his head eventually took it in. Why would Father Mason leave him so much? How had he managed to accumulate that amount of money on his meagre salary?

The second piece gave something of a clue as to how the money should be used. It contained a name and address: Mehmet Ozric, Marmaris, Turkey.

Both papers drooped in Duncan's hands and he stared at the door, none the wiser as to what it was all about, or what he had got himself into. Instead of getting answers he found himself in possession of a large sum of money and yet more questions needing to be answered. And he had the strangest feeling Mehmet Ozric was the key to open the truth.

Leaving the torn envelope on the table, Duncan pocketed the draft and the address and rose to walk to the door on legs that felt like they belonged to another. His head was scrambled and all he knew was he had to get out of the room.

The young man who had brought him the package appeared moments after Duncan pressed the buzzer. On opening the door he said, "Would you like us to re-secure the package for you?"

Duncan shook his head and glanced back to the now empty envelope. "There's no need."

Nodding in acknowledgement, the young man held the door open for Duncan to exit. "If you would like to follow me, I'll take you down to the lower level."

On walking the perimeter they passed the office occupied by Chris Broadhead, who looked up and raised a hand in farewell.

Duncan paused in his stride to respond, and stared in. Whether it was a trick of the light or the smoked effect of the glass, he was not sure, but he was certain he had seen a dark shadow flicker across the man's eyes, as though two pairs were studying him, one pair with undisguised malice. The sensation was much like when the boy had stared in at him from the crossing. Duncan blinked and shook his head, but the banker had turned away and reached for his telephone.

Duncan's heart thudded against his rib cage as he hurried after his escort, his nerves on edge. This was the second time in as many days he had seen shadow eyes. Although part of him was convinced he hadn't imagined it, he decided that perhaps it would be wise to see a doctor after all.

# 9

**P**ausing outside the terminal building of Dalaman airport, Duncan took a few moments to get his bearings. Compared to the dreary, overcast weather he had left in Gatwick, the sensation of warmth on his back and the sight of clear blue skies was heaven. Heat haze shimmered in the distance, distorting his view of faraway hills, and the pleasant aroma of flowering shrubs and bushes tickled his nostrils. His first sight of Turkey should have been idyllic, but was mixed with unease.

He felt adrift, cut off from all he knew, and had no idea what to do other than locate the mysterious Mehmet Ozric. But then what? Having studied the texts on the Apocalypse of Thomas during the flight he was none the wiser how any of it could tie in with any type of research Father Steff would have been involved with, or with the actions of Regent Kearson, and no clues suggesting Turkey as a destination. He hoped Mehmet Ozric could shed some light on matters or his trip would be a complete waste of time.

Peering down to the main car park on the level below, he spotted the taxi rank. With any luck the car arranged by the hotel was waiting there to take him to Marmaris. The little plastic wheels of his case rumbled along behind him as, with his trench-coat slung over a shoulder, he walked towards the ramp leading down. On reaching the Y-shaped junction he turned to the right, and collided with someone walking up.

The man he'd bumped into turned and fixed him with midnight eyes that twinkled in amusement. For some reason, his presence filled Duncan with something akin to awe and he found himself staring, slack-jawed, as though wanting to say something but having no idea what.

As though sensing his unease, the man smiled in reassurance.

Perhaps it was his exquisite beauty that struck Duncan dumb, but he doubted it. He felt as though he knew him from somewhere, even though he was sure they'd never met. But before he could broach the question a sharp poke in the back had him swivelling. Annoyance rose to the surface at the intrusion, which he swiftly quashed.

Standing behind him was a swarthy Turk, short and pot-bellied, shadowed growth on his chin, a stained white T shirt hanging loose over baggy trousers, the total antithesis of the man in the black overcoat.

"You Connors?"

Duncan nodded, wanting to get rid of him so he could find out more about the tall, dark stranger.

"Good. You come with me. I have taxi."

"Can't you see I'm busy?" Duncan snapped. Turning, he made to apologise to the dark man, but he had gone, and there was no sign of him nearby. Duncan scowled, and switched his attention back to the taxi driver who, arms crossed, foot beating an impatient tattoo on the concrete, glared at him.

"You coming, or you want to walk?"

After one last look for the stranger, Duncan followed the driver to his battered taxi and climbed in, annoyed by the untimely interruption.

It was when they were leaving the car park that Duncan spotted him again. He stood beside the exit, and smiled as they passed. Duncan's heart faltered as he returned the smile and raised a hand in acknowledgement, and again he wondered where he knew him from. Perplexed, he settled back for the journey, confident that the answer would come to him in due course, when he least expected it.

During the drive the taxi driver said little, content to accelerate along the road to Marmaris as though he were in a race, and curse any motorist who had the temerity to get in his way. After the first fifteen minutes of listening, the litany of abuse went over Duncan's head and he found himself ignoring it, and settled for watching the passing scenery, which helped push thoughts of the enigmatic stranger from his mind.

To his surprise, Turkey proved to be more picturesque than he expected. Instead of a land harsh and craggy, this part of the country at least was lush and verdant. The red-brown rock of the hills and mountains was covered in bushes and trees, and in the fields there were houses set amongst lime and lemon groves. But as they neared Marmaris, the landscape changed.

More and more houses appeared, and they entered an industrial area on the outskirts of the town. Shops, garages and outlets took over from green fields, and the amount of traffic increased, much to the driver's annoyance. His mutter-ings became more irate as he found himself dodging scooters that weaved in and out of the two lanes that entered the urban sprawl.

Eventually they reached the hotel, which was situated on the seafront, and the driver pulled over. Resting an arm on the back of his seat he swivelled to stare at Duncan. "We here. You get out now. I have money to make."

"I love you, too," mumbled Duncan, opening the door to let himself out and dragging his case from the seat beside him. He had no sooner shut the door than the taxi sped off, narrowly missing a collision with a scooter carrying more people than it was designed for.

"Welcome to Turkey," Duncan muttered, turning to peer up at the hotel.

Separated from the beach opposite by the busy main road, the Ketenci was a simple, modern building, five stories high with balconies dotting its frontage. To reduce the glare of sunlight off white walls, Duncan shaded his eyes with a hand as he looked up. The place looked impressive from the outside and, after a moment's inspection, he stepped up a short flight of steps and through the doors to enter the large lobby.

His room, booked over the internet, proved bright and airy with a sea view. After tossing his coat onto the bed and dumping his case he strode across the marble floor to throw open the doors leading out to the balcony. Once outside he closed his eyes and took deep, long breaths of warm air. The salty tang of the sea cleared his mind and caused a smile to form on his face. It was the first time he'd felt truly relaxed for what seemed like an age.

To his annoyance his mobile rang, and he headed back indoors to grab it from his coat, wondering who could be ringing him. He had few friends and rarely did anyone contact him; he had bought the phone in the first place because it worked out cheaper than installing a landline at his bed-sit. As far as he knew, only Father Mason had access to his number.

Thumbing the answer key, he said, "Hello?"

"Where are you?"

He instantly recognised the voice of Regent Kearson, and his mouth went dry.

"H-how did you get my number?"

"University records, Mr Connors. Now, where are you? I need to speak with you urgently, on a matter of importance to the Church."

Unprepared for questioning, especially by the likes of the Regent, he was at a loss as to what to say. "I-I'm out of the country." He winced at his answer.

There was a pause before the Regent spoke again. "Exactly *where* are you, Duncan?"

There was an undertone to the Regent's voice that set the hairs on the back of his neck to bristling. Instead of answering, he pressed the 'end call' button. For good measure, he turned off the mobile and tossed it onto the bed, then flopped down beside it, hands clasped at his belly, to lie back and stare at the ceiling, knowing it would only be a matter of time before the Regent found out where he had gone.

✶✶✶

Sitting behind his desk, Regent Kearson replaced the receiver and leaned back in his chair, long, delicate fingers steepled in front of his face.

"He's left the country."

In the chair opposite, Father Tumbletee frowned. "So soon? He told me it would be a couple of weeks before he left." Shaking his head, he pursed his lips, and then said, "The impetuosity of youth. I just hope he has made the right decision. I was rather hoping he would change his mind and continue with his studies. He had a bright future within the Church, you know."

The Regent snorted. "Really?" Rising, he moved to the small desk beside the door and dragged out the computer that was stored beneath. After placing it on the desk he turned to the priest. "Are you sure your contact can gain access to any hidden files on this?"

Father Tumbletee smiled and dipped his head. "Computers are his passion. Whatever has been hidden he can find." Arching a brow, he asked, "Anything in particular you wish me to search for?"

The Regent met his gaze, and said, "Anything that should not be there. And you are to tell no one of this. Understood?"

Father Tumbletee nodded. "You can rely on my discretion, Regent."

"I hope so."

The implied threat was not lost on the priest, who grimaced, but said nothing by way of reply.

# 10

The flicker of flames from the open fire caused shadows to dance in the dimly lit room. Situated in the catacombs beneath the most ancient sector of the Vatican, the small library that housed the Church's knowledge on the occult was cool at the best of times, and the permanently lit fire served both as a heat source and as a combatant against condensation. Although the room was fitted with the latest technological equipment to ensure constant air temperature and humidity there was nothing like an open fire to create the warm air movement that helped to keep the books in perfect condition. Also, as 'Keeper of The Knowledge', Monsignor Louvière liked the ambience the fire gave to the small, windowless room. To him, its presence helped keep Shadow at bay, and other evils that conspired against the Church.

Rising from his seat, he leaned against the table, fingers splayed, and scanned the faces of the three Bishops sat before him. Like him, they were specialists in the occult and 'Protectors of The Knowledge' and, like him, were aware of the reasons behind the World's rising level of violence, both natural and man-made.

"The Missio has left the seminary."

His words, softly spoken, had the desired impact and, as he let his gaze rest briefly on each of them, saw the shock he had felt when given the news.

"So soon? But he's not ready." Bishop Bambera glanced

to his colleagues. His small, deep-set eyes, sunk within fleshy features, flicked between them as though seeking support for his statement.

Bishop Ramerez ignored him and fixed the Monsignor with a gaze as sharp as his features. "Where is he?"

Louvière sighed, and reclaimed his seat. As ever, it was Ramerez who came straight to the point.

"We do not know where he is –" he raised a hand to forestall any questions "yet, but can surmise he will answer his calling."

"But he is untrained." Again it was Bishop Bambera who stated the obvious. "Considering his lineage, he could … he could …"

Bishop Ramerez looked across the table, a lopsided smile on his face, and said, "Bring about the End of Days?"

"Stop tormenting him, Ramerez." Sitting between them, Bishop Adams glared at him before leaning forward to rest his forearms on the polished oak surface. "Do we have any idea where he is heading for?"

Monsignor Louvière shook his head, and said, "No, but we should have that information shortly."

"But why now?" It was Bambera again. "Why up and leave before his studies were completed?"

"God moves in mysterious ways." Ramerez chuckled, and then swung his gaze to Louvière. "But he does have a point. Why now?"

Louvière bit back an angry retort, and said, "His tutor was killed in a car crash. It would appear the two were close, and that his death raised issues of Faith."

The only response from Ramerez was the raising of a brow.

"We have to protect him," said Bambera.

"Or eliminate the potential threat." Adams held Louvière's gaze, and waited for a response.

Without flinching or backing down, Louvière said, "Both options have been catered for."

★★★

Father Tumbletee pressed the 'end call' button and pocketed his mobile. Looking across the desk that separated them, he said, "He is in Turkey."

Regent Kearson leaned back in his chair, fingers steepled, and gazed at the ceiling. "And you know this how?"

Father Tumbletee shrugged. "From Father Mason's computer. Apparently he was corresponding with a Mehmet Ozric, collector of curios, who is based in Marmaris."

The Regent leaned forward and pinned Tumbletee with his gaze. "About what, precisely?"

Although his jaw worked, it took a moment for the words to spill forth. "Ab-ab – about the Apocalypse, as told by Thomas."

A thunderclap erupted as hands slammed onto the top of the desk, and the Regent rose to lean forward and glare down at his victim. "I already know this from my own feeble efforts, now tell me something I don't know."

Father Tumbletee sunk into his seat under the verbal onslaught. There was a madness lurking behind the Regent's eyes that instilled terror.

"Light! He was talking about descendants of Light!"

"Was he, now?" The Regent released the priest from his gaze and stared into the space above his head. "Anything else?"

Father Tumbletee swallowed the ball of saliva that had built up at the back of his throat. "Shadow. They spoke of Light and Shadow."

The Regent pinned him with his gaze.

"That is all I know. My contact is forwarding their emails as we speak."

The Regent nodded, and then sat back in his seat, whereupon he leaned back, hands clasped behind his head, to continue his inspection of the ceiling. "I trust you will furnish me with copies as and when they are available?"

Father Tumbletee nodded. "Of course. But there is

something else you need to know."

"Which is?"

"There are encrypted files hidden on the hard drive."

His interest piqued, the Regent turned his head to peer at him. "How long until they can be deciphered?"

The priest shrugged, and then shrank back in the seat as the Regent's gaze hardened. "I cannot say. It could be hours, it could be days. My contact is the best in the business, but even he has limits."

The Regent mulled over what he had been told for a second before saying, "You have a current passport?"

Father Tumbletee nodded.

"Good, because you will be accompanying me to Turkey." He grinned the grin of a predator. "Oh, and you had better get packed. We will be leaving at the end of the week."

Standing, the Regent clasped his hands behind his back and moved to one of the windows to gaze at the world below, and said, "So you had better organise your replacement."

# 11

Sipping a tepid cappuccino, Duncan sat at one of the outer tables of the Leidzeipleine, a cafe-cum-restaurant situated in Old Marmaris at the foot of a lane leading up to the ancient fort. He had stumbled across the cafe the previous day and loved its location. It was some way from the hustle and bustle of the main shopping area but within walking distance of his hotel, and it suited his current requirements. The effects of unaccustomed exercise carried out in temperatures nudging twenty-six degrees was taking its toll, and he felt in need of a more leisurely start to the day.

The warming rays of the early morning sun worked its magic as he sat and watched the area come to life. He had forgotten how uplifting warm, sunny days could be, and the pleasure to be gained in watching others go about their business.

Across the road shops were being opened, more people appeared on the narrow lane by the minute, and the cafe was starting to fill. Across from him, a family of four tucked into a full English breakfast, while on the outer tables small groups of Turkish men drank coffee and passed the time arguing or chatting in their native tongue. Everything appeared in harmony. After two days spent traipsing around Marmaris, a morning spent doing nothing was exactly what Duncan needed.

Up to now he had managed to locate three men called Mehmet Ozric, none of whom recognised the name Steff

Mason, or seemed likely candidates to be the priest's confidant, but there were still another two in the local telephone directory to try. They both lived on the other side of town, which would involve a lengthy taxi journey; not something he was looking forward to. From what he had seen and experienced, Turkish drivers were afflicted with lunacy.

He had been sitting at his table for over half an hour and was on to his second cup of coffee when he saw her. Dressed in a pale, knee-length skirt, sandals and tight-fitting blue T shirt, her long blonde hair tied back into a ponytail, she walked across the frontage of the cafe to make her way up the lane towards the fort. It was not just her delicate features that drew his attention; she seemed to glow with an inner fire, her sun-bronzed skin shining from within. The cup in his hand hovered in the air, halfway between the table and his mouth as he followed her every step. For some reason, his inner being cried out for him to make contact, and he set his cup on its saucer, intent on following her up the hill.

The impulse surprised him, but the need to get to know her was strong upon him. Rationality fled at the thought of losing sight of her, and he hurried to follow.

"One moment, Sir!"

Duncan swivelled at the call.

A table boy scurried towards him. "You are not paying?"

Thrusting a hand inside a trouser pocket, Duncan fumbled for his wallet, glancing over his shoulder in time to witness the girl disappear around the corner. He pulled a twenty lira note from the bundle and slapped it into the boy's hand, then turned to stride away.

"This too much, Sir," the boy shouted after him.

Duncan waved a hand in his direction and called, "Keep the change. Nice coffee."

"No need to run, Sir," the boy shouted. "Pretty lady only live up hill!"

Momentarily distracted by the lad's obvious amusement, Duncan narrowly avoided a tumble over a chair as he sped around the corner. Up ahead, the girl strolled around a curve in the lane, and Duncan increased his pace. On reaching the curve an elderly lady materialised in a doorway to his left and grabbed his arm, hauling him to a halt with a grip surprisingly strong for one so old.

"You English, yes? You come see Mamma Cass?" A skeletally thin arm emerged from beneath a black shawl to point at racks filled with bead necklaces, bracelets and ornaments on leather thongs. "Mamma Cass cheaper than Aldi, cheaper than Tesco, cheapest in Marmaris. Mamma Cass cheapy, cheapy. You like?"

The girl disappeared into a shop doorway farther up to Duncan's left. Mentally marking the spot, he turned to face the old crone whose face contained more wrinkles than he thought possible on a visage so small.

She smiled as he looked down, revealing a mouth devoid of teeth, her dark, beady eyes alight at the prospect of a sale.

"Mamma Cass cheapy, cheapy. Cheaper than Aldi, cheaper than Tesco, cheapest in Marmaris." She pointed to her rack again, and grinned.

Duncan sensed he would not get away until he bought something, and inspected the wares.

A sign beneath the beaded necklaces proclaimed, 'one lira each, or three for two lira'. Selecting three garishly beaded necklaces, he delved into his wallet and pulled out a five lira note, thrusting it into the women's outstretched hand. She made no effort to give him change. Instead, she dug in a pouch strapped around her waist and pulled out a brass safety pin with three beads on it, the middle one having a white blob with a black dot in the middle. The brooch looked like a small fish.

Mamma Cass pinned it to the breast of his T shirt, where it gleamed in the morning sun. After patting the brooch, she stepped away and smiled her gummy smile. "Mamma Cass cheapy, cheapy. Cheaper than ... "

Duncan held up his hands. "Cheaper than Aldi, cheaper than Tesco, cheapest in Marmaris."

A cackle of amusement escaped her lips, and she waved him away before turning to look for more victims.

Duncan shook his head and continued up the hill, eager to catch a glimpse of the girl again.

The door she had disappeared through stood ajar. Pausing outside, he looked up to read a sign which read, 'Mehmet Ozric, dealer in curios'. His jaw dropped. Could this be the place he was looking for? If so, spotting the girl had to be fate. He had seen a number for Ozric Curios in the book but discounted it from his search as no first name had been given.

His thoughts returned to the girl and, wanting to catch a glimpse of her, he walked past the doorway to halt at the shop's only window. Although the interior was gloomy, he spotted her, and his breath caught in his throat, all thoughts of Mehmet Ozric pushed to the back of his mind.

She was kneeling in the middle of the floor pulling stuff out of boxes to pile beside her, radiating that same healthy glow he had noticed when first he had seen her. His pulse raced and he felt suddenly warm. Damp patches sprang to life beneath his armpits, and he knew it was not solely due to the heat of the day.

As though sensing she was being observed, the girl looked up. Her eyes went wide as she spotted him and her mouth opened as if she were about to cry out.

Duncan waved his hands and stepped back. He had spotted the guard at the entrance to the fort, holstered gun at his side, and did not want to end up on the receiving end of some Turkish justice.

"It's okay!" he called. "I'm only looking for ..." his mind raced "curios!" He gave a hesitant grin.

The girl scrambled to her feet and dusted herself down before staring at him, her expression neutral.

"We're closed."

Duncan arched a brow in surprise at her American accent. For some reason he'd assumed she was European. Moving to the doorway, he popped his head through and smiled. At least he hoped it came across as a smile; now that he was this close to her his heart beat faster and he feared it would look more like a grimace.

The girl's eyes rested on the brooch pinned to his T shirt, and a wry smile appeared on her face. "I see you've been grabbed by Mamma."

"Hmmm?" Duncan looked to where she stared, and laughed. He held out the beaded necklaces he had bought and, mimicking the old lady's voice, said, "Cheapy, cheapy! Cheaper than Aldi, cheaper than Tesco, cheapest in Marmaris."

The girl giggled; the sound as bright and cheerful as the weather, and Duncan found it difficult to breathe. He could not understand it. Not usually at ease around women, he had never had one affect him this way before. And he'd actually made her laugh. What was happening to him? He had no answer to that question, and did not care. All he wanted was to speak to her for a while, get to know her. If she would let him.

"Would you mind if I looked around?"

"We're not open for another month." She glanced to the boxes littering the floor. "As you can see, I've not even stocked the place yet."

"I won't get in your way, I promise. Only, it's my third day in Marmaris and I've run out of things to do, and I've always had an interest in –" he glanced around the shelves and displays "curios."

Smiling, the girl shook her head, then glanced to the boxes again. "Well, if you've nothing better to do than poke around genuine fakes, you can help me unpack these."

"Genuine fakes?"

"Come now, you're in Turkey, the genuine fake capital of the world. These guys have things copied and made before the rest of the world knows about the original – including curios."

Her laughter was infectious and Duncan found himself laughing along with her. Stepping inside, he held out a hand.

"Duncan Connors."

"Louisa Cooke, late of Arkansas, now of Marmaris."

Her small, delicate hand felt warm and comfortable in his and he found himself reluctant to let go. Before she could consider him impolite, he released his grip, and said, "A pleasure to meet you, Louisa of Marmaris."

For some reason his comment set them to laughing again, and Duncan realised it was the first time he had ever felt comfortable in the presence of a woman. There was that special something about Louisa Cooke that warmed his spirits, and it was a feeling he liked.

\*\*\*

As the door closed on Duncan's exit, Louisa found herself staring at it in bemusement, and wondered why she had agreed to meet him for dinner that evening. Her confusion was not because she hadn't been on a date for goodness knew how long, or because she found herself *wanting* to dine with him. It was the fact that she felt drawn to him. For the first time since Brad, her ex, she was actually attracted to someone. It was stimulating, and her skin prickled with exhilaration. She had not felt this good in years. Her humour was in stark contrast to that of the previous few days, when she had been feeling strangely subdued.

The inexplicable appearance and disappearance of the man with the white hair had her feeling as though something were missing from her life. In some strange manner, his presence had filled the shop with an amity that lingered, and she longed for him to appear again, if only to prove he existed and was not some figment of her imagination.

Mehmet had seemed convinced he was real enough, especially after seeing the symbol drawn on the box. After ripping off the flap with the drawing on he had ushered Louisa upstairs and into the apartment, sitting her down and saying that he had to go someplace special, that the man posed no threat and that she should not be worried by his appearance. She tried to explain that the manifestation had not filled her with concern – quite the opposite, in fact – but Mehmet was too wrapped up in his own thoughts to take in what she was saying. After promising to return within a couple of days he told her to tell no one of the visitation, and that he would explain everything when he got back.

That had been two days ago and he still had not made an appearance, and she was eager to hear his explanation. But that would have to wait. Right now she had a date to ready for.

Turning from the door, she walked across the cluttered floor to the shop and pushed aside the beaded curtain to make her way up the stairs. The three hours spent chatting with Duncan while they unpacked, stacked, laughed, drank coffee and discussed life in Turkey had helped fill the void of the day and, although neither had spoken of their past lives, she got the impression that he could be damaged goods. But what the hell; she was old enough to take care of herself, and it wasn't as though they were serious or anything. It was only a meal, for chrissakes. If after tonight she decided he was a jerk, then nothing lost.

She was onto her fourth outfit when a voice from the living room had her flinch.

"Louisa?"

It was Mehmet.

"In here!"

Scrambling over the small mound of discarded clothing strewn over the floor, she made her way to the bedroom door and stepped out into the living room.

The raise of an eyebrow showed Mehmet's surprise at seeing her in a dress, the plunging neckline of which revealed more cleavage than she would normally show.

Grinning at the look on his face, Louisa did a twirl, arms outstretched, enjoying the feel of the light material as it swished against her skin. "Like it?"

Mehmet said nothing.

Louisa spun to a halt, having noticed the weary cast to his eyes and the haunted expression on his face. Her smile faded and she frowned. "What is it? What's wrong?"

The half-smile Mehmet conjured did little to disguise his unease. "We have to leave."

"What?"

"Right now."

"B-b-but why?"

Stepping towards her, he lightly grasped her arms and stared into her eyes. "Please, do not question me. Trust me. There are things that need to be done, need to be said, that cannot be discussed here." Unconsciously, his eyes flicked to a corner of the room before resting again on Louisa's. "Where we might be overheard."

Louisa wriggled from his grasp and folded her arms across her chest, where she rubbed at the goosebumps that had sprung to life on her bare biceps. She had never seen him like this before, agitated and wary, and it set her pulse racing for all the wrong reasons. Forcing calm into her voice, she said, "Why? What could be so important that we have to drop everything?" And her date with Duncan, she realised.

"You have to trust me like you have never trusted anyone before. Believe me, our lives are in peril should we stay. More I cannot …"

"Peril?"

Now he *was* scaring her.

He held up his hands to ward off further questioning, and said, "Please. No more. I will explain when we get to where we have to go."

Being dictated to by men was something Louisa hated, and the last thing she expected from Mehmet. She had taken years of it from Brad before she finally snapped, and she was not about to be pushed around again. Eyes narrowed, she told him so, and was shocked to see anger crease his features.

It only lasted a moment, and then he threw his arms in the air while cursing the ceiling in his native tongue. "Are all American women so stubborn?" he demanded, turning fever-bright eyes on her.

Louisa arched a brow, her lofty response a cover for the panic that bubbled near the surface.

Mehmet saw the look, sighed, and then shook his head.

"Ay yeii yeii! Louisa Cooke, you are a wilful lady." He paused for a moment, seeming to struggle with an internal dilemma before saying, "Where we have to go is where you will find out about our visitor. More, I cannot say. But is that enough for you to trust me in this?"

The mere mention of the man in black was enough to capture her interest and calm her fears. But for their lives to be at risk because of him? Her mind drifted to the mysterious manner in which he had appeared and subsequently disappeared from the shop, and she realised there were things going on that were way beyond her understanding, and that Mehmet seemed to be in the thick of it. For the second time in as many days, the hairs on the back of her neck stood on end. Only this time, they refused to lie back down.

# 12

Duncan whistled to himself as he strode along the busy quay, heading towards his hotel. To his left, gulets and launches bobbed on a gentle, sun-dappled swell. The slap of rigging and mooring ropes accompanied the cries of boat owners as they attempted to cajole passers-by to try a cruise, but he ignored their entreaties and threaded his way through tourists and locals alike, his thoughts firmly fixed on Louisa. There was something about her that ousted his usual timidity. Time had literally flown by in the short time he was with her, and he found himself looking forward to meeting with her that night. He had amazed himself when he'd asked her out for dinner, and was even more stunned when she readily accepted.

Moving aside to allow a rather large lady and her two screaming kids to pass, Duncan realised he'd forgotten to ask about Mehmet Ozric. He accepted the woman's thanks with a smile and a nod, and decided to broach the subject later – over dinner. The thought of meeting with Louisa again had him smiling, and he increased his pace, eager to get back to the hotel, even though he had a good four hours in which to prepare.

Once back in his room he grabbed a pile of books from the bedside table and moved out to the balcony, intent on whiling away an hour or two in research before getting ready. Sitting on a wicker chair, he placed his books on the glass-topped table and opened *The Secret Gospel of Thomas*, and flicked to the chapter on the Apocalypse. However, he could not get his head around it. The passages were too deep and he found himself skimming over material he should have been absorbing. For an all too obvious reason, his attention was not what it should be, and he decided to look for something lighter to read.

The book he grabbed from the table was a book on Gnosticism, and the opening chapter, entitled 'Messengers of Light', immediately grabbed his attention. Hoping for inspiration, or at least something that would keep him interested for an hour or two, he began to read, little realising that the content would keep him enthralled for far longer than he expected. Concepts were put forward that connected with the core of his being, concepts that touched on what he believed, but delved deeper.

According to the book there is but one True God that is beyond all creation. He never created anything in the sense *create* is understood, but brought forth from within all there is in the world, implying that all is in itself, a part of the One True God. As a result, every person has within them a spark of Light; a spiritual component which is a fragment of the divine essence. Although most are ignorant of this spark, salvation can be brought about through the guidance of Messengers of Light, who, through their teachings, stimulate the rise to awareness.

Although this teaching was in direct odds with all Duncan had been taught, it made perfect sense, and also cleared the reference that had been made by Steff Mason in his letter. To Duncan, it came as no surprise to learn that Christ was the foremost Messenger in history who, aided by his apostles, attempted to raise awareness for the good of the world.

Closing the book, Duncan laid it reverentially on the table and stared out to sea. In the distance, the hazy outlines of faraway mountains merged with both sea and sky, and he found himself longing for a Messenger of Christ's charisma to appear, to enlighten those whose basic nature had firmly quashed the spark of Light within. Or even men such as the apostles; men who had found their spark and could help bring to an end the ever growing chaos that was abroad in the world.

His thoughts turned to the dark stranger. In him Duncan had sensed an aura of peace and calm, a person who was at ease with himself and the environment. Could he be a Messenger? The thought had him half-smile. It would be too much to ask that it happen again. Instead of wishing for a miracle it would be better to grab the Church by the throat and shake some sense into it, get it to continue where Christ left off.

But he knew that would never happen, which was one of the main reasons he could no longer continue with his studies. Like the apostles of old, his belief was that he should be out there making a difference. He snorted in amusement at the thought. Who did he think he was; the new messiah?

Even so, as ludicrous as the idea was, he felt as though he had furthered his knowledge into what Father Mason had been researching, that by gaining a different perspective on the meaning behind religion he had glimpsed into what had lain behind the man's thoughts.

Absentmindedly, he glanced to his watch, and lurched upright. Two hours had passed and he ran the risk of being late for Louisa. Hurrying inside, he stripped off and jumped in the shower. World salvation could wait until after his date.

In a little under an hour he was sitting once again at a table in the Leidzeipleine, cradling the same cup of coffee he had been nursing for the past ten minutes. Now that he was so close to seeing her again, time dragged. But they had agreed seven, so seven it would be.

The sun had started to dip behind the hill and long shadows were creeping across the tables, but, unlike back home where it would turn cold once the sun began to set, the evening remained warm and balmy. The smell of spiced meat hung heavy in the air, aromatic and enticing, and already there were diners at the tables, eating and drinking while they chatted and laughed. To add to the ambience, the tables now sported candles, their bright flames flickering behind the coloured glass of their bowls. The smell of melted wax mingled with that of the food, and the atmosphere was one of warmth and relaxation, even though Duncan felt anything but. He was a nervous wreck.

"You find pretty lady?"

It was the table boy from earlier in the day.

Duncan smiled and nodded. "Yes, I found the pretty lady." He glanced to his watch. "In fact, I'm about to meet her again." Rising, he fished in a pocket for his wallet.

The table boy laughed. "You lucky man. Mehmet, he must be blind."

At the mention of Mehmet's name, Duncan paused to meet the lad's twinkling gaze.

"Three years she has stayed with him and does he make with her?" He pursed his lips and shook his head. "I say again, he must be blind." On seeing the wallet in Duncan's hand, he grinned and waved him away. "No, you not pay. You give too much already. This night, coffee is – how you say? – on the roof."

Duncan laughed, the action easing his nerves. "On the house."

"Ah, yes. On the house. Now, you go and enjoy. Maybe we see you later? We do good food."

"Maybe," said Duncan, smiling. He raised his wallet in thanks, and then made his way to the lane.

The walk to the curios shop did not take long. He was standing at the door within three or four minutes, adjusting the hang of his shirt before knocking. Too late, he realised he'd brought no flowers, and had no time to track down a florist to purchase some or he would be late instead of early. Raising a hand, he cursed his oversight and knocked loudly on the wooden door. But no light came on within to indicate Louisa had heard him. He knocked again, this time more loudly, to no response.

Stepping back, he peered up to the first-floor windows, but all was dark, the curtains pulled shut. Perhaps she had fallen asleep. He looked down to search for a small pebble to throw at the window.

A tug at his shirt had him flinching. He swivelled and stifled a curse of annoyance as he spotted the wrinkled face of Mamma Cass peering up at him. The last thing he needed was 'cheapy cheapy' trying to sell him more of her rubbish.

"Louisa gone."

Duncan scowled, not quite believing what he had just heard. "What?"

Meeting his gaze, Mamma Cass repeated, "Louisa gone." She tugged at his shirt again, her dark eyes unblinking and serious. "You come."

Duncan pulled away from her grasp. Louisa was gone? He could not believe it. Did not want to believe it. His gaze returned to the first-floor windows. But why else did she not answer his knock?

"Louisa gone!" There was irritation in the old woman's voice, and she tugged at his shirt again.

Snarling an oath, Duncan swatted her hand away, instantly regretting his action, but before he could apologise she grabbed at him again.

"*You come*!" There was a sharp, edgy rasp to her voice.

"*Mamma!*"

Mamma Cass swung round, and released her grip.

In the doorway to Mamma Cass's shop stood a young Turkish girl he judged to be around eighteen. She was dressed in black trousers and a loose-fitted, blousy top and wore her hair short. Her arms were folded across her chest as she looked on in disapproval. Once she had Mamma's attention she spoke to her in their native tongue, her tone containing more than a hint of reprimand.

Accompanied by much arm waving and gesturing towards Duncan, Mamma Cass responded in words that were short, sharp and clipped. Duncan could not understand a word of what was going on, but hoped the girl succeeded in preventing her from harassing him further. With the realisation he had been stood up his good humour had evaporated and he wanted to be alone with his thoughts, as maudlin as they were likely to be.

When the rant was over, the girl looked to him, her hesitant smile an indication of nervousness as she said, "Please. Mamma Cass needs to speak with you. Her English not good, so I will speak for her. Please?" She gestured towards the shop.

Mamma Cass peered up at him, eyes bright. As though coming to the conclusion he would follow, she shuffled to her shop and disappeared through the doorway. Sighing, Duncan trailed after her, even though it was the last thing he felt like doing. With Louisa gone not only was his evening ruined, but he had lost his lead to a meeting with Mehmet Ozric.

The inside of Mamma Cass's shop proved to be tiny. Crammed with crates and boxes, it was more of a storage room, the only light being that which spilled in through the doorway. It was warm and stuffy inside, and bags of herbs hung from hooks to the floor joists that supported the floor above. Their pungent aroma overrode the smell of dust and leather. In the rear wall, a beaded curtain similar to the one in the curios shop screened a door opening.

"Please sit." The girl indicated a wooden crate on the stone-slab floor.

Duncan looked at it for a moment, wondering what Mamma Cass wanted with him, then sighed and perched on a corner.

Mamma Cass pulled a canvas chair from behind a stack of boxes, unfolded it and sat opposite to peer at him, eyes unblinking. After a moment she settled back, a smile playing about her lips. Beside her, the girl shuffled her feet and looked anywhere except at Duncan as the silence dragged on.

Still raw from being stood up, and growing impatient by the lack of communication, Duncan snapped under the intense scrutiny. "What's this all about? You obviously didn't ask me in here just to stare at me." Pent-up anger bubbled forth in his words.

The girl flinched at his tone and, after a moment's pause, translated what Duncan had said.

Mamma Cass nodded as she listened, then spoke in Turkish.

"Mamma Cass says Louisa is gone," the girl translated. "With Mehmet. They left this afternoon. Mamma says they go to Mehmet's village."

Duncan's shoulders sagged at the news, and he sighed. So, they were more of a couple than he had been led to believe. That would explain a lot. But why string him along like she had? There was no point.

The old lady spoke again.

"Mamma says she tell you where village is, then you go help."

Duncan frowned. He looked to the girl, and said, "With what?"

The wait for her to interpret what Mamma Cass said was frustrating, more so as she seemed to struggle with the translation.

"Mamma Cass say you are of Light and Shadow and what you seek is not what you find. And what you discover will not be what you seek. Without your help, Shadow will rule Light, and this cannot be. Mehmet knows this, but not how to keep balance. He is of Truth. He needs you. You help. The spirit of Life in Louisa is not enough. You must go also."

The mention of Light and Shadow brought the hairs on the back of Duncan's neck to standing. The book on Gnosticism had broached the very same subject, and he began to wonder if he had inadvertently stumbled onto the crux of Father Steff's research.

Mamma Cass spoke again, and the intensity of her gaze as she directed her words at him sent a shiver down his spine.

In translation, she'd said, "Both Light and Shadow want you. In you is power. In you is Light and Shadow. In you is balance."

77

Breaking free of her gaze, Duncan massaged his eyes with his fingertips while trying to make sense of what he had heard, but it was akin to collecting water in a sieve. As soon as he attempted to hold onto the concept, it trickled away. He sensed it had something to do with the divine spark. But what?

Mamma Cass spoke again, and he looked up. There was something about the reverential manner in which she said the words that set his pulse to racing.

"Mamma Cass says to take heed of the Guardian. In him is true Light," said the girl.

His fingers slid down to pull at his cheeks as he stared at the old woman. The man at the airport – she had to mean him. Could he be a Messenger; a modern-day Christ?

On seeing his reaction, Mamma Cass dipped her head, the glint of understanding in her eyes. She spoke again, this time with words of instruction.

"Mehmet and Louisa gone to Olukbasi. It is far and you will need car. They are in danger and need your help. If you do not go, they will fail."

Duncan let go of the breath he never realised he'd been holding. Adrenaline coursed through his body. Even though he had only known Louisa a short while, he knew he must go to her aid. His gut feeling was that the Guardian would expect him to do so. The emotion was strong and compulsive, and could not be denied.

The smile on Mamma Cass's face deepened, and the wrinkles on her face turned into furrows at the expression. She rose to her feet, nodded once in his direction, and then moved outside.

Duncan switched his attention to the girl, and in a quiet, determined voice said, "Any idea where I can get the best deal on a car?"

Once outside he strode down the hill to the main town and headed for the car rental showroom the girl had recommended. Too wrapped up in his own needs, he remained blissfully unaware that he was being followed.

# 13

With one hand grabbing the handle over the door, booted feet braced against the dash, Louisa winced as the jolt from a pothole sent a jab of pain up her spine. Convinced the suspension of Mehmet's old jeep had collapsed at the impact, she turned and cast him a worried look.

Unconcerned, he grinned. In the half-light of dusk it looked almost feral. Or insane, she amended, given the speed he was gunning the battered vehicle up the tortuous mountain track. The jeep was barely fit for the road, and since they had left tarmac some twenty minutes ago, it showed. Behind them, a dirty-brown dust cloud marked their passage.

To the left of the hive-lined track, rugged hills rose sheer. Twisted pine, shrubs and olive trees clung to the scree-strewn slopes as though fearing a sharp gust of wind would send them toppling, while to the right, a precipitous drop lay in wait for the careless driver, falling to the shadowed valley far below. Lights winked amongst lime and lemon groves at its base, a positive sign of civilisation. Although what classed as civilisation up here was sure to be far removed from what Louisa was used to.

She glanced at her watch, and her thoughts turned to Duncan. She wondered how he had taken being stood up. It was seven-thirty and she should have been with him now, the only man she'd felt physically attracted to in years, enjoying an evening of good food and good company. Instead of which she was stuck on a road leading to the back of beyond having spent three hours travelling, most of it in silence. It would not have been so bad if Mehmet had told her what the trip was about, but he had said little, if anything, since they'd left the apartment. Knowing how stubborn he could be, she'd decided it best to leave the matter alone until they reached their destination. She hoped the wait was worth it, otherwise he would be on the receiving end of her frustration at having to miss her date.

A shiver coursed through her, and she hugged her light-weight jacket closer. The pine-scented air had a definite chill to it.

In a screech of brakes, the jeep ground to a halt, throwing Louisa forward to send her unbound hair whipping around her face.

"What the … " Pushing errant locks behind her ears, she stared through the dust-caked windscreen at the road ahead. "Goats!"

Tapping the horn, Mehmet eased his way through the twenty or thirty goats that milled along the track. Reluctantly, they scrambled out of the way.

"That a good sign. Five minutes and we will be home."

Louisa grimaced. His home, not hers. Whatever it was that had driven Mehmet to leave the warmth and comfort of their apartment behind must be serious.

But how was she involved? Why did she have to come away with him? Mehmet had told her it was to do with the stranger she'd met, but how could that be so? She had not felt any threat from him, certainly nothing to warrant such alarm. Quite the opposite, in fact. Was it because she had seen him that she had to leave as well? She didn't understand it, and the more she thought about it the more elusive the answer appeared to be.

The trail wound through two rock piles, after which it continued for a further mile before opening out in front of a cluster of shacks perched on the slopes of the surrounding hills. Terraced pastures bordered by hives surrounded the ramshackle buildings, some fenced to keep chickens, donkeys and livestock in, and others to keep them out. A number of homes had satellite dishes fixed to the walls and Louisa was sure she spotted at least two Volvo Estates tucked away behind some hedging.

As they drove through, the few inhabitants out working their pastures looked up. On seeing Mehmet they waved, smiles creasing their sun-browned faces. Mehmet waved back, his features relaxed and at ease for the first time since they'd left Marmaris. And she had to admit that the village exuded a sense of peace and tranquillity, not dissimilar in fact, she thought, to the atmosphere created by her friend, the manifestation.

For some strange reason Duncan also sprang to mind. Then again, perhaps it was not so strange. She would like to meet both men again, and sometime soon.

"My house," said Mehmet, pulling up beside a wooden shack that looked much like the rest.

"You have Sky?" Louisa asked, peering across him to stare at the distinctive white dish.

"Of course." He smiled in amusement, and pointed to a line of poles that dotted the hillside opposite. "Electricity. You think because we live in the mountains we are backward?"

Louisa's spirits rose further at the discovery he had power and TV. Grabbing her overnight bag from the footwell, she followed him into the building where, to her disappointment, inside, it looked much what it was from the outside – a wooden building with a corrugated tin roof. The smell of fusty air had her wrinkling her nose.

"Welcome to my country home, Louisa Cooke." Mehmet bowed theatrically, and beckoned her in with a wave of an arm.

She stood at the threshold for a moment, not knowing whether to laugh or cry before she stepped haltingly forward to flick her gaze around the primitive accommodation.

As though sensing her disappointment, Mehmet straightened, and shrugged. "I know it is nothing special, but it has been in my family for generations. I do not come here much

81

so it is …" he looked around, "a little uncared for."

Louisa smiled. "It's fine – really."

She scanned the sparsely furnished room again in an attempt to convince herself it was not that bad, but failed. With its moth-eaten sofa, tin sink, pantry cupboard, antique cooker, rickety table and chairs, it was the direct opposite of what she was used to, and hoped they did not have to stay for too long. She found her eyes drawn to the plasma TV and Sky box in the far corner. They looked so out of place nestled in the recess between the soot-blackened hearth and the wooden wall. But at least they were something from the modern world to remind her of what she had left.

Moving across the building's only room to the stone chimney on the right gable wall, Mehmet delved in a pocket of his black combat jacket for some matches. He stooped, struck a match and then held it to the kindling beneath the pyramid of twigs that had been laid in the hearth. As soon as it caught he turned to Louisa. "Please, sit down. I will turn on the TV and it will soon feel like home. Yes?"

Although she was sure nothing could ever make the place seem like home, she did feel more comfortable once seated.

After tossing her the remote, Mehmet continued to feed the fire, placing on larger branches and chunks of wood from the pile beside the hearth until it blazed, releasing the pungent aroma of burning pine.

"Now I will make coffee."

Rising, he moved across the room to the cupboard.

Louisa began to flick through the channels on the TV, absently surfing in an attempt to find one that was not in Turkish. Eventually she settled for Sky News, which was showing footage of riots in France. Images of cars burning, kids throwing rocks, police being shot at and a body lying on the road did little to lift her spirits, so she moved on. Another news channel and yet more bloodshed. This time in Afghanistan, where war was in full flow, the underlying headline informing the viewers that a meeting of the world's superpowers was to be held later that month in Istanbul to discuss the prospect of the conflict spreading. Fed up with images of war, she flicked through to a music channel and then shuffled out of her jacket.

"Ah, music. That is good," said Mehmet. He cocked an ear in appreciation to listen to Coldplay before thrusting a steaming mug into her hands, and then settled, cross-legged on the floor in front of her.

"It's a darn sight better than watching people kill each other," Louisa murmured before taking a sip of her drink. She closed her eyes and savoured the flavour of the coffee as it worked its way down to her stomach to warm her from within.

"You are right, Louisa. There is too much killing and violence in the world, and it is getting worse."

Only half-interested in continuing the topic of conversation, she asked, "Why's that, do you suppose?"

Mehmet shrugged. "It has always been man's way. What one man has another man wants, so he takes."

"That simple, eh?" She smiled as she said the words, to show she was teasing.

"No, it is not that simple. Maybe once, long ago, but not now."

"Hmm?" Louisa peered across her half-raised mug, and frowned. There was something about the way in which he said 'not now' that caught her attention. "What do you mean?"

He smiled. The expression chased shadowed concern from his features. "Nothing that cannot wait until the morning." He rose to his feet, and said, "I have to go now. If I do not visit my uncle he will never forgive me. I would take you but he is not comfortable with strangers, and can be very rude." He shrugged in acceptance that that was the way it was, then said, "There are blankets in the cupboard, and wood to keep the fire burning. I am sure you will be fine until morning."

"Why? Aren't you coming back?"

Mehmet laughed. "There is only one bed, and you are sitting on it. So I will sleep at his home. He will not mind.

There is plenty of food if you feel hungry. Get some rest; we have far to walk in the morning."

With that, he took his mug to the sink and then moved towards the door.

"Wait!" Louisa rose from the sofa to face him. He could not leave her just like that, without even a hint as to why they were here.

Mehmet paused with his hand on the latch. "You will be safe here. No one will harm you."

Louisa sighed. "Why are we here? Why am *I* here? You haven't told me a darn thing since we left Marmaris."

His features darkened, but not through anger. Louisa recognised the wariness he had shown when telling her they must leave.

"Tomorrow, Louisa. Answers best left until we are both rested and less tired. Please, you have trusted me this far, just wait a little longer and I will tell you what you want to know."

Without waiting for her to respond, he ducked out of the door and closed it softly behind him. The sound of his footsteps receded as he walked away.

Louisa scowled and ran to the window to watch as he crossed the track to walk deeper into the village. Noting the house he eventually entered, she decided to follow. Somehow, she doubted he *had* to go see his uncle and she wanted some answers. This was one mushroom that hated being kept in the dark.

Grabbing her coat from where she had tossed it on the sofa, she opened the door and padded out. The air was even colder now that night had fallen. By the time she reached the shack Mehmet had entered she was frozen, and wished she had thought to put on a sweater.

The sound of raised voices drove away such concerns and she ducked to work her way closer to a partially open window. On peering in she saw Mehmet gesticulating as he shouted. His dark eyes were flashing in anger, and his shoulder-length hair danced in outrage as he shook his head.

Unbowed by Mehmet's verbal onslaught an aged man sat at a slatted wooden table, elbows planted in defiance, chin resting on clasped hands. Although old, his eyes gleamed brightly with intelligence while, behind him, an elderly woman ignored the commotion and prepared supper.

Louisa cursed herself for a fool as she listened in. Although she had picked up some Turkish in the time she had lived in the country, they spoke too fast for her to interpret what they were arguing about.

After a couple of minutes spent ranting, Mehmet appeared to run out of steam and slumped in a chair to bow his head and run hands through his hair. Voice subdued, he asked a question. Although spoken in Turkish, Louisa recognised the words.

"Are you with me in this?"

The elderly man nodded, and then rose to grab a bottle of whisky and two tumblers from the worktop near his wife. He slid a tumbler to Mehmet and poured two generous tots.

Not sure what she had just witnessed, Louisa crept away, knowing that any answers would have to wait until the morrow, whether she liked it or not.

***

The smell of coffee and someone banging around the stove roused Louisa from a deep, dreamless sleep. She ran a hand through tousled hair and opened her eyes to blink them into focus before stretching. Even though her thoughts had been in turmoil when she'd settled onto the sofa the night before, she felt surprisingly refreshed.

"Something smells good," she said, covering her mouth with a hand to stifle a yawn before tossing aside the blanket to swing her legs to the floor. The touch of wood on bare feet had her wriggling her toes. The feel was rough compared to the marble floors of the apartment back in Marmaris.

Sunlight streamed in through a window and she could see dust motes in the air; sparkling as they drifted, and even though the fire had burned down hours ago, the warmth from the early morning sun had heated the shack to a comfortable temperature.

Mehmet appeared from around the back of the sofa and thrust a steaming mug of coffee into her hands.

"Thanks."

"Feeling better now you have slept?" he asked, pulling a chair round from the table and taking a seat.

Louisa nodded, and took a sip of her drink.

"I have prepared breakfast of sweet bread and meat. It is on the table when you are ready."

Louisa smiled her thanks. "What time is it?"

"Six-thirty, and we must be away soon. There is much to do, and to explain."

Mehmet held her gaze and she felt her heart quicken. The time for answers loomed.

"My uncle is coming with us. He knows these hills as well as I, and it is always best to be prepared."

Prepared for what he did not say, but anyone who could stand up to Mehmet in full rant was welcome along, in her view.

Within the hour they were knocking at the door to Mehmet's uncle's shack. At Mehmet's suggestion, Louisa wore jeans, a sweatshirt and heavy walking boots while he, dressed in similar fashion, had a coil of rope thrown over a shoulder.

The old man came to the door within moments and, after a curt call of farewell to his wife, stepped outside. Like Mehmet, he too had a coil of rope looped over a shoulder and was prepared for walking. Unlike Mehmet, however, the look he gave Louisa was not overly warm and friendly.

Seeing the old man's sour expression, Mehmet said, "Louisa Cooke, meet Hiki Ozric." Leaning forward, he whispered loudly, "Do not worry, he is not as feeble as he looks."

Hiki grimaced. "Not so feeble I can't slap you." Turning on his heel, he led the way out of the village, northwards, in the direction they had arrived from late the previous day.

Mehmet grinned. "Ignore him; he is always grumpy in the morning. But he gets better as the day goes on."

Louisa was not so sure. Having witnessed their heated discussion the previous night she knew his mood had everything to do with her and not the hour of the day. Yet another puzzle to add to her lengthening list.

Upon leaving the confines of the village they entered woodland. The smell of pine was heavy in the air and the drone of bees a constant companion. Warming rays of sunlight filtered through the leafy canopy as they walked, to cast a green-tinged light to the overgrown, meandering trail they followed. After twenty, tiring minutes of walking, Mehmet decided to open conversation.

"Where we go is a place of great secrecy."

Ahead, Hiki paused to look back, and shook his head.

"My people have known of it since … forever, and have been guardians of it for as long."

"Guardians?"

Mehmet held up a hand to silence her, then used it to hold back a branch that was in danger of whipping back across the track.

Walking on, he said, "The Cavern of Rebirth. It is a mystic place, and some say it is the centre of all that is good about the world. That it was at this place mankind first learned of love and the balance."

Now she was confused. What had love and balance to do with any of this?

By way of explanation, Mehmet said, "Without dark we cannot appreciate the light, and love is the same. In a world without fear and hate how could we appreciate love?"

Louisa interjected, unsure what he was getting at. "But surely a world without fear and hate is what we strive for, isn't it?"

Mehmet turned to her and grinned. "That is my point exactly. It is what we strive for. It is a balance. We need the bad to attain the good, for without the bad what is there to seek?"

Ducking beneath an overhanging branch, she said, "I-I don't understand. What has that to do with … anything?"

"It has everything to do with it. Now, we are nearly there."

Ahead, Hiki halted and unlooped the rope from his shoulder. After tying one end around a tree he threw the free end through a screen of bushes. By the time Louisa and Mehmet arrived he had already eased himself through and commenced his descent.

"It is not far to climb," said Mehmet. "Only ten or twelve feet."

What he had not said was that below the ledge they were descending to the sheer face of the boulder-strewn slope dropped for a further hundred feet, to a dried-up riverbed. The water-worn rock called to Louisa as she peered down, and she felt her pulse quicken. Moisture slicked her palms, and she licked at lips suddenly dry.

Scrambling away from the edge, she remained on her hands and knees, breathing deeply in an attempt to quiet the beating of her heart.

Mehmet stooped beside her, an arm resting lightly around her shoulder. "What is the matter?"

Aside from the constant drone of bees, there was nothing to disturb the quiet, and Louisa imagined her scream of terror echoing through the hills as she slipped and fell to the rocks below.

"I-I can't do it. I can't go down there. I-I'll fall."

Gripping her shoulders, Mehmet held her gaze, and said, "You can do it, and you will. For inside that cavern is the answer to what you wish to know."

From below, Hiki's voice boomed out. "Where are you?"

"Coming!" Mehmet shouted, holding Louisa's gaze. "Come. I will help you."

He rose to his feet, lifted the coil of rope from his shoulder and then held out a hand to help her rise. Once she was standing he tied the rope around her waist and then moved to wrap it around a tree trunk near to the slope's edge.

"Take the rope my uncle fixed and grasp it, then begin to step backwards to the edge. The slope is not that steep and you will be able to walk down. Do not worry, because I have you. You cannot fall."

Louisa grasped the rope, and froze. She could not do it. There was no way she could lower herself over the edge. Her legs felt weak, her grip slippery.

"You must do it, Louisa. You must. There is no other way."

She swallowed the bile that had risen in her throat and, one faltering step at a time, moved towards the edge.

"Keep looking at me, Louisa. Hold onto my eyes. My eyes are everything."

Her right foot slithered over the edge and she screamed. For a split second the drone of the bees stopped, then recommenced as if nothing had happened.

"I have you. Do not fear. You cannot fall."

Louisa fixed on to his gaze and planted her foot firmly on the slope, then brought her left one to bear, surprised when she did not slip.

"There. You have it. See? It is not so hard. Slowly, slowly, and you will be there in no time."

To her astonishment, he was right. Even taking into account her excruciatingly slow progress, her feet hit solid rock in under two minutes, and Mehmet landed lightly beside her less than thirty seconds later.

Grinning, he said, "Easy, hey?"

Her smile was forced as she stood rooted to the spot, afraid to move in case she slipped from the ledge, which was wider than it looked from above. In her mind, she could still picture the dried riverbed below, and imagine the injuries caused by impact.

Mehmet untied her rope and moving to his left, held on to her arm and tugged her after him. After four paces the ledge opened out into a hollow in the rock. Three metres wide and two high, it was plenty big enough to enter, and Louisa flopped through. Relief that she was still alive washed over her. The noise of her landing echoed hollowly around her, and she looked up to gape in amazement.

The echo of Mehmet's laughter bounced off the cavern walls.

"Welcome to the place where all of your questions will be answered, Louisa Cooke."

# 14

Although the cavern was no larger than a tennis court, Louisa felt dwarfed as she stood at its entrance. Sunlight reflected off limestone, giving the craggy rock an eerie quality, and there was a pervading aura of peace and tranquillity that made her feel small and inconsequential. She walked farther in, opened her arms, looked up to the low ceiling, closed her eyes and slowly spun, absorbing the essence of the place. Her eyes opened at the sound of Mehmet's low chuckle, and she halted her twirl to raise a brow in query.

Smiling, Mehmet stepped forward to grasp an arm and turn her. He nodded towards a small opening in the rear right corner, and said, "Through there is better surprise."

Her nose twitched as she stared at the dark entrance. Something was burning. The smell reminded her of the oil-soaked straw her father would use to ignite the bonfires back home on the farm.

"It is Hiki," said Mehmet, by way of explanation. "He has gone to prepare. It is dark further in."

Louisa had forgotten all about the old man. Keeping close to Mehmet, she let him lead the way, and stooped to enter the low opening. The smell of burning was stronger inside the tunnel, and her eyes began to water.

"Not far to go," said Mehmet, looking back over his shoulder.

She saw his shadowed smile of reassurance in what little light filtered through from the first chamber, and nodded.

Enclosed spaces she was fine with, it was heights that gave her the jitters.

Accompanied by the echo of footsteps and the sound of their breathing, they walked on, and the acrid smell of smoke grew stronger. A sound began to impinge on her awareness and she detected dampness in the air. The noise was water, she realised, rushing over rocks.

When they emerged into a cavern three times the size of the first she saw the reason why, and stood immobile, mesmerised as Mehmet stepped to the side to allow her an unrestricted view.

Torches spluttered in sconces set in the rock every four or five metres around the perimeter. Their flickering flames caused shadows to dance to a rhythm only they could hear, while the craggy roof arched high overhead, cloaked in darkness, a natural well for the rising smoke. But it was the stream that bisected the cavern that grabbed her attention. The water was crystal clear. It spewed from a hole in the far wall to cascade into a winding channel worn smooth by countless years of erosion before disappearing down a crevice to her left. A bridge consisting of five planks spanned the two-metre-wide tract of water, giving access to the slab on the other side, and on that slab stood Hiki, arms folded across his chest, a glower on his wizened features. But even his obvious displeasure could not detract from the sense of harmony she felt.

Oblivious to Hiki's antipathy, Mehmet smiled and threw wide his arms. "Welcome to the Cavern of Rebirth." He stepped forward and indicated for her to follow. "Come, there is more to see."

Intrigued, Louisa asked, "How did this place get its name?"

Mehmet halted and turned to face her. "What do you see?"

Louisa again looked around the cavern, luxuriating in the tranquillity. She had never felt so at peace in her life. "Where do I start?" she asked, her voice an awestruck whisper.

Mehmet laughed, the laugh of a man pleased at her reaction to his surprise. "Partly it is the stream that gives the cavern its name." He pointed to where the water spurted out of the rock. "Like life itself, pure, it enters in a rush, to run its course before leaving this world, contaminated and moving to another plane. There is another reason, one that will become clear in a little while." His warm smile forestalled any questioning, and he walked towards the bridge. "Come. There is something I want to show you. Something that will raise as many questions as it answers."

His voice echoed hollowly around the cavern as she followed him. A frown of puzzlement tugged at her brow. She had far too many questions already without any more being tagged on.

As if frozen in place, Hiki still stood on the slab of rock. The glower on his face had not lessened and remained fixed in position when he moved to the side to allow her to step off the makeshift bridge. As she made to nod her thanks, her eyes fastened on a semi-circle of small mounds she had not noticed before. The mounds looked like stalagmites; white calcium spires tinged with orange from the glow of the torches. There were thirteen of them, spread equally around the rock wall that circled the slab. Four of them had what appeared to be necklaces around their trunks; medallions held in place on leather thongs.

"What are they?" asked Louisa, gazing at them. The small discs looked to be made of copper, and each had slots set in a series of patterns.

"Why not go and see?" said Mehmet, with a sweep of an arm. "And tell me which one calls to you."

There was an underlying excitement to his words that caused her to hesitate, and she threw him a puzzled look before flicking her gaze over the pillars with the medallions. Behind her, Hiki growled like someone with catarrh in their throat.

"There is no danger. Please, move closer and tell me which one calls to you."

This time the tone in his voice was one of soothing persuasion. Stepping forward, she moved towards the first of the pillars, stooped to inspect the slots on the disc, and gasped. They formed the same design as that drawn on the box by the dark man; a stylised drawing of cupped hands and a bird flying free. She looked to Mehmet, who nodded once, eyes hooded.

She reached out to touch the disc, her fingers brushing the cold surface to trace the design. It seemed to glisten with an inner fire under the light from the torches, but no sensation other than the coolness of metal came to her.

"That one is not for you." Mehmet's words were calmly spoken, and he bade her move to another.

The slots on the next medallion formed a circle with a crescent moon floating above. Again, the only sensation she felt as she traced the design was the coolness of its surface, so she moved on.

This time, the design was that of an arrow pointing up, the tip shaped to resemble a fir tree. Even as she approached, she felt drawn to it. Her heart beat faster and her flesh tingled, as though adrenaline coursed out of control through her body, and she felt faint. As she reached out to trace the pattern with her fingertips her arm shook, and she could feel an aura of expectation in the air. The surface of the disc was hot to the touch and she snatched back her hand, and almost lost her balance.

Unseen by Louisa, Hiki's eyes widened at her reaction, and he stepped forward to grasp Mehmet's arm, his grip strong, his gnarled fingers digging into flesh.

"Reach out and grasp it, Louisa Cooke. It is yours to take."

Although softly spoken, Mehmet's words roused her from her shock. She licked at dry lips and cast him a swift, nervous glance before plucking the courage to reach for the medallion again.

"Remove it from the pillar, Louisa."

She grasped the thong, slid it free, and then rose to her

feet to hold the medallion in front of her face. She stared at the simplistic beauty of the piece. How could something so innocent cause such a reaction?

"Now place it around your neck and let the disc rest against your flesh."

Seemingly of their own volition, her arms rose to place the leather loop over her head, despite an inner reluctance to do so. Protected by her sweatshirt she could feel nothing, and released the breath she had been holding. Then, after easing her ponytail free of the leather, one hand moved to the disc while the other loosened the sweatshirt to allow it to drop through. She winced as the metal rested against skin, expecting searing heat to burn into her, to brand her, but instead, a warming glow asserted itself. It flowed from the disc to spread through every fibre of her being. She closed her eyes in ecstasy and leaned back, arms wide, body arched to the cavern roof as though some invisible hand supported her weight. Her whole being was alive, glowing with sensation, tingling with expectation. She could feel the brush of a breeze against bare flesh, smell the acrid reek of fire, taste the mineral scent of water, hear the gurgle of the stream, all with heightened senses. It was unlike anything she had experienced in her life, and she knew there could be nothing to match it.

Her very core opened up to the power, and her body strained with overwhelming sensation, threatening to burst like an over-inflated balloon. With eyes screwed shut, she fought to retain her identity. On reaching the point where she thought she could take no more the sensitivity lessened and the rush of elation subsided. Drained, she fell to her hands and knees and gasped for breath. Tears sprang unbidden to her eyes. Now that the rush of elation had gone she felt as though part of her had been ripped out, that something was missing, and a hand flew to feel the shape of the disc beneath her sweatshirt. It warmed at her touch, and she sobbed in relief.

An arm wrapped around her shoulder, and she flinched.

"The spirit of Light has not left," Mehmet whispered into her ear. "It will always be there. It is a part of you. What you felt, in here –" he tapped an index finger to her chest, "was rebirth. Like me, you are of the Light."

Although she heard his words, they made no sense, nor explained what had happened to her. Wiping tears from her eyes with the back of a hand, she met his gaze. "W-w-w …"

"Shhh!" Mehmet placed a forefinger to her lips. "Say nothing. Hiki has prepared something to eat. We will talk soon."

He guided her to where Hiki sat on the ground beside the bridge and bade her be seated. Once she was settled the old man handed her some bread and a bottle of water.

"You will feel better once you have eaten," said Mehmet.

Too many questions crowded into her head, questions that needed answers, but Mehmet forestalled them with the palm of a hand. "Eat, and I will talk. You listen.

"Remember when we were in my home and you asked why there was so much killing in the world?"

Mouth crammed with bread, Louisa nodded. She was ravenous.

After a quick glance to Hiki, who – to her surprise – nodded encouragement, Mehmet continued. "It is all to do with balance; of Light and Shadow. Or, as most would understand, good and evil. We need one to appreciate the other. Without evil how can we recognise good? And without good, how will we know what is evil? Sometimes good is stronger and the world is filled with peace and understanding, and other times evil takes control and the world is filled with fear and war. But always the Light will draw back the balance. Whereas Shadow seeks to dominate, to rule, to crush, Light seeks to keep the balance and prevent such a state.

"In the world today, Shadow dominates and Light is losing the battle. This I can feel. For too long mankind has harboured the shadows, and now they take form, creating war where once there was peace, famine where once there was feast, and hatred where once there was love. Light is losing the battle, and darkness looms."

Mehmet grinned without humour. "I see I have confused you. Let us imagine a corner in your home; a bright, sunny corner next to a window where you place your favourite chair. You fill this corner with flowers, your favourite photographs and only think good thoughts when you sit there. In time the corner becomes a place of love and peace, somewhere to go when harmony is needed. In days, weeks, or even years, this love and peace will spread to encompass the room, so whenever you go to the room it fills you with gladness. But what if you carry this feeling out of the room and into the hallway, and when that is filled, to the next room, and so on until the whole house is filled with good feelings? And what if you then move out into your neighbour's house and fill that with love? Will not the whole world eventually be filled with love?"

He shook his head, lips compressed. "If it were not for the frailties of mankind that would be so. But it is too easy for people to see the bad in things, to desire that which others have, to take that which is not theirs. As with Light, Shadow is in us all, and will seek to dominate those who are weak, who cannot resist temptation. It only takes one voice of discontent for it to begin its work, and undo all that Light has created. And so darkness spreads, casting shadow onto harmony. But no matter how many shadows take hold there has always been the Light to create a balance. Only now, that balance is tilting too far towards darkness. In much the same way that love and harmony can spread, darkness has taken hold, and will not stop until it has what it desires. Total control."

A torch crackled and Louisa flinched, roused from the hypnotic effects of Mehmet's words. "I-I don't understand. What has that to do with what happened to me?" A hand reached for the now familiar shape of the disc beneath her sweatshirt. Mehmet's words had explained nothing, only created more questions, as he had forewarned.

Hiki gazed at her with newfound respect in his dark eyes, and said, "You are of Light, Louisa Cooke. In you is Life."

Mehmet rose to his feet and walked to the pillar which held the disc engraved with the scales. Reverentially, he lifted it and placed it around his neck, closing his eyes for a moment when it rested against his skin. To Louisa's eyes he appeared to shudder in pleasure at the contact.

Once seated again he met her querying gaze, and said, "In me is Truth."

Wanting more, Louisa asked, "What are we?"

"That is a difficult question to answer fully. We are of Light." He shrugged. "Descendants of the original thirteen."

"O-original thirteen?"

Mehmet nodded, his face solemn. "In ages past there was a messenger and his twelve disciples of Light. It was they who thrust back the last attempt by darkness to dominate, and they who perished for the cause. But their job was done. They succeeded in resurrecting the spark that lies within here" – he placed a hand on his chest for emphasis – "to bring salvation to the world. And, in doing so, created a legend."

The reference was too obvious to miss, and Louisa gasped. "You mean …"

"We are direct descendants of Christ and his twelve disciples. In us lies the power to repel Shadow. In us lies the well-being of our world."

"Us? Just us?" she looked to the pillars. "But there are still two medallions left, and the others have been taken, so there must be more." She felt a well of panic rise within her breast.

With a shake of his head, Mehmet met her troubled gaze. "Besides we two, only two more are left to carry the fight. The lines of the others have come to an end, and with their passing, their cipher also." A momentary shadow clouded his eyes, gone in an instant. Leaning forward, he said, "How did you choose Marmaris as your destination?"

The question confused her for a moment, and she

stammered as she tried to reply. Partly because the question had come straight from left field, and partly because she feared the way she had chosen would come across as childish. "I-I-I opened an atlas at the page showing Europe, closed my eyes and stabbed a finger on the page. The country it pointed to was Turkey, so I did the same on the page for Turkey." She gave a hesitant smile. "And here I am."

"You were drawn here, Louisa. Do you not see? The Light called you, and you answered. It was your destiny. As soon as I saw you I knew why you were in Marmaris, even though you did not. And I knew that the shadows were loose in the world." His eyes glazed over, "And that we would be called. Like you, the other two will also be drawn here, and then our work begins."

The medallion pulsed against Louisa's chest, reminding her she still clenched it through her sweatshirt. "What are these shadows?"

The question snapped Mehmet back from wherever his thoughts had taken him. "They are a physical form of pure evil. Remember the room? And how it can be given harmony and love? Well so can badness. When enough evil exists in one area, it gathers force until it takes form."

"You mean, like people? Shadows are people?"

Mehmet shook his head. "No. Not people. Within people. Darkness is an essence; something you can feel but cannot touch, sense but cannot see. But it is there, waiting for rebirth." On seeing her grip tighten on the medallion, he nodded. "Much like with Light, only worse. Rebirth for a shadow is what it says. It is possession at birth. Only it does not enhance the balance within the newborn." He slapped a hand to his chest for emphasis, "It destroys it. There is no balance, only dominance. Only Shadow."

If she had not experienced the effects of the disc she would have dismissed Mehmet's explanation as the stuff of fantasy, but she knew it to be true. "But why?"

It was Hiki who answered.

"To bring about the ultimate evil."

Mehmet expanded. "If enough badness is carried out in the name of evil, then that too will gain form. And if that happens nothing can stop it from taking control. We will become its playthings, its pets. War, rape, famine, disease and conflict will rule, and Light will be extinguished. We, and two others, are the last of the pure line. It is we four who must confront the shadows and prevent the End of Days."

Silence settled on the cavern at his words. Even the gurgle of water and splutter of torches appeared subdued. The image of the stranger in the shop sprang to life in Louisa's mind and she gasped, eyes wide in sudden knowledge.

"The dark man! He is one of us, too!"

Her excitement faded as Mehmet shook his head.

"Louisa, he is not one of us. He is of us. He *is* the Light. The Guardian is the one we were born to protect."

# 15

Sarah screamed. She was in agony. It felt as though her insides were being torn apart. With eyes screwed shut, her fingers scrabbled at the tiled floor of her kitchen as she willed it to be over. Another spasm rippled through her gut, and another scream came from a throat made raw. Where in hell's name were they? She'd phoned what felt like hours ago and the girl on the other end said they would be there right away. She had even told them she was on her own and that there was no one nearby to help, and detailed the exact route to her cottage in case they got lost in the lanes. Where were they, the bastards?

The face of another bastard flashed into her head; the too handsome, too perfect bastard who had got her into this mess and then ran as soon as he found out she was pregnant, back to his bitch of a wife! Whatever happened to his promise of 'never-ending love', and "I'll tell her soon, don't worry. You're the one for me. I'm just waiting for the right moment"?

Her back arched off the floor as a wave of intense pain pushed down from her belly. The baby was coming.

Sarah started to cry. She had not wanted it to be like this, on a cold, tiled floor, surrounded by a cooker, a fridge, some kitchen units and a washing machine, the smell of last night's lasagne in the air. Where were they? Didn't they care?

A cool breeze washed over her face, and the eyes she'd screwed shut snapped open. Someone was in the house!

Fighting back the pain, she raised her head from the floor. Her vision swam as she stared at the doorway. There *was* someone there! She could see him, dressed in black, distorted and blurred through her tears.

"About bloody time," she growled through gritted teeth.

Another wave of pain had her gasping, back arched and fingers scrabbling.

A hand, cool and gentle, rested on her forehead, pushing her down, and she flinched, but with its touch came easement. Although awareness remained, she felt detached, remote from the ravaging of her body, which she knew continued the process of birth. Had he given her drugs? If so, how?

Soon after, she felt a tugging between her legs. Liquid pooled beneath her buttocks to be absorbed by her bathrobe and she knew she had given birth. She opened eyes she never knew were closed and raised her arms to receive her child – *her* child. Not the bastard's – *Mine!* – and met the smiling gaze of the doctor. This time the tears that fell were tears of happiness.

The man's dark eyes crinkled, and his snow-white beard parted to reveal teeth equally as white. Inclining his head towards the baby, he smoothed a bedraggled lock of hair from her eyes, and then rose, his smile radiant against ebony skin.

A pounding at the front door demanded Sarah's attention. "It's open!" she called through the kitchen, wondering whether it was the doctor's colleagues come to help. If so, they were too late. But when she looked back to where he had been standing, he had gone.

# 16

The hens scattered from the rutted track in a flurry of wings, and clucked their annoyance in loud, raucous squawks as Duncan slowed the Fiat to a halt just where they had been pecking at the dirt. He paid no heed to their complaint, and hunched over the steering wheel to stare out of the dust-streaked windscreen at the array of ramshackle buildings that clung to the hills like limpets to a rock. Heat shimmered off corrugated roofs and he could see livestock in fenced paddocks, but there was no sign of any human inhabitants.

Like ghouls from the mist, men in baggy shirts and trousers and women in floral dresses, shawls draped around their shoulders, began to materialise on the hillside above to stare down at him. There wasn't a hint of welcome in their gaze, and he shuddered. It was like a scene from a Hammer horror film. Wary, he eased the car forward, looking for sign of Mehmet's jeep.

He spotted the car matching the description given by the girl after travelling some thirty yards, and pulled up alongside it. Like the shack, it had seen better days, but proved he had arrived at the right village. Now all he had to hope was that both Mehmet and Louisa were at home so he could find out what he had got involved in.

The door to the car creaked as he opened it, as did his back on swinging his legs out. He winced, and eased slowly upright, pushing a fist into the small of his back as he did so. It had been years since he had last driven and the hours spent behind the wheel had taken their toll. Ignoring the pain and stiffness in his joints, he made his way up the short flight of timber steps and hammered at the wooden door of the shack with the heel of a hand. There was no response, and he could feel the gaze of the villagers boring into him. He sensed they had moved closer and it set the hairs on the back of his neck bristling, but he refused to turn and face them. Instead, he raised a hand to hammer at the door once again.

Just as before, there was no answer, and he sighed. He would have to await their return. Turning, he made to walk back to the car, but halted on the edge of the timber veranda. Twelve of the villagers stood on what classed as the main road. They formed a semi-circle some twenty feet away, arms folded across barrel chests, and stared at him.

Involuntarily, Duncan swallowed, and then forced a smile. He raised a hand in greeting, but need not have bothered. Not a flicker of emotion crossed a single weathered face. In an attempt to exude a confidence he did not feel, he forced the smile to remain as he walked back to the Fiat to grab the bottle of water from the passenger's seat. Then, sitting on a nearby wall, he took a sip and settled for what he hoped would not be a long wait. Although he sensed no immediate threat from the men surrounding him, he guessed they were unlikely to let him leave, even if he wanted to, and hoped his air of confidence showed his apparent lack of concern.

It was close to an hour later when he realised something was happening. The heat had been getting to him and he was starting to flag, so it took him a while to realise that more villagers had joined the men who surrounded him. Standing, he swept his gaze over the gathering. He could see nothing untoward, but there was an undercurrent in the air that set all his nerves on edge. His flesh tingled, his mouth went dry, and he found himself flicking his gaze to the car, his mind working out whether he had time to get in, start it and make good his escape. But before he had chance to move a muscle an avenue opened in the throng and three figures walked through.

He gasped.

Between and slightly behind two men walked Louisa. Her face was drawn and dark circles shadowed glazed eyes. She looked as though she carried the world's woes on her shoulders; the total antithesis to the girl he had been chatting with in Marmaris.

One of the two men who flanked her was old and wizened like the inhabitants of the village, and a scowl creased his craggy features. The other was a similar age to Duncan, dressed in jeans and a sweatshirt, two coils of rope slung over a shoulder and a canvas roll tucked under an arm. His skin glowed with the same inner hue he'd seen in Louisa, and Duncan immediately knew it was Mehmet Ozric, the man he was supposed to find. It was he who spoke.

"What are you doing here?"

The sound of Mehmet's voice roused Louisa and her eyes snapped into focus. She gasped in recognition, and her words echoed that of Mehmet. "W-what are you doing here?"

Mehmet swivelled. "You know this man?"

Louisa reddened, and nodded hesitantly. "His name is Duncan Connors and – and we had a date for last night. One I had to miss."

Mehmet scowled. "With *him*?" He fixed Duncan with a baleful gaze while still aiming his words at Louisa. "You do not know who he is!"

Frowning, Louisa said, "I told, you, he is Dunc –"

"Can't you see it?" There was suppressed anger in Mehmet's every movement as, tensed, he swung to face her. Patting his chest, he said, "Use your soul, Louisa. Use the Light."

The expression puzzled Duncan, but before he could think on it he found himself drawn to Louisa's gaze, and stepped forward.

The villagers stiffened, and the old man began to edge

towards him around the far side of the Fiat.

Louisa's eyes widened, and a hand flew to her mouth. Although whispered, her words carried the short distance to where Duncan stood.

"He's one of us?"

Duncan frowned.

"Yes, and no." Gone was the passion with which Mehmet had previously spoken. Instead, he sounded saddened. Turning, he met Duncan's querying gaze.

"In him is both Creator and Destroyer. In him is both Light and Shadow. In him lies betrayal."

Sensing movement from behind, Duncan swivelled, too late to prevent a rock from crashing against the side of his head.

***

He was in a tunnel and had no idea how he came to be there. Torches set in sconces lined the walls. Their orange flames flickered on rock and caused shadows to writhe on the roughly hewn surfaces as though in agony. Acrid, oily smoke stung his eyes and seared his throat, and he began to sweat. Turning, he looked behind him, but saw only darkness, complete and absolute. There was only one direction to take; he stepped forward and followed the tunnel, the echo of his footsteps his only companion. After two hundred paces, and with no final destination in sight, he stopped to look back, and swore. The darkness followed. There was no sign of the corridor he had travelled.

Fear gripped him and he increased his pace, until he almost ran down the torch-lined avenue that stretched ever onward, curving slightly so that the end could never be seen. Within a couple of minutes he arrived at a circular slab of stone that blocked his path, and he slid to a stop. He glanced over a shoulder and saw that the darkness had paused in its advance. It hovered fifteen paces away, as though it waited for the right moment to pounce.

Panic set in and he turned his attention to the slab. A frantic inspection revealed it rested in carved grooves that ran across the tunnel, leading to a recessed room to one side. It was apparent the slab could be rolled clear, but he doubted whether he had the strength to move it. Even so, he knew he had to try.

Stepping to the side, he pressed both hands against the rim, braced his legs against the tunnel wall and pushed against the stone. Every sinew and muscle bulged, but it refused to move. He redoubled his effort. Sweat stung his eyes, his muscles burned, and, ever so slowly, it began to roll. At first he didn't realise, but when he felt the stone judder he knew he was succeeding, and the knowledge granted him additional strength.

In a shower of dust and small stones the rock door suddenly rolled clear to crash to a halt against the far wall, and he scrambled through the opening. To his relief, the darkness did not follow. He exhaled noisily and turned to see where he had been drawn to, and his eyes widened in surprise.

He stood in a huge amphitheatre. Stalactites hung from a lofty roof, the uneven floor was covered in rocks and boulders. A sickly, green-tinged light emanated from the craggy walls giving the impression of sickness and corruption and, above the sound of his breathing, he could hear a harsh, guttural voice raised in chant. It came from somewhere ahead, but he could not understand a word of what was being said. Using the boulders and rocks for cover, he worked his way forward.

It did not take him long to get to the other end of the cavern, by which time the voice was louder, but the words still incomprehensible. With his back pressed against a large boulder, he gathered his courage and prepared to step from cover to see who it was that spoke and, after taking several deep breaths, moved into the open, where his courage fled.

Sweat slicked his palms, his heart raced and he felt the blood drain from his face as his gaze fixed on an altar, for that is what sprang to mind on seeing the immense wheel of rock set in the ground. At its centre a clear bubble floated above a stone plinth. A haze of red-tinged light emanated from the wheel of rock to cushion it, like albumen to a yolk sac, and his gaze was drawn to the grotesque caricature of life contained within. Strangely humanoid, the unborn child radiated an evil so palpable he could almost taste it, and he backed up a step.

The hooded figure that knelt before the altar ceased his chanting at the movement and rose to his feet. An open book flanked by two black candles lay on the ground between the man and the altar, and was obviously the tome from which the words were being read from. Duncan's eyes fixed on the wording, but they were in an unfamiliar language.

"Welcome, Missio. I knew you would come."

Duncan's gaze snapped to the speaker, whose features were concealed within the voluminous hood of his robe.

The hood moved as the figure glanced to where Duncan had been looking, then twitched again as he became the focus of attention. "The Book of the Dead is an acquired read, especially the doctrine of eternal life, and not something you will be overly familiar with. Yet!"

The surface of the bubble rippled and the foetus within moved its head. Eyes darker than night peered out to suck him into their hypnotic gaze. Unable to resist the pull, he found himself walking towards the altar, to what he knew would be his death.

As he passed the man in the robe a hand shot out to grip his shoulder. Fingers gouged into flesh and numbing pain coursed through his body. Hauled to a halt, he had no option but to stare into the nothingness within the hood.

"You will serve us well, Betrayer."

The man chuckled and dug his fingers deeper into his skin.

The pain was excruciating and he dropped to his knees.

"But not yet. The time is not right. Soon, you will be summoned, and then you shall fulfil your destiny, and the Word that gives life will be heard."

The fingers dug deeper and the pain intensified, becoming unbearable. At the point when he thought he could take no more, the world turned dark and, thankfully, he passed out.

# 17

At Duncan's cry of pain, Mehmet leaned over the arm of the couch to grip him by the shoulders and force him back down, and then glared across the room at Hiki. "You hit him too hard."

Hiki shrugged. "He deserve it. I would do again, no problem."

Mehmet growled low in his throat. "He is not *the* betrayer, old man."

Hiki spat on the bare boards of the floor and sneered at the comatose form of Duncan. "He will destroy us." Turning, he moved towards the door. "I go now. Stench in here is strong."

From where she sat on the floor, arms wrapped around her knees, Louisa watched the door close on his exit, and then swung her gaze to Duncan as she tried, yet again, to figure out what was going on. Despite the presence of the disc against her flesh and the feeling of 'completeness' since possessing it, her confusion over Mehmet's explanations and the unknown role he expected her to play in banishing Shadow had numbed her mind. And, with the appearance of Duncan, who was also of Light, her confusion had deepened. Of the four descendants Mehmet said survived, three were in the same room. It could not be coincidence. There had to be truth in what he told her.

The thought brought a wry smile to her face. 'In me is truth,' Mehmet had said when slipping his medallion over his head. 'In you is life.' But what was in Duncan? Why was he a threat, as Hiki had so vehemently stated? He had called him betrayer, and Mehmet had said Duncan was both Creator and Destroyer. What did it all mean?

Without warning, her medallion warmed and an image of the Guardian appeared in her mind's eye. Her eyes widened in surprise and she gasped. The aura she had felt when he had appeared in the shop enveloped her and she knew, in an instant, the image was real and not conjured by her fraught imagination. He was with her now, in her head, letting her know they would not be alone, that he would be with them, in spirit if not in body.

As though hearing her thoughts, the Guardian smiled, and then looked down at the bundle of cloth he held cradled in an arm. He raised a hand and pulled free the swaddling to reveal the face of a babe. The smile on his face deepened, and his mouth moved to form a word. That word was 'Faith'. Louisa heard it loud and clear, although it had not been spoken, and could feel the love he held for the child.

"He wakes."

At the sound of Mehmet's voice the image of the Guardian disappeared, and with it, Louisa's sense of harmony.

"But he will have a sore head." Mehmet rose and looked across to her. "You want some coffee?"

Louisa nodded, and raised a hand to grasp at her medallion. The Guardian's presence lingered in the touch, and she smiled.

"W-w-where am I?" Duncan's eyes flickered open, and he raised a hand to probe gingerly at the bloodied cloth that bound his head.

Louisa released her hold on the disc and rose to her feet. "In Mehmet's shack. How are you feeling?"

"Like half a mountain fell on my head. What happened?"

Louisa gave a half-smile and knelt on the floor beside him. "Hiki. He hit you with a rock."

He looked at her quizzically, and said, "B-but why?"

She shrugged. "You'd have to ask him."

"He does not like you."

Mehmet handed Louisa a steaming mug of coffee, and then said to Duncan, "You want one?"

Louisa winced. The dislike evident in his voice was too obvious for Duncan to miss. Wanting to diffuse the situation, she said, "White with one sugar."

Mehmet scowled and moved away.

Duncan probed at his bandaged scalp again, and winced. "Seems like Hiki isn't the only one that doesn't like me."

Louisa smiled, and reached across to pull his hand from his head. "I do. Now stop playing with that or it will never heal."

"Bad dreams gone now?" Mehmet stood beside them, a mug clasped in his hands.

A haunted look entered Duncan's eyes, and he looked away, and swung his legs off the sofa to sit up. He accepted the mug of coffee and nodded, his expression guarded.

"Now you tell us why you are here."

Annoyed by Mehmet's apparent lack of concern for Duncan's well-being, Louisa rose and sat on the sofa beside him in what she hoped would come across as moral support. "Can't it wait until he's rested?"

Mehmet shook his head, and fixed her with a look that showed no sign of compromise. "You know there is not time, Louisa." He turned back to Duncan and repeated the question.

After a moment's pause, and a sip of his coffee, Duncan said, "Steff Mason."

Mehmet frowned. "The priest?"

Duncan nodded. "My tutor."

Taken aback, Louisa could only stammer, "Y-y-you're a priest?"

"Was. After Father Mason's death –"

"Father Mason is dead?"

There was more than a hint of horror in Mehmet's voice, and Louisa immediately picked up on it. "Was he one of … ?" She left the question hanging, not wanting to voice her fears.

In answer, Mehmet shook his head. "No. But he believed in us."

Duncan frowned. "Believed in you? I thought you were helping him in his research."

Ignoring the question, Mehmet began to pace the floor, elbow cradled in a hand as he rubbed at his chin. "How did he die?"

"A car crash."

"When was this?"

"A couple of weeks ago. Why?"

Mehmet paused in his pacing and stopped to stare at Duncan. "Because it was just over two weeks ago I last spoke to him. He said he had some information for me, information that would upset the Church, information concerning ..." he glanced to Louisa, "us. He told me he was going to drive to the university to email his findings, but the email never came. I tried to contact him, but ... " He shrugged. "Now I know why he did not keep his promise."

"Email!" The mug of coffee slipped from Duncan's hands to hit the floor with a clatter. A chocolate-brown puddle formed.

Instinctively, Louisa rose from the sofa to grab a towel to mop it up, but Mehmet stayed her with a wave of a hand. "It can wait." Directing his question at Duncan, he said, "What is so important about email?"

Duncan's face blanched, his words coming out in a rush. "Not the email; the computer. Father Mason's computer. After his death I visited his office to see for myself that he wasn't there, and his computer had gone. The Regent had taken it, it was in his office when ..."

Mehmet held up his hands. "Please. More slowly. Tell me what happened. I do not think Father Mason's death was an accident and what you say may be important."

Mehmet's certainty that Steff Mason's death was no accident confirmed the fear that had been gnawing at Duncan since his discussion with David Crabtree, and the subsequent ransacking of his flat. Whatever was going on here, a deadly game was being played and, like it or not, he was in the thick of it. Giving as much detail as he could remember, he told them of the events subsequent to Father Mason's death. His commentary acted as therapy. It felt good to talk about it and have people listen who appeared to understand what he had been through, was still going through. By the time he finished his throat was dry and the dull throb in his temple had escalated.

"Is that everything? Mehmet asked.

Duncan nodded, then wished he hadn't. His head felt like someone was stabbing it with sharp needles.

Louisa placed a hand on his arm. "I'll go get you something to ease the pain." She returned moments later with a glass of water and two painkillers. "Take these. They're strong."

Slumped in the chair he had dragged over from the dining table, Mehmet shook his head. "So it would seem the Regent is of Shadow." He pursed his lips. "Even now they grow strong, and have infiltrated the Church. Where else have they done their damage?"

Louisa scowled. "Everywhere."

The talk of Light and Shadow as entities only served to compound Duncan's confusion. Not helped by the headache, he was struggling to come to terms with how the information he had given Mehmet and Louisa linked in with whatever they were.

"You have left nothing out?"

Duncan made to shake his head, but stopped. He had not quite told them everything, and was certain Mehmet sensed as such.

"When I left the airport I met someone." He paused, his inner being swathed in remembered harmony.

"Who?" Mehmet prompted.

Meeting his gaze, Duncan said, "A dark man with white hair."

Louisa gasped. "You've met him too?"

Duncan did not know whether to be pleased or down-hearted that his meeting wasn't unique. Not wanting to aggravate the throbbing in his head now that it had begun to recede, he said, "At the airport, as I was making my way to the taxi rank I bumped into him. I made to apologise but he just smiled." A small smile formed on his face. He could feel the aura of peace and tranquillity even now.

"Did he say anything?"

"No. The taxi driver turned up and interrupted, and when I looked back he'd gone. He was at the exit, though. I saw him as we drove through. And I sensed we would meet again, sometime soon."

Mehmet's eyes lost their focus as he stared at a point over Duncan's head, until Louisa spoke, at which point they fixed on her.

In soft, hesitant tones she said, "The dark ... the Guardian came to me just before, after Duncan had settled and I was sitting on the floor. At first I thought I was daydreaming, but I felt that same sense of peace I felt when he came to the shop, and I knew he was there, in my mind. He had a child in his arms. A babe, really. Not more than a few days old. He showed her to me, and called her Faith."

"Faith? Are you sure? Was he not just telling you to have faith?"

Although carefully shielded, Duncan sensed a wistful undercurrent in Mehmet's voice.

"That's what I thought at first, but now I'm sure he was naming the child." She stared at Mehmet. "The child that is the fourth and final descendant." Her gaze flicked to Duncan and then back to Mehmet. "Behold, this is your army of Light."

A frown tugged at Duncan's brow. "What are you, and who is this Guardian?"

"What are *we*, Duncan Connors. What are we."

Mehmet's statement should have surprised him, but it didn't. Ever since reading Steff Mason's letter and the reference to Light and Shadow, and that Duncan should trust the Light within him, he had felt something change. Not something he could point a finger at and identify, but he felt different. More so after his meeting with the dark man they called the Guardian.

"What are 'we', exactly?" The sureness of Duncan's tone was at odds with his inner turmoil.

An intensity entered Mehmet's eye that Duncan could only put down to total belief. "We are children of Light. Direct descendants of the thirteen."

The analogy did not fit into anything Duncan could grasp. "Thirteen what?"

His question had Mehmet laughing. A twinkle entered his eye as he said, "And you a man of the Church, you ask me that?"

For a brief moment Duncan sat and stared at him as if he had taken leave of his senses, then sank back into the sofa, frowning in disbelief. "But you can't mean ... That would be impossible."

"Why would it be impossible, Duncan Connors? Out of the billions of people on earth, why should not just a few be able to trace their past directly back to biblical times?"

"Because ... because ..." He had no answer. "But what has this to do with the Apocalypse of Thomas? Isn't that what Father Mason was researching?" He was grasping at something solid in the hope he could better understand what Mehmet so obviously hinted at.

Mehmet leaned back in the chair. "That is what first brought us into contact; his research into the gospel and my talent for tracking down religious artefacts. The gospel is one of many that the Church, in their wisdom, omitted from their version of events. Thomas knew that evil would rise again once they had banished it, and that people of Light would be needed to banish it again, and so wrote the apocalypse as a warning. Hidden in the desert for centuries, it was found when it was needed. But only a few knew its true meaning, and I am one of them. The others ..." He shrugged, his eyes momentarily hooded. "They are no longer here."

Rising, he said, "And now I must go to speak with Hiki." He raised a hand to forestall Duncan's question. "Tomorrow. You need to rest. We have a long walk and you will need your strength."

Wishing them a good night, he left, leaving Duncan with more questions than answers.

With Mehmet gone, Louisa rose from the sofa. "I don't know about you, but I'm starved. What do you fancy?"

"Louisa, who –"

She turned and gave a weak smile. "Tomorrow, Duncan. Leave it to Mehmet. Believe me, I am as new to this as you are. Any explanation I could give would only confuse you even more. But what I can tell you is that you must trust Mehmet. He is the key to all this. He is the one who knows what's happening out there. Your Steff Mason believed in him, and so must you."

# 18

A part of Louisa wished she were going with them as she watched Mehmet and Duncan walk the dusty road towards the woodland, but she knew the experience within the cavern was one Duncan needed to feel for himself. She half-smiled, wondering which medallion would prove to be his. She had no doubt he was of Light, like her. And Mehmet. Surprisingly, considering her usual cynical outlook on life, she'd accepted the fact without preamble, her primary concern being the role she would have to play in preserving the Light, the whole concept of which was beyond her at the moment.

When they disappeared behind a screen of bushes she made her way back into the shack. It was a fine, warm morning and she fancied sipping a cup of coffee while sitting in the sun, watching the villagers go about their daily chores, and maybe making some sense of all she had learned. And of all she had not.

She had just poured her drink when there was a knock at the door. Instinctively, she knew it was Hiki, and called for him to enter.

The door opened and he strode in, the wrinkles on his sun-browned face deep with concern. A momentary twinkle entered his eye when he saw her, and he nodded in greeting. Remembering her first encounter with the wizened old man, this was something of a turnaround, and she smiled in welcome.

"Coffee?"

He nodded. "That would be good."

Not wanting to change her plans about sitting outside she asked him to bring two chairs, and carried the mugs into the pine-scented morning.

They sat in companionable silence for a while, listening to the drone of bees and the call of birds. Louisa, eyes half-closed, leaned back in the chair, enjoying the warmth of the sun on her face, while Hiki, leaning forward, nursed his coffee and stared at the ground. Eventually, he said, "You want to know why I not go with them?"

Louisa straightened in her chair as he glanced her way. "The question had crossed my mind."

Hiki stared at the ground again. "Because I not like that man." His words were hard and cold. "He is from long line of betrayers. He will destroy us."

He used the same words he had used the previous night, and Louisa had already half-guessed the name of the disciple to whom he referred. "You mean Judas," she said.

Hiki hawked and spat. "His ancestor betray the Light once, he will do it now. I know this." Looking up, his eyes locked with hers. "I know this. But Mehmet?" He shook his head and looked away. "He is like the bee. He sees everything with honey. He not listen to me."

"But it's not as though he has a choice. Whatever it is we have to do will be hard enough with the three of us, never mind if it were only the two."

"You forget about the other, Louisa Cook. There is one still to come. We do not need *him* to help us."

Louisa sighed, and told Hiki of her visitation, and of the babe.

He wilted at the news. "It would seem centuries of my people guarding the secret will be for nothing. Such a waste." Rising, he handed Louisa his half-finished coffee. "Best I go now. I have fields to work."

Louisa rose and gripped his arm. Standing, she was the same height as he, and stared him in the eye. "All is not lost.

Where I come from we don't admit defeat, and never give up before we've started."

"But what have we got, Louisa? Two of you true to the Light, one who is corrupt, and another who is a child." He shook his head. "We are too weak." He thumped his barrel-chest for emphasis, and said, "We need strength."

Annoyed by his unexpected attitude, she said, "Tell me how the disciples defeated Shadow. Surely Shadow was as strong back then. How did they manage it all those years ago? Are you telling me we're weaker? Not worthy? Because if you are …" Her voice shook with emotion and had risen as she spoke. The thought of Hiki thinking them too ineffectual to preserve the Light sparked an anger that she found diffi-cult to quell. It was a sensation she had never felt before.

Instead of bowing under the onslaught, Hiki grinned, his first genuine show of amusement that morning, and Louisa faltered in her tirade.

Chuckling, he patted the hand that gripped his arm. "With you, I think we will win. Mehmet right about you. He say you were strong lady, and I not believe him. Now? I do. You want real coffee? Not like rubbish Mehmet buys." Without waiting for an answer he moved away, dragging her with him.

It was cool in his kitchen. His shack, shaded from the morning sun by the slope and forestry behind, was larger than Mehmet's and had three separate rooms. Four if you included the small outhouse that acted as a bathroom. The kitchen was at the point closest to the slope and positioned to catch the sun from midday through to sunset. The smell of freshly ground coffee hung heavy in the air, reminding Louisa of the coffee shops back home, but had the added fragrance of pine, brought in on a zephyr.

Sitting at the large timber table she sipped at the bitter-tasting brew, black as obsidian, and waited for Hiki to speak. It was obvious now that his apparent defeatism was his test of her mettle, and that Mehmet had already told him abut the Guardian and the child. Somehow she had passed his test, but why had he needed to test her in the first place?

Sitting opposite, Hiki, eyes closed, breathed deeply of his coffee before taking a sip. "Ahhh! Is good. You ask me how Shadow defeated in past. Now I tell you."

The small cup paused on the way to her mouth, as if it too awaited his words.

"By spreading the word. Remember how Mehmet tell of good room spreading to house and on to next house?"

Louisa nodded.

"That is how."

"I-I don't understand. What has that got to do with us?"

"You are the good. You are of Light. People believe in you, in what you say. You can help them find their own Light." He placed a hand over his heart. "In here. That is what you have to do. My people will help. We serve Light, but are not of Light. You are. You release that Light in others. That is what you must do, as Thomas did to us."

"Thomas?" Louisa frowned, confused.

Hiki laughed. "It was he who set my people free of Shadow, and set us to guard cavern and its secret. It was he who wrote clues to help those in future." He smiled. "How you think farmer know where to find clay bowl that held gospels?"

"You mean the Nag Hammadi Library?" Louisa remembered reading something about supposed translations and how the Church frowned upon the findings, but she had been more interested in something so old being found after centuries of being buried under sand.

Hiki nodded. "He hid writings with others in case they be discovered too soon and ignored. Even now, with so much bad in the world, his words are not believed." He shook his head, then brightening, said, "What you think we should do?"

Startled by the question, she could only stare at the old man over her raised cup. "I-I-"

Hiki laughed. "No, do not answer. I was only – how you say? Teasing. Now, I must work." Rising, he placed his cup on the side before moving towards the door. "Finish coffee. Enjoy. I will see you later, when Mehmet returns."

The sun had commenced its descent by the time Mehmet and Duncan came back. Louisa was sitting outside Mehmet's shack, trying to read a book she had found inside, but was finding it hard to concentrate and could not get into the story. When she saw them, she tossed the book to the ground and sprang to her feet, aware that the villagers had also noticed their arrival. Scores of them ghosted in from the fields, woodland and shacks to gaze at the two men.

The change in Duncan was noticeable well before he reached her. With head bowed, shoulders hunched, he walked three paces behind Mehmet, deep in thought. But it was his aura that took Louisa's breath away. The glow she had seen in him previously had intensified.

They halted as they reached Louisa, and Mehmet grinned. "He is one of us."

"I can see that." Looking over his shoulder, she glanced in concern at Duncan. "Is he – is he all right?"

With a flick of his head, Mehmet indicated they should go inside. "I think he could do with some coffee. Like you, he has learned much, but has many questions."

Seated on the sofa, Duncan accepted his drink without a hint of a smile, took a sip, and then resumed staring at the floorboards. Louisa, not knowing what to say, shook her head and sat cross-legged on the floor, back resting against the timbered wall as she nursed her mug. Mehmet had left moments earlier, to see Hiki, he had said, but Louisa knew he had left her with Duncan in the hope they would help each other come to terms with who they were.

The silence dragged on and still Duncan made no effort to speak, or to finish his drink, and she was starting to feel uncomfortable, not least because her backside was going numb. She had almost opened conversation a number of times, but had talked herself out of it, reluctant to pry when it was his story to tell. As much of a shock as rebirth had been to her, she had the feeling it had been more so for him.

"It was my fault, you know."

The words were softly spoken and she was unsure as to whether Duncan had uttered them or not.

"Say again?"

Duncan looked up to meet her gaze. Dark shadows had formed beneath his eyes, which were bloodshot and world-weary. With the blood-stained 'turban' wrapped around his head, he looked slightly demented.

"My parents." He shook his head. "It was my fault."

Louisa frowned. "I'm sorry, Duncan. I have no idea what you're talking about."

"They died, when I was eighteen." He snorted, then sipped at his drink, and grimaced at the taste of cold coffee.

Louisa rose and gently eased the mug from his hands. "Let me get you a hot one."

Duncan nodded his thanks, and gave a wan smile before resting back on the sofa.

"We were arguing, you see."

Now he had started to talk, Louisa realised he had something building up inside he needed to get out, and prompted him to continue as she made two fresh drinks.

"About me wanting to join the army. They didn't want me to do it, but my mind was made up. And they had no right to stop me. I wasn't theirs."

Louisa paused in the act of pouring the drinks. "What do you mean?"

"I was adopted. They weren't my birth parents. I only found out when clearing through the junk in the attic and found an old case full of photographs and stuff, from when I was a baby. Underneath it all were the adoption papers."

Louisa moved to the sofa and handed him his drink before resuming her position on the floor. "What was the problem? They were the only parents you ever knew. Maybe they were worried that if they'd told you the truth you would want to look up your biological parents and they would lose you. I know I'd be pretty darn worried about that if it were me."

A pained look crossed Duncan's features, and he sighed.

"I know that now, but back then … I was just a kid, and reacted as kids do. I did the one thing I knew would mess them up – enlisted. They were strict Catholics, you see. Mass every Sunday, helped at the church, involved with God knows how many charities, and they hardly had two pennies to rub together themselves. So me joining the army went against everything they stood for."

"Wouldn't it have been easier to track down your real parents?"

"I tried. Apparently, my mother was a drug addict and dumped me soon after I was born. There were no records as to who my real parents were, and by the time I realised my mum and dad had rescued me from a life in foster homes it was too late." He grimaced. "And the more they tried to per-suade me not to join the forces the more determined I was to go through with it."

Pausing, he took a sip of his drink.

"How does that make it your fault they died?"

Duncan didn't answer for a moment, content with staring into the contents of his mug, which he swirled.

"We were arguing. We were on the motorway. Dad was driving and Mum was twisting in the front seat to have a go at me for doing something so out of character and telling me I should have spoken with them before making such a drastic career choice." His eyes misted over and he took another swallow of coffee before continuing. "She started to shout at me and I shouted back, said a few things I shouldn't and the whole thing got out of hand. Dad twisted round to have a go back at me and – Wham! – the car veered across the road and into the path of a lorry. I was thrown clear, but my parents …"

Duncan turned to look across to Louisa. A watery glimmer coated his eyes. "So, you see, it's my fault they died. In typical Judas fashion, in trying to do right I do wrong, and carry the guilt for eternity. Hiki was right, I am the destroyer." Averting his gaze, he shook his head. "As a soldier of Light, I may turn out to be your worst enemy."

Rising, Louisa moved to his side and dropped to her knees, grabbed hold of his hands and forced him to look at her. With Hiki, the sense of defeatism was an act intended to test her, but with Duncan it was real, and she detested defeatism. She had wallowed in it herself for too long and would not sit back and let others suffer as she had.

"It was an accident, Duncan. Okay, so you were arguing with them, but you never caused the car to crash. It was a sad, tragic accident. Nothing more, nothing less. Understand? And what do you mean you may become our worst enemy? In you is Light, Duncan, not Shadow. I can see it. Mehmet can see it. And since you've come back from the cavern it burns brighter within you. Forget about guilt, you are one of us, one of the Light. We *need* you!" Her voice had risen and her hands had tightened like clamps. "Don't you dare give up before we've even started."

Eyes haunted, Duncan met her gaze.

"I can see you, and you shine with Light. Mehmet sees you and in him is the truth. You will not betray us, Duncan. I would stake my life on it."

She realised what she'd said as soon as the words were out of her mouth, and hastily apologised, but Duncan merely grimaced and pulled his hands free.

"I need to go for a walk."

In rising, his medallion dropped free of his shirt, and Louisa gasped. The slotted pattern was the same as the one the Guardian had drawn on the box what seemed like an age ago, the design of cupped hands and a bird flying free.

"I'll be fine. I just need to clear my head." Turning, he made his way to the door and left, closing it softly behind him.

Louisa stared at it for a moment, resisting the urge to follow and further apologise, before raising her eyes to the ceiling and breathing a heavy sigh. It was Duncan who the Guardian had meant was coming. It was he who was the link in all of this, and now he was off chasing his own demons instead of concentrating on the ones that mattered.

Heaving another sigh, she moved to the kitchen area. She needed something to do, and making a meal would keep her occupied. Also, it would give her chance to prepare for Mehmet's questions when he returned to find their army of Light diminished by a third.

# 19

The shadows had lengthened and the heat of the day had begun to dissipate. The lowering sun would soon disappear behind the hills, leaving a crescent moon to cast what little light it could muster to illuminate the valley. Only vaguely aware of his surroundings, Duncan, hands thrust into the pockets of his jeans, head bowed, walked out of the village and made his way down the track he had driven along the previous day. He had no idea where he was aiming for, but needed time to himself, to attempt to come to terms with what he had learned since donning the medallion.

The medallion, handed down to him from the one person history despised, had woken within him his true heritage, and he felt unworthy to be of the bloodline. Although the Bible painted Judas as the betrayer, the cursed, the reviled traitor, it was wrong. The Church was wrong, he knew that now. When the Light blossomed within him a great truth was also revealed. A truth the Church had fought long and hard to expunge, by whatever means it thought fit.

Judas had betrayed Jesus at Jesus's own request.

Of all the disciples, Judas was the most pure of thought and deed. His inner Light burned the strongest and it was he who understood the true meaning behind his leader's words, and it was he who understood that the only way the world would enjoy freedom from Shadow was to release the Light. Jesus knew that with his passing a legend would be born. One that would eventually encompass the world and quash

Shadow, and that the only disciple capable of understanding was Judas. Trusting in his words, Judas had complied with his wishes, taken the *traitor's* gold, and lived the remainder of his short life being hated, but sure in the knowledge that his deed had been carried out for the safe future of mankind.

Despite his newfound knowledge, the feeling of being tarnished remained, and Duncan fully understood Mehmet's and Hiki's reactions to him. In doing right, Judas would forever be remembered as doing wrong. In creating he had destroyed, and, thanks to the Church, he would never be forgiven.

Twilight had fallen as he walked and there was a definite chill in the air. He shivered and burrowed deeper into his jacket, contemplating turning around and walking back to the shack, but did not feel ready for company just yet. Another ten minutes of walking saw the twin silhouettes of the rocky peaks he had passed the previous day loom out of the darkness, tall and sinister, and he stopped. He had travelled further than he thought and knew it was time to return. It would soon be fully dark and the light from the moon would be too weak for him to negotiate the track safely.

He kicked out at a small rock and listened to it skitter across the ground before he turned to make his way back. At least the walk had given him time to realise he must carry on where Judas left off – help Light vanquish Shadow. Only this time he would not underestimate the power they faced, and ensure Light prevailed. Although he may not be able to rewrite history and clear his ancestor's name, he could make sure his legacy lived on, and help clear the path for future generations.

He staggered as a sudden, sharp pain lanced through his head. He screwed shut his eyes and, teeth clenched, doubled over to press hands against his temples. The agony he felt was exactly the same as when the boy had stopped on the crossing to stare at him and when Chris Broadhead had peered at him from the office, and he knew Shadow was nearby.

As suddenly as it appeared the pain vanished. He staggered back at the release, his breaths coming in ragged gasps, and feverishly scanned the darkness for any sign of movement, but all remained still. Too still. The breeze had dropped and the ever present noises of the night had quietened.

The sound of a branch snapping came from somewhere ahead. Its sharp retort reverberated through the trees, and Duncan swivelled. Stone ground noisily beneath his booted feet as he shouted, *"Come out, you bastard! Show yourself!"*

In answer, someone laughed. It sounded child-like, and was filled with malice. A small rock landed on the ground close to where he stood, causing him to jump. The laughter sounded again, its evil undertones echoing in the night, and Duncan felt rage build within him.

A stabbing sensation attacked his temples again, less sharp than previously, and he winced

"You're one of us, Duncan. Why fight it?"

The words had been whispered into his ear. In fear, he spun, but no one was there, and he was convinced that whoever had spoken had been right beside him.

*"Where are you?"*

Duncan's loud cry shattered the quiet, and night sounds rushed back. A gust of wind raced past him and he staggered back a pace, as though he were caught in the pull of a speeding lorry.

"You're one of us, Duncan. Do not fight it."

The words, carried on the wind, ended with a peal of laughter.

Ahead, the track back to the village stood out as a silvered trail under the dim light of the moon, and Duncan began to run. An unquenchable fear gripped him, and a need to get back. He had to warn the others that Shadow knew where they were.

At his back, manic laughter hung in the air, mocking his terror.

Its sinister tones spurred him on and pushed his weakened body beyond its usual capabilities. By the time he reached Mehmet's shack his lungs burned, his clothing was soaked with sweat, his bloodied turban had worked loose and his legs felt like lead weights. Knowing that if he stopped he would collapse, he crashed into the door, which flew inward at the impact to smack against the timbered wall. Once inside the threshold he fell to his knees and retched.

Strong arms gripped him and hauled him to his feet and he heard a voice ask what had happened. In response, he mumbled, "They know where we are," before darkness claimed him and all his aches and pains were forgotten.

When he eventually came to, Duncan struggled to recall where he was. His vision swam and everything was a pale grey blur. His legs ached and it felt as though someone had hammered at his head with a hammer. He groaned, and hands gently gripped his to prevent him from raising them to his head.

"Don't touch."

His eyes flickered open and an oval patch of brightness gradually focused into a face.

"Louisa?"

Louisa smiled and nodded. "How are you feeling?"

"Dry." His voice came out hoarse and croaky. His throat felt parched.

"I get water."

Duncan frowned. "Hiki?"

Louisa grinned. "The very same. He's feeling somewhat guilty for your condition."

At his look of confusion, she said, "Your head. Apparently, the wound was worse than we thought. It became infected."

Although she smiled at her next words, Duncan sensed there was anxiety barely hidden.

"We nearly lost you."

"I-I don't understand."

"You don't need to, and best you don't. Hiki is feeling bad enough about it already."

He made to speak but she silenced him by placing a finger

over his lips. "Later, when you're rested."

Taking the glass from Hiki, she helped Duncan to take a few sips before placing it on the floor. "That better?"

Duncan nodded, and settled back onto the sofa. Memories of his walk came rushing back and his eyes flew wide. He struggled to rise.

"They're here!"

Louisa pressed against his chest and pushed him back down.

He did not have the strength to fight back and sank into the soft cushions. As though repeating a mantra, he said, "They're here."

"We know."

"H-how?"

"You tell us," said Hiki.

The old man moved around the sofa and came into Duncan's line of sight. "In your bad dreams you cry out and tell us of Shadow. Mehmet, he gone with men of village to look." He shrugged, his lips compressing into a thin line. "But he not find. Shadow gone by now. They learn what they come for, so no need to stay."

Hiki's words, spoken so matter-of-factly, scared Duncan more than his encounter with Shadow, the underlying implication being that they had been tested and found to be no threat. He closed his eyes and sighed. "They don't fear us, do they?"

The sound of Hiki's chuckle caused him to open his eyes and stare at him. A smile split the old man's weathered features.

Glancing to Louisa, he said, "They do not know you yet. If they did, they would know fear." Still chuckling, he made his way towards the door. "I go find Mehmet. Tell him to come back. He of better use here, where you can plan down-fall of Shadow."

As the door closed on his exit, Duncan murmured, "What was all that about?"

A crimson flush coloured Louisa's cheeks as she rose to her feet. "I'll go grab you something to eat. You must be starved. There's some lamb broth on the stove. It won't take a moment to heat through."

Duncan eased himself to a sitting position on the sofa, and the room began to swim. His vision blurred and he felt sick. Resisting the urge to throw up, he closed his eyes and cradled his head in his hands until the sensation passed, then slowly eased his eyes open. The smell of lamb broth carried across the room and he felt his mouth begin to salivate again, though not through hunger.

"How long have I been out?" he asked, aware of how frail his voice sounded.

"Hmmm?"

"How long?"

Louisa moved across the room, carrying a steaming bowl of broth and a plate containing a couple of slabs of bread on a tray. "Two days."

The news had him groaning. Two days? That was two days too long. He looked up as she placed the tray on his lap. "But we should be doing something."

Louisa shrugged. "You're in no condition to do anything right now, and what is it you want us to do? I, for one, have no idea." She ran a hand through her long hair, unbound and unkempt, and looked away.

He noted the haunted look to her eyes and realised she was as much afraid as he.

Louisa folded her arms across her chest and moved to the room's only window to stare out in abstraction. Framed by the patch of brightness her hair took on the appearance of burnished silver. Her skin glowed, and Duncan found himself holding his breath as he gazed on the beauty that was her Light. She was the one person he would risk everything for.

At that moment, however, he did not have the strength to save himself, let alone anyone else. He had never felt so weak and drained in his life before. Without warning, the room began to darken. His eyelids fluttered as he fought a losing battle to remain conscious, and he slumped to the side. Unsettled by the movement, the tray containing the broth slid off his legs to crash to the floor.

Mehmet's long, lopping strides carried him closer to the shack. A layer of dust coated his boots, jeans and jacket, and although his Light blazed, the dark rings beneath his eyes indicated his tiredness. Beside him, Hiki had to jog to keep apace. Despite her concern over Duncan, Louisa found herself smiling at the sight. The crash of the tray hitting the floor, however, brought those concerns to the fore, and she spun away from the window to race towards the sofa.

Duncan lay slumped to the side. The flesh on his face appeared to have shrunk, to stretch taut against his skull, and the dark stubble on his cheeks and chin stood stark against pale, translucent flesh.

The door to the shack burst open and Mehmet stepped inside, closely followed by Hiki. On seeing Louisa stooped over Duncan, his eyes widened and he hurried across the room, his boots clumping solidly against the timbered floor.

"He lives?" he asked, placing an arm around Louisa's shoulder and staring down.

"Barely."

Grasping one of Duncan's hands, Louisa placed fingertips against his wrist to feel for a pulse. She found one. Weak and erratic, it confirmed that all was not well. She looked up and met Mehmet's questioning gaze, and said, "But, for how long … "

"He need a doctor. Quickly. He is no good to us dead."

Whether it was a trick of the light, Louisa could not be sure, but it seemed as though Duncan's Light faded even more at Mehmet's words.

"Take too long," said Hiki. "We need to take him, before it too late. I go get car." Turning, he hurried out of the shack.

Louisa helped manhandle Duncan up and into Mehmet's arms before running outside to open the doors to Hiki's battered old Volvo estate. Crouched behind the wheel, the old man peered at her, his brow furrowed in concern, the creases building on the many wrinkles.

As Louisa slipped in and along the rear seat, he turned

to face her. Although his lips moved, no words came out. Sensing he was attempting to apologise, she reached out and grasped his shoulder. Before she could say anything, Mehmet reached the car and stooped to lower the comatose form of Duncan through the doorway.

Louisa reached out to grasp his shoulders and help ease the unmoving body onto the back seat. No sooner had he been settled, his head resting in her lap, than Mehmet slammed the rear door closed and ran round to the passenger side to jump into the front seat.

Hiki gunned the car forward before he had managed to fully close his door. "Careful, old man. We would all like to live to fight Shadow."

Hiki grunted an acknowledgement, ignored Mehmet's scowl, and floored the accelerator. The car lurched forward, scattering a flock of hens in its wake. Their loud squawks of outrage were drowned by the roar of the car's engine, and their wing-beating forms became hidden in a cloud of dust.

Louisa gazed out of the grime-streaked window as the car sped out of the village, the car's ancient suspension struggling to cope with the nuances of the pot-holed dirt track, her thoughts sombre. Duncan had to live. The Guardian would not let him die, would he? Duncan was vital to their cause; he had to be. Or why would he tell them he was coming? He couldn't die before they'd even started on whatever it was they were supposed to be doing.

Looking down, she gazed once again at the taut flesh on Duncan's face, and sensed a further lessening of his Light, and knew the opposite could be true. She grabbed hold of one of his hands and held it tightly, aghast at how cold and clammy it felt, and willed life into his still body. One thing was for sure, she would not let him die without a fight.

# 20

Father Tumbletee tossed his suitcase onto one of the two beds and then walked across the room to open the window. Immediately, he was assailed by the heat of late afternoon and the sounds of a busy city, and frowned, wondering yet again why they had travelled to Istanbul when he had informed Regent Kearson that Connors was in Marmaris.

He pursed his lips and stared at the city's skyline in abstraction. Minarets vied for attention with looming high-rise buildings against an azure sky, but they barely registered. His thoughts were firmly fixed on the Regent, and what he was up to.

The door opened and he turned away from the window to nod in greeting as the subject of his thoughts strode into the room. "Anything important?" he asked, referring to the phone call the Regent had received soon after they had registered.

A scowl briefly marred the Regent's face as he placed his small suitcase on the bed. It was there and gone in an instant, and Father Tumbletee could have been mistaken about what he saw, but he doubted it. Regent Kearson was hiding something.

The Regent stooped to place his leather bag on the floor and then shoved it under the bed with a foot. He turned to Father Tumbletee and gave a lop-sided smile. "Senior Church matters, and not something you should be bothering your mind with." He pulled at the sleeve of his jacket to reveal his watch, which looked much like a Rolex to his companion, and glanced at the time. "Speaking of which, I have a meeting to attend."

Father Tumbletee opened his mouth to speak, but the Regent silenced him with a look.

"And no, I do not require your company. But I do require the information your computer *specialist* has failed to supply. I suggest you make contact and inform him of the urgency in the matter."

"But … "

The Regent held up a hand. "No excuses. We have to know where Connors is ultimately heading." He turned to walk away, but halted to peer at Tumbletee over his shoulder. "Otherwise it will have been a complete waste of my time bringing you along."

The heat of anger at the condescending tone coloured Father Tumbletee's face and, fists clenched at his side, he stared at the door after the Regent's exit. Then, calling him a most ungodly name, he strode to the door and yanked it open, but paused at the threshold. If there was one thing he prided himself on it was his ability to be in total self-control, no matter what the provocation. To give in to anger was to make mistakes, and he hated making mistakes.

He sighed, closed his eyes, dipped his head and took deep breaths to calm his rage before going back into the room and dropping to his knees beside the Regent's bed. Reaching underneath, his questing hand grasped the handles of the leather bag and he pulled it out. It looked much like a doctor's bag, and was sealed with a lockable clasp that flipped over the top. Out of curiosity he tried it, but it was locked. He snorted in derision and struggled to his feet, the bag clasped in a hand. To his surprise, it was heavier than it looked and he wondered what it contained. At that moment, however, the contents were the least of his concerns. He intended to find out where the Regent had gone and the bag gave him the cover he needed.

On enquiry at reception, the receptionist had no idea of the Regent's destination, but, after Father Tumbletee explained the reason behind his request, offered to call the taxi company he had used to find out. As he had hoped, his plan worked to perfection and in under five minutes he was also in a taxi, heading towards Ayasofya, the city's ancient bastion of Christianity.

As soon as he stood outside the huge building he knew he would have a problem. Now used as a museum, the domed citadel was immense and bound to be full of tourists, so where would he start? Sighing, he walked to the tourist entrance, the Regent's bag clasped in a hand, paid his entry fee and entered the vaulted outer vestibule.

Deducing that the obvious place for the Regent to hold a secret meeting would be in an area popular with tourists, where he could blend in with the crowd, he made up his mind to seek such an area once he entered the museum proper.

He took little notice of the gold mosaics with their floral patterns as he made his way through the inner vestibule, nor the one of the Christ Pantocrator above the Imperial Gate as he passed through, but the sight that greeted his eyes as he entered the main church took his breath away.

The area was vast, covering at least four acres, and was dominated by a soaring dome that rose some fifty-six metres above his head. Along with others who had entered behind him, he paused at the threshold, mouth agape, and stared up in awe. Light filtered through a crown of windows that dotted the circumference of the base of the dome, and glistened off golden tiles that covered the entire interior of the convex surface. He felt inferior, miniscule, and realised that that was the whole idea.

Someone barged into his back in passing and broke the spell. Father Tumbletee stumbled forward, and accepted the man's apology with a brief nod of his head. Then, striding out, his eyes flicked from nave to gallery, from gallery to side aisle, from side aisle to apse, in search of the recognisable figure of Regent Kearson.

He was almost halfway across the floor immediately beneath the dome when he spotted him, and halted. The Regent was deep in conversation with another man on a square of marble flooring known as Coronation Square, and he was too close for comfort. If they turned now they would see him, and he did not think the Regent would believe him if he told him he was out doing a spot of sightseeing, especially as he had his bag clutched in his hand.

Surreptitiously, he made his way to the south gallery and hid behind a pillar, wanting to see who it was the Regent spoke with. The Regent's back was to him as he stared out, and partially obscured the features of the man he was speaking to. Even so, there was something familiar about him. He had the feeling he had met him before. As he looked on, the man leaned back to peer around the Regent, and dark eyes fastened on him.

Father Tumbletee gasped in recognition and ducked out of sight, to flatten himself against the pillar, hoping that he, in turn, had not been recognised. His heart hammered against his chest and he held his breath, not daring to breathe. The man Kearson spoke with was Monsignor Louvière, one of the most senior members of the Vatican. They had met once, a couple of years ago, when he had attended a mass in St Peter's Square and been given a tour of the Vatican afterwards. Louvière had been one of those whose task was to greet the select few. But what was Kearson doing meeting with the likes of him? As far as he was aware, Kearson did not rate high on the ecclesiastical ladder.

Knowing whom it was that the Regent was at pains to keep secret added further mystery as to why they'd taken a detour to Istanbul, and to what Kearson was up to. Clutching the leather bag to his chest, he scurried away, eager to get back to the hotel before he was discovered missing, along with an item of property that did not belong to him.

# 21

L ouisa hated hospitals, she always had. The austere buildings, sterile and unwelcoming, rooms containing pain and suffering, filled her with dread. As an eight-year-old, her parents had forced her to visit her cancer-ridden grandmother. She had witnessed her slow, painful journey to death, watched as the flesh appeared to melt from her bones, and sobbed as she eventually slipped away. As she walked beside the gurney on which Duncan lay, grasping one of his hands in her own, the similarity of his condition to her gran's struck her, and she choked back a sob, hoping he would not suffer the same fate.

The clean, antiseptic smell of hospital grew stronger as the porter pushed the gurney along the maze of corridors to only he knew where, the sound of its rubber-shod wheels rumbling across the tiled floor an ever-present companion. With ease borne from familiarity, the young Turk negotiated the intersections and turns at a speed commensurate with their urgency until, eventually, they entered a narrow, windowless side corridor and pulled up beside a small, teak reception desk.

The nurse behind the counter looked up and, after a brief conversation with the porter, disappeared through a doorway behind. Within moments she reappeared, accompanied by a doctor. Stepping from behind the counter, the doctor ushered Louisa away before removing a stethoscope from around his neck to listen to Duncan's chest. After a brief examination, he frowned.

Sensing his concern, Louisa glanced to Mehmet, who pursed his lips and shrugged. Standing beside him, Hiki looked to the floor and would not meet her gaze. Before the sense of helplessness she had felt when watching her gran die could take control, the doctor spoke urgently in Turkish, and the porter pushed the gurney towards the double doors at the end of the corridor. Louisa made to follow, but the doctor thrust out an arm to stop her, and shook his head.

The light grasp of Mehmet's hand on her arm had her turning.

"They take him for examination. We have to wait here."

Briefly, Louisa thought of pulling free and chasing after the fast-disappearing gurney, but, realising the futility of the action, looked on in helpless frustration as the double doors swung closed, and with them, her contact with Duncan.

"He will be fine. They have the best doctors here. You will see."

Still staring at the doors, she murmured, "I hope so."

Behind them, Hiki cleared his throat. "I go get coffee. I find good stuff, not rubbish they sell in this place."

In spite of her fear for Duncan's life, Louisa smiled at his customary gruffness.

"He will be fine."

The smile that formed on Mehmet's face appeared forced, but she appreciated the words and reciprocated with a weak smile of her own. In a voice that sounded more relaxed than she felt, she said, "So what do we do now?"

His smile widened, this time with genuine feeling. "Now? Now we sit and wait." Taking her by the arm he guided her to the seats lining the wall opposite the reception desk. "They will not keep us waiting long."

In spite of his confidence it was over three hours before the doctor reappeared, the pile of discarded paper cups on the floor beside the chairs testament to the length of time it had taken. Despite Hiki promising them real coffee they'd had to make do with the processed rubbish available from the hospital's vending machine. Although barely drinkable, it had helped ease their tension.

On seeing the doctor reappear through the doors, now dressed in green scrubs and with a face-mask dangling around his neck, Louisa, Mehmet and Hiki rose as one from their seats.

"How is he?" Louisa demanded, hurrying forward to meet him.

To her frustration, the doctor gave her a fleeting glance of annoyance before stepping past to stop in front of Mehmet. The slight, unintended or not, roused an anger within. Scowling, lips compressed, she reached out and grabbed the doctor's arm to haul him round.

"I asked, how is he?"

She met the doctor's look of astonishment with steely resolve. This time she would not be ignored.

Smoothly, Mehmet intervened. Speaking in Turkish, he said something to the doctor whilst stepping forward and gently peeling her hand off his arm.

After Mehmet had finished talking, the doctor cast Louisa a brief look of compassion before dipping his head in what she took for an apology. It was then the realisation hit her: he didn't speak English. With head tilted back, she closed her eyes and sighed.

As Mehmet and the doctor conversed, Hiki's face drained of colour. He wilted before Louisa's eyes, and slumped back to sit on one of the seats. With elbows resting on his knees, he buried his head in his hands.

Louisa's heart faltered. She felt faint. Duncan was dead, she knew it. Reaching out, she grasped Mehmet's arm. Instinctively he covered her hand with one of his own, but continued to listen to what the doctor was saying. Once he had finished and moved away through the double doors he had emerged through but minutes before, Mehmet looked to her.

"He's dead, isn't he?" She heard herself ask, her voice barely above a whisper.

141

Mehmet raised a brow and shook his head. "No. He is not dead. He is not good, but he is not dead."

Like Hiki before her, she sagged at the news, and had to be guided to one of the seats.

Kneeling, Mehmet continued, "His skull is cracked. The doctor had to operate to make sure the broken bone had not caused bleeding in the brain."

Beside her, Hiki groaned. "It all my fault."

Mehmet fixed the old man with a look of compassion. "The doctor said that Duncan has thin bone to his skull, which is why it broke so easily. Any knock could have caused it to crack. And who is to say he had not already cracked it before you hit him with the rock."

Looking up, Hiki glared at him. "And that supposed to make me feel better?"

"He is not dead, old man."

"Yet!" Hiki snapped.

"Enough!" Louisa yelled, jumping to her feet, causing Mehmet to fall backwards. Hands on hips, she glowered at Hiki. Her body tingled with suppressed emotion. The last thing she needed was to hear words of negativity, especially from Hiki after what he had put both her and Duncan through.

In a voice filled with passion, she said, "It was you who said we must be strong, and now it is you who are being weak. Duncan is one of us. He will survive. He will live. It is the will of the Guardian, and I will not have you, or anyone else, cast doubts as to him pulling through. You – you ..."

Taken aback by the outburst, Hiki could only sit and stare, mouth open, wide-eyed in amazement.

Close to tears, the sound of Mehmet chuckling had Louisa spinning to glare at him.

He rose to his feet, dusted himself down, and then said, "It has been a long time since Hiki has been set right. But you are correct; he is being weak. You are also correct in that Duncan will survive. The doctor said it should be so."

The news was a welcome relief, especially after Hiki's

outburst, but Louisa sensed there was a 'but' coming, and could not summon the elation she knew she should feel.

She was right. The smile faded on Mehmet's face and he griped her shoulders. "The doctor also said he is not sure whether the bone has pressed on the brain, causing injury."

"Injury? You mean Duncan could be brain-damaged?"

Mehmet attempted to smile, but failed, and let his hands drop to his side. "The doctor said it could be so. He needs to run a scan to find out. That is where they have taken him now."

"H- h-how long before they know?"

"Two hours, three." Mehmet shrugged. "I do not know. But I do know that Duncan is a fighter. So I believe he will be fine." He fixed his gaze on Hiki. "And so should you."

After holding Mehmet's gaze for a moment, Hiki nodded.

"And so should you," Mehmet continued, speaking to Louisa.

Although softly spoken, his voice held belief, and that filled her with more confidence than anything the doctor could have told her. If Mehmet believed, then so would she. She had to, otherwise her faith in the Guardian and the power of the Light would be dealt a severe blow. One that she would struggle to come to terms with.

A prickling sensation affected the flesh to her chest, and she reached up to grasp at her medallion. As if it too were in agreement, warmth and vitality flowed through her body, reinforcing her conviction and, for what seemed like the first time in an age, she managed a smile.

"That is better, Louisa Cook," Mehmet enthused, returning her smile with one of his own. "Now, let us go and get some food. I think we could do with some fresh air, and I know my belly needs to be fed." He patted his washboard stomach for emphasis.

Her mood lightened and she managed a chuckle. Whilst not feeling particularly hungry, she could do with being outdoors for a while, and linked an arm through his. "I agree."

Calling over his shoulder as they walked down the corridor, Mehmet said, "And you, old man."

"What did you say to the doctor?" asked Louisa, thinking back to the moment when Mehmet had stepped between them.

The question caused him to laugh. "I told him what he needed to hear, that you were his wife."

Eyes wide, Louisa paused in her stride to slap him on the arm.

Mehmet grinned. "You are in Turkey, remember, and only woman of the man can be with him in a place like this. You understand?"

Louisa did, but could not shake off the fact that the word marriage had not filled her with dread. Putting it down to her fear of losing one of their comrades, she pulled on Mehmet's arm. All of a sudden she felt very warm, and needed some fresh air.

***

Gently, the hand that gripped her shoulder shook her to wakefulness. Even so, Louisa woke with a start, momentarily disoriented before realisation of where she was filtered sluggishly through to her consciousness. The hospital bed that Duncan lay on gradually came into focus, as did the tangle of tubes that attached him to a drip and the monitoring equipment, visible within the dimness of blind-filtered sunlight. Her eyes snapped to the screen opposite which, it seemed to her, hovered vulture-like beside the bed, keeping an eager and anticipatory watch over its prey. To her relief, the blip of Duncan's heartbeat appeared regular and strong.

She could tell by the gentle but firm grip on her shoulder that it was Mehmet who had woken her. Easing herself forward, she pushed clear the blanket that had been draped over her and then rubbed at eyes that felt dry and filled with grit. "What time is it?" she murmured, attempting to stifle a yawn.

Mehmet squeezed her shoulder and then stepped around the chair she'd been sleeping on to lean back against the hospital bed, arms folded against his chest. "Eight-thirty, and time to get something to eat. Hiki has gone to get breakfast. Come," he pushed away from the bed and held out a hand, "It is a beautiful morning and, like me, I am thinking you need to clear your head of hospital."

Mehmet was right. It had been over a day since Duncan had been brought back from theatre and in that time she had rarely left his side, let alone ventured outside. Returning his smile, she tossed aside the blanket, grasped the proffered hand, and rose to her feet.

"He will still be here when we get back," urged Mehmet.

"I know. It's just …"

"Duncan is doing fine, the doctor said so. In a day or two he should come round and all will be well again."

"Will it?" Louisa fixed Mehmet with a penetrative gaze. "Will it … will *he* be well again?"

Sighing, Mehmet shrugged. "The doctor said the scan showed no sign of injury to the brain, so all will be well. You will see."

Although the words were intended to inspire confidence, Louisa could sense the uncertainty behind them, and also see it in his eyes. It was that same uncertainty that gnawed away at her, that threatened to shatter the thin veneer she had created to keep out despair.

"Then why has he not come round already?"

"The body is repairing itself. When it is strong, he will wake. Even now he looks better. His Light grows. Now come, some clean air will do you good, as will some food."

As though in agreement, Louisa's stomach rumbled. Looking over her shoulder, her gaze was drawn to Duncan's features, relaxed and seemingly at peace. Mehmet was right; his skin had a healthier glow about it and had lost that yellowed, parchment-like quality. He looked more 'alive' than he had done since they had rushed him to the hospital. If it were not for the shaved scalp and stitches running in an arc behind his right ear, he would look like he merely slept.

Her eyes flicked once again to the monitor. The blip

145

remained strong and regular. Reassured, she turned her attention back to Mehmet and nodded her agreement to the break.

They had barely left the room and were only halfway down the corridor leading to the stairwell when a cold shiver ran down her spine. She stumbled to a halt, suddenly fearful, and swivelled to stare back down the way they had come. A numbness built within, one that developed at the base of her spine and expanded until it enveloped her whole upper body. Every nerve was tingling and on edge. Something was wrong.

"What is it?" Mehmet demanded, stopping to stare at her.

She never heard the words, was merely aware of their intrusion at the edge of consciousness. With eyes fixed on the doorway they had so recently emerged from, the numbness spread from her torso to her limbs and, immobilised, she realised what it was. Fear. Cold, unadulterated fear.

A ripple of air formed around the doorway, like a shimmering of heat haze, that caused her to flinch, and the paralysis fled. Like a dam had been breached, blood pounded through her veins and previously leaden limbs sprang into life. The slap of her boots echoed loudly in the corridor as she ran, determined to reach Duncan before it was too late.

\*\*\*

He was back in the cavern again and, for some inexplicable reason, was dressed in what appeared to be a hospital gown. He knelt in front of the altar, facing the foetus suspended within the yolk sac. But something had changed. The red tinge to the albumen had deepened and both the foetus and sac had grown; the albumen a narrower, denser cushion. He gasped in fear in realisation, and attempted to surge to his feet, to flee, but strong hands gripped his shoulder and forced him back down.

"I would advise you to not to move, Duncan. Head injuries can prove troublesome, especially to someone in your somewhat weakened condition."

He attempted to wrestle free, but the robed man's grip was too strong and he did not have the strength to fight him.

"Tut, tut, Duncan. You should know better than that."

For emphasis, fingers dug deeper into flesh. The pain was excruciating, and he winced.

"That's better."

The pain vanished as the grip on his shoulders disappeared. Footsteps echoed hollowly in the cavern. He opened his eyes and the man stepped into sight, standing to one side so as not to block his view of the altar, his features concealed by the voluminous hood.

"How does it feel to be kneeling before your God, Duncan Connors?" He inclined his head towards the altar.

Duncan glared up, unwilling to gaze on the monstrosity he referred to. "That's no god of mine."

The man stepped forward until a mere two paces separated them. Despite the close proximity, Duncan could not see inside the dark confine of the hood, and a ripple of fear thrummed through his body.

"I think you will find that it is."

As menacing as the man's words were, they did not prepare Duncan for the hand that shot out from the robes to grasp his head at the joint between the neck and the chin. Fingers, claw-like and strong, dug into flesh and twisted his head until he had no option but to gaze at the obscenity before him.

"Now gaze upon your God and beg forgiveness for your sins."

Wet, slimy, spittle flecked Duncan's cheek, burning into flesh, but the pain barely registered. His eyes were fixed on the child. For that is what it was. Whereas the last time he had been there it had been a foetus, now it was nearing naissance. Limbs were clearly defined and the body near fully formed. Loose, grey flesh rippled over a framework that was complete, and the latticework of veins had direction and fluidity. It would not be long before the being, whatever it was, had life, and with that life would come the End of Days: The cataclysm of which Thomas foretold; that which he was trying to prevent.

A ripple disturbed the flaccid flesh and the child's head began to move. Memories of what had happened the last time he had gazed on eyes blacker than night forced their way to the fore and his fear deepened

"Behold, your God is about to greet you." For emphasis, fingers gauged more deeply into flesh.

Through clenched teeth, Duncan repeated his previous words; "That is no god of mine. I am of Light, and no being of Shadow will ever consume me."

The grip on his throat tightened. It restricted his breathing, and he fought for breath.

"That is what your ancestor said when faced with the ultimate being, and we all know where his allegiance fell."

The flesh of the child pulsated and its veins bulged, red and angry. A vibration plucked at the air within the cavern, harsh and discordant. Startled, the man in the robe let loose his grip on Duncan's throat to turn and gaze, wide-eyed, at the altar. He suddenly swivelled, and yelled, "What have you done, Connors?"

Duncan rose to his feet, and said, "I am of Light."

A pulse of heat blazed at his chest, the cavern winked out of existence and he found himself floating above a town square. Market stalls, their flaps tied shut for the night, stood as darker shades against moon-silvered cobbles, while dogs, free from daytime beatings and chastisement, foraged. The dark maw of a cave entrance, flanked by a stone surround and set back in an avenue of stalls pulled at him, but he refused to be taken. Instead, he floated higher, away from the source of his discomfort. In doing so, something caught his attention. Its moon-kissed surface glowed like a beacon amidst the darkness, and he floated closer.

It was a bell tower, its cross-adorned dome topping three tiers of arched, open windows which were set upon a solid base of dressed stone. In the background was a church, a Christian church, built of similar stone, having cross-shaped openings to its gables. The whole was enclosed by a low, stone wall. But it was the bell tower that drew him closer. It blazed in the gloom, a citadel of Light amongst Shadow, the church a mere adornment for its glory. Before he had chance to investigate further, it winked out of existence and he was pulled from the scene by a power too strong to fight.

\*\*\*

Louisa was only fifteen paces away from Duncan's room when an explosion sent shards of glass and timber blasting into the corridor. She was hurtled from her feet, and sent skidding across the tiled floor to collide with the wall opposite. After what seemed like hours, but must only have been seconds, the bombardment ceased, and the wail of an alarm began to sound in long, ear-splitting bursts. The air thickened with dust and the acrid taint of smoke and she coughed, coarse and rasping.

"Louisa, Louisa, are you all right?"

Mehmet skidded to a halt beside her, dropped to his knees and eased her arm away from her face. After helping her to sit, he wiped a bedraggled lock of hair away from her eyes. His fingertips came away stained red.

"You are hurt."

Grasping each side of her temple, he tilted her head forward to inspect the wound.

Louisa could see the look of concern on his face, but any words she may have uttered were swept away in a bout of coughing.

Once her fit subsided, Mehmet eased aside her hair to examine the wound. "It is not deep. Only a scratch. The blood makes it look worse than it is."

"Duncan!" Pulling from his grasp, she lurched to her feet and sprinted the short distance to what remained of the doorway to his room. On reaching the shattered opening she slid to a halt. A hand rose to her mouth as she gazed in at the devastation.

The room was trashed. The monitor lay bent and twisted against the far wall, the window blinds hung drunkenly from one fixing, the glass of the window had been blasted out to leave jagged splinters protruding from the frame, and dark soot patches marked the walls and ceiling. The drip stand and trolley cupboard were twisted and distorted, as though caught by an intense wave of heat, and glass and debris littered the tiled floor.

Central to the devastation, however, was an oasis of calm. An area untouched by chaos. An area with Duncan knelt at its centre. The bed, white and pristine against the backdrop of soot-blackened mayhem, was untouched by whatever had caused the cataclysm. Duncan, seemingly oblivious, knelt on the bedding, arms outstretched, head tilted back, eyes closed, the tube of the drip trailing from an arm, looking like it was he who had caused the explosion.

Mehmet arrived beside her, and his eyes widened at the sight that greeted him. *"Ben benim ne gördüðüme inanmam."*

Barely aware of Mehmet's slip into Turkish, Louisa stepped slowly into the room, her eyes fixed on Duncan. Debris crunched beneath each footstep as she made her way towards the bed.

"Duncan?"

Her softly spoken word elicited no response.

"Duncan?"

Although spoken more loudly, there was still no reaction. She had reached the bed now, and stopped to stare in amazement. There was not a mark on him. No sign of a scratch or a bruise to show he had been in the middle of what had happened. He appeared calm, composed and, most worryingly of all, still in his coma.

Mehmet halted beside her and sucked in a sharp breath. "Louisa."

Although whispered and barely audible above the siren, she sensed the urgency in his tone and twisted her head to stare at him. But he did not return her gaze. Instead, his eyes were fixed on Duncan.

"Can you not see it?"

Her brows furrowed into a frown. "See what?" she asked.

"The glow," he answered, and raised a tremulous hand to point at Duncan's chest.

Fearing what he meant, Louisa's eyes widened, and ever so slowly, she turned her head to look for whatever he referred to.

She gasped. Why had she not seen it before? Visible beneath his gown, Duncan's medallion blazed with white light.

Without warning, Duncan's arms dropped to his side, his head turned towards her and his eyes snapped open. The intensity of his gaze had her flinching, and she raised a hand to stifle an unbidden scream.

Duncan's lips curled back in a feral grin. Then, with head tilted back, he laughed. Short, sharp and tinged with more than a hint of madness.

A wave of fear swept through her and she stepped to Mehmet's side, subconsciously seeking protection. An arm wrapped around her waist to pull her tight.

As quickly as it had erupted, Duncan's mirth subsided and the light of insanity faded from his eyes. This time the gaze that fixed on her was one of sureness, of power, of confidence in who he was. The words that he then spoke drove any thoughts of him being mad far from her mind.

"I am of Light."

As soon as the words were spoken, the light that blazed from the medallion dulled, consciousness faded from his eyes, and he slowly toppled forward on the bed.

Before Louisa had chance to rush to his side, the tramp of booted feet pounding on debris had her swivelling. Within moments, ten armed Jandarma stormed into the room, and each had a weapon trained in their direction.

In warning, Mehmet grabbed her arm to stay any movement that could be mistaken for intent. "Now is a good time to stand still and say nothing," he whispered, raising his hands slowly to level with his shoulders.

One of the Jandarma stepped forward and waved his gun towards the corridor whilst speaking in Turkish. Two of his colleagues stepped aside to allow a clear passage to what remained of the doorway.

Looking to Mehmet, Louisa raised a brow in query.

Mehmet sighed. "Now we have to go with them. It would appear they think we are responsible for this." He flicked a glance around the ravaged room.

Using a Turkish swear-word Louisa recognised, the Jandarma who had ordered them out stepped forward and jabbed the barrel of his gun into Mehmet's side.

Mehmet winced, but said nothing, and turned to walk towards the jagged opening in the rear wall. Sensing the danger they were in, Louisa allowed herself a lingering look at Duncan before meekly following.

Standing amongst the doctors, nurses and orderlies that lined the corridor outside she spotted Hiki. His face was white and he looked as though he were about to burst through and plead their case. Mehmet also spotted him, and shook his head.

Hiki sagged at the instruction. In passing, Louisa caught his attention and mouthed, 'Look after him', before being marched away to whatever fate awaited them. Whatever it proved to be was bound to adversely impact on their mission. And from what she had recently witnessed, that was the one thing they didn't need.

# 22

Sitting on a bench opposite the hospital entrance, the man dabbed at his perspiring brow with a handkerchief and looked on with mild interest as two police vans, sirens blaring, screeched to a halt. Within seconds, armed Jandarma jumped out and raced inside. Intrigued, he leaned back and settled himself for the show. The past few days spent baking in the sun waiting for his quarry to recover and make his next move had been as boring as hell, and he was quite looking forward to the diversion.

He had been watching the doors for further activity for some minutes when his mobile rang, and he delved in his shirt pocket. With eyes still glued to the hospital entrance, he held the phone to his ear and said, "Still no change. I'll let you know when they make a move." His eyes narrowed, and he snapped a response: "How was I supposed to know the silly old bastard would smash him over the head with a rock? What did you want me to do? Take on a whole bleedin' village? Listen matey, your boy is still in the land of the living, so stop worrying. I'll call you when I get some news. Okay?"

He made to lower the phone and cancel the call, but paused to listen further, and a frown tugged at his brow. "You want *who* dead?" A slow smile spread across his face. "Nope. That will be no problem at all. And seeing as he is making his way to me, so much the better. You still want me to keep an eye on this Connors guy?"

There was movement close to the police vans and he rose to walk closer to better see what was happening, and only half-listened to what was being said.

"Whoa. Hold on a moment. Something's gone on. They've arrested Connors' partners in crime, by the looks of things." He rolled his eyes. "The bloody Jandarma, that's who. The police. They've just pulled them out at gunpoint and loaded them into separate vans."

With a screech of tyres, the vans speeded away, and he increased his pace.

"I'll call you back once I've checked out what's gone on."

He did not wait for a response and ended the call, his curiosity piqued.

***

The small cell she had been thrown into stank. Countless years of stale sweat, urine and goodness knew what else had seeped into the stone walls and concrete floor, leaving a pungent memory of previous occupants. The narrow shaft of light that entered through the small, high opening in the rear wall did little to illuminate the gloom within, or supply enough air to remove the tangible aroma of filth. However, sitting beneath the window, arms wrapped around raised knees, back to the wall and with head bowed, the cell's shortcomings were far from Louisa's mind.

They had taken her medallion.

She felt bereft without it, as though a part of her had been forcibly removed, and it hurt. Along with her boot laces, belt, and anything else that could be used to self-harm, the medallion on its leather thong had been taken and casually tossed into a basket, warranting no more scrutiny than a cheap trinket.

Her thoughts turned to Mehmet, and she wondered if he felt as helpless as she did. Although she had no idea where he had been taken, she guessed he'd suffered the same fate. They'd been separated as soon as they'd emerged from the hospital and taken to different armoured vehicles. Then, after what felt like hours, the stuffy, enclosed van she travelled in slid to a halt and she was taken out and thrown into the cell; no phone call, no lawyer, no interpreter, no nothing. Not even an explanation of why they had been taken. And there had been no sign of Mehmet.

Now, sitting on the cold, hard concrete, she felt alone. Trapped. And was powerless to do anything about it. Questions and anxieties mounted. She had never felt so low.

Unbidden, the voice of Hiki sounded in her head, scolding her for being weak and, deep within, a core of determination began to build. Rising, she winced as cramped muscles protested at the movement, but a steely resolve had ousted her angst and she set aside her pain to stride towards the door.

Her hand was raised to pound on the metal slab when she heard the recognisable tramp of booted feet in the corridor outside. The footsteps were coming towards her cell, and her mouth twisted into a grim smile of determination.

Using all of her strength, she pummelled the door. The dull, metallic pound reverberated around the small cell, the echoes accompanied by her shrill cries to let her out, that they couldn't hold an American citizen captive without due cause. She had no idea what reaction her outburst would create, and was momentarily dumbstruck when the footsteps halted outside and she felt rather than heard the rattle of a key being inserted into the lock. A shiver of panic ran through her then, and she stepped back. Licking at lips gone dry, she flinched and stepped further back as the door burst open. Loose mortar fell to the floor as it slammed back on its hinges.

The hairs on the back of her neck rose as, outlined in the doorway by the harsh light of the corridor's fluorescent lighting, she saw the silhouette of an armed guard, his gun drawn and pointing towards her.

She took another step back, and yet another when he moved inside to step into the shaft of light from the cell's window. His narrow, tanned face was impassive as he glared at her. Dark and unblinking, his eyes seemed to bore directly into her very being; as though she were something unpleasant he'd just stepped in. Seconds passed as hours beneath his harsh scrutiny until, eventually, he gestured with his gun for her to step outside.

Too shocked by events, she didn't move.

The guard's eyes narrowed in annoyance and he began to shout in Turkish, and his gesturing with the gun became more pronounced, as though he were trying to sweep her out of the cell. Not wanting to further antagonise him, she hurried past and into the confines of the windowless corridor, where another guard waited.

On seeing her emerge he flicked his head to the left to indicate that she should follow him. The heavy clump of booted feet behind indicated that the guard who had entered the cell had stepped into line behind her as they walked towards the exit at the far end of the corridor. Rusted metal doors like the one to her own cell lined either side of their route. All were ajar, and all revealed dark maws of openings, sinister and brooding. The stench of uncared-for humanity hung heavy in the air, and her stomach churned.

She counted four openings either side of the corridor between her cell and the exit before the rattle of a key in the lock indicated the leading guard had opened it. Both she and her escort had passed before he followed, locking the door behind him. The resonant clang of it closing had a finality she found alarming, and she swallowed the saliva that built up in her throat. With head held high, she attempted to exude a confidence she did not feel as she walked towards the patch of daylight showing at the barred, half-glazed door at the end of the hallway, beyond which she knew to be the reception area.

The wait at the locked door seemed interminable while the guard to the rear sorted through the assortment of keys on his large key-ring. She was convinced he knew which key it was and was merely playing with her emotions by feigning ignorance, and ignored his leering smile as he finally opened the door and held it ajar for her to walk through.

On stepping into reception her purposeful strides faltered, and she halted. Her gaze fixed on a dishevelled figure sitting on a wooden bench secured to the whitewashed wall opposite. With his hands clasped and elbows resting on his knees, he stared at the floor before him in apparent dejection.

"Hiki!"

On hearing her cry, Hiki looked up from his inspection of the stone flags, just in time to be smothered by her embrace. Hesitantly, his arms rose to encircle her and, with a reverence bordering on awkwardness, he began to pat her on the back.

Relief on seeing the old man released pent-up emotions, and Louisa felt her eyes prick with unshed tears. Not wanting to appear weak, she extricated herself and stepped back to dab at them with the sleeve to her sweatshirt.

"It is good to see you, Louisa," said Hiki, rising to his feet. The many lines on his face deepened at his smile.

Louisa was almost at a loss for words. "But how ... why?"

Hiki shrugged, and then grinned. "Only one woman's prison in area, so obvious you get taken here. As to how, I explain about your husband and his illness." Leaning forward, he whispered, "And I have help." He inclined his head to indicate a doorway behind and to his right.

Through the glass of the upper section of the door she saw the doctor from the hospital, the one who she had grabbed when he would not tell her what was wrong with Duncan. He was talking to someone she could not see. Her eyes widened in surprise.

Hiki laughed. "He is telling Jandarma what happen to Duncan. That you could not be blamed for explosion. That it was fault in electricity. They agree to let you go. Doctor is respected man and they believe him." He shrugged again. "Me, they would not believe. But him?"

"What about Mehmet?"

157

The smile left Hiki's face, and he grimaced. "We not know where they take him yet. Doctor find out and then we go and get him also. Important we get you first, yes?"

Louisa glanced around the reception, the whiteness of freshly painted walls in sharp contrast to the stench and uncleanliness of the cell she'd left behind, and had to agree. Her freedom had been timely, and probably prevented her from doing something that would have seen her remaining in the locked room for a good deal longer than ...

A frown furrowed her brow. "How long was I in there?"

"Five or six hours. I not sure. But come. Do not think about that. You are free now. And now is time to make plans. Yes?"

His optimism was contagious and she found herself smiling.

The door behind Hiki opened and the doctor emerged, the basket containing her belongings in his hands. After nodding back to whoever it was he had been speaking to, the door swung closed behind him and he stepped forward to stand beside Hiki. Smiling, he dipped his head in acknowledgment and offered her the basket.

Her gaze fixed on the medallion, nestled amongst the folds in her belt, and she gingerly reached out to take it. Whether it was a trick of the light, or her imagination gone wild, she was sure it glowed in welcome at her touch. Although every fibre of her being urged her to immediately place the medallion over her head, she resisted. She knew her reaction to its touch would send shivers through her being, and had no inclination to allow any watching guards or the doctor to witness their reunion. That was one act that would be done in private. Instead, she pocketed it before claiming the rest of her belongings.

"Thank you, you have been very kind."

A puzzled frown formed on the doctor's face and he looked to Hiki, who translated. In response, he gave a small shrug, smiled, and turned to deposit the basket on the bench.

Louisa sensed more than saw the Light burning within

him, and instantly knew they would not be alone in their fight, that people like the doctor existed elsewhere in the world, people whose inner balance had Light in dominance, people who would help them banish Shadow. Fresh optimism swept through her, and she realised there were good people in the world who would resist the lure of Shadow.

Turning to Hiki she smiled, and said, "And now we make plans."

# 23

The sound of something scraping, sharp and shrill, against a hard surface impinged on his awareness and he tried to open his eyes. But although his lids twitched, they refused to part. He hadn't the strength. They were too heavy and he felt so very, very tired. Like a guttering candle, awareness flickered and then faded, and darkness claimed him once again.

Some time later, he had no idea how long, muted flesh-coloured light pierced the pitch blackness of his sanctuary, lighting his consciousness with filtered luminescence. Although causing him some discomfort, he felt no pain or fear, more annoyance his harmony had been disturbed. Then, as though a switch had been flicked, the light disappeared and he welcomed the return of the black. He was safe now.

Without warning, an eyelid was peeled back and a shaft of brilliant white light drove through his head. His back arched and he screamed out in pain. It felt like a white-hot poker had pierced his skull. With eyes screwed shut, he fought to return to the safety of unconsciousness, but couldn't. Something prevented him. Even though the shaft of light had gone, the pain in his head remained. His breathing came in ragged gasps, and he could feel sweat prickling his body. Would Shadow not leave him alone?

A hand grasped his arm, its touch warm and firm, and he heard his name being called.

"Duncan! Duncan!"

It was a voice he recognised, and his breathing calmed.

"Duncan. It's me, Louisa. Can you hear me?"

Louisa. The name came readily to him, and a picture formed in his mind of a tall, slim girl dressed in a light summer skirt and blouse, her long blond hair scraped back into a ponytail. She was smiling at him and her tanned skin glowed with Light from within.

"Louisa?"

The voice sounded so unlike his that it took him a moment to realise it was he who had spoken.

The pressure on his arm momentarily increased.

"How are you feeling? Can you open your eyes?"

Duncan turned his head towards the voice. He could sense her presence now, and knew it not to be a trick of Shadow.

The mere thought of Shadow caused submerged memories to flood back, and images assailed him. Of the altar, the humanoid suspended in the sac, pulsing red veins, and of his sudden flight back from wherever it was that Shadow had taken him. And of his overwhelming sense of fear. His body tensed and clawed hands once again scrabbled at sheets. His back arched off the bed as he fought to suppress the images, and strangled growls emerging from between clenched teeth.

"Duncan! Duncan! What's wrong? What's happening?"

Duncan could detect the panic in her voice, but it barely registered against the torment of knowing Shadow had grown so strong, that malice and destruction was taking physical form.

"Doctor! Isn't there anything you can do? You've got to help him!"

Pain, sharp and sudden, stabbed him in the arm. Gradually, his panic lessened, and with the lessening the images of horror faded. As the sanctuary of darkness threatened to take him again, another image formed in his mind. Standing strong and bright against despair, this image gave strength

161

when the others had taken it, gave hope when the others had quashed it, blazed like a beacon when the others had sought to suppress Light. He had last seen it when fleeing from the cavern of Shadow and now, like then, it stood for all that was right in the world and he knew he could rest in peace. If only for a short while.

Louisa's grip on Duncan's arm relaxed as his chest began to rhythmically rise and fall and his features composed in sleep. Looking across the bed, she smiled her thanks to the doctor, who nodded in acknowledgement before placing the syringe he had been holding into the disposal bin beside him. After a quick check of the heart monitor and ensuring the drip had not come loose in Duncan's arm, he left them alone.

Louisa watched him as he left. Unlike the tall, imposing, handsome doctors you would see on TV, Adem was nothing remarkable. He was fiftyish, maybe five-foot-ten, slightly overweight and losing his hair, but had been a marvel since helping Hiki get her and Mehmet free.

Turning her attention back to Duncan she studied the scar behind his ear, and rose from the chair she was sitting in to lean across and move aside a lock of hair that had fallen over it. The wound was healing neatly. The hair around it had started to grow back and it was less angry-looking, even though the black stitches remained. His physical wounds appeared to be doing well, despite the traumatic events of three days ago, his mental ones, however, needed more time.

Sighing, she sank back into the chair. Still holding onto Duncan's arm, she closed her eyes and settled into the cushioning to make herself comfortable. She had no idea what Adem had given him, but it was bound to be strong, so it could be some time before he regained consciousness.

"Louisa?"

She stirred in her sleep at the sound of her name being spoken.

"Louisa?"

162

Back arched, she stretched, and winced as the arm of the chair dug into her ribs. She exhaled noisily at the jab of dull pain.

A hand lightly grasped her arm, and her name was spoken again.

Instantly awake, she jerked upright, and her eyes fixed on Duncan.

On seeing her awaken, he smiled, and squeezed her arm.

"Where am I?"

His voice sounded weak and rasping, and she could see pain etched on his face.

"In hospital." She leaned forward, and covered his hand with her own. "How are you feeling?"

His eyes widened. "Hospital? Why? What's happened?" There was panic in his voice.

"Easy, Duncan. You're doing okay." She moved to sit on the side of the bed. "It seems you have thin bone to your skull, and when you were hit by the rock …" She paused and gave a wry smile. Then, wanting to deflect any criticism away from the old man, said, "It wasn't Hiki's fault, the doctor said it could have happened at any time."

Duncan grimaced. "I'm not blaming him, don't worry. I would've done the same thing in his position. He was only doing what he thought right." His gaze flicked around the room, briefly resting on the heart monitor before returning to her. "H-how long?"

"Four days."

"Four days!" He made to surge upright, but winced in pain and flopped back onto the bed, eyes screwed shut, beads of sweat forming on his forehead.

In panic, Louisa slipped from the bed, ready to head out of the room to find Adem, but Duncan reached out to grab her arm. There was desperation in the gaze he turned on her.

"I'm fine, really. I just feel so … so weak and useless. I – we – should be doing something, and we've wasted so much time. Shadow is getting strong."

Duncan's eyelids fluttered closed and the grip on her arm slipped free.

"So strong."

Although the two words were barely audible, a frisson of apprehension prickled her skin.

"Louisa?"

Her heart faltered at the call of her name, and then nearly thumped its way out of her chest when it restarted. Eyes wide, she spun towards the doorway.

"Louisa, what is the matter?"

"Mehmet?"

On seeing him standing at the doorway, rucksack in hand, brow furrowed in confusion, she sighed in relief, the tension slipping free of her muscles.

"Did I scare you?" Not waiting for an answer, he stepped inside the room and tossed the rucksack beside the chair before peering down at Duncan. "He has not woken yet?"

Her composure restored, she raised a hand to run it through her hair, more of a reaction to her fright than a need to tidy it. "Briefly. A moment ago." She smiled a tight-lipped smile, and then moved forward to sit on the bed again to look at Duncan, so relaxed in sleep despite his whispered proclamation. "But he is so weak." Looking up, she knew that the fear Duncan's two words had inspired showed in her gaze.

Mehmet misinterpreted, and sat in the chair, leaned back, stretched out his legs and steepled his fingers. "He is young and strong. He will soon get his strength back, and then we fight Shadow."

"But how? We have no idea what we're going to do, and Duncan said …"

At her words, Mehmet tensed. "What did Duncan say?"

The look he gave her was searching, as though he expected him to have given an instruction on what their next move was to be. Louisa had the strangest feeling that leadership of their group had changed hands, that Mehmet, after being the guardian of the truth for so long, yearned for Duncan to take control and give them direction. Unfortunately, she doubted her answer would satisfy that yearning. Almost reluctantly, she repeated his words, not wanting to dash Mehmet's hopes.

Instead of being taken aback, however, Mehmet merely grunted, nodded in acceptance, and tapped the rucksack with a foot. "Good job we went back to get these. With his books, Duncan will know what we must do."

Louisa was stunned. She stood to glare down at him. "How can you know that? Look at him!" She flung an arm in Duncan's direction. "It could be weeks before he is ready to get out of bed, never mind decide what we have to do. Even if the answer is in the books, what makes you think he can find it?"

"Could you keep your voices down? Someone is trying to rest here."

Although faint and rasping, Duncan's interruption was timely, and prevented Louisa from saying something she would later regret. On swivelling to stare down at him, the shock of hearing him speak must have shown on her face. His lips curved into a smile, a smile that did not reach his eyes. Something still bothered him.

The mattress settled beneath her weight as she perched on its edge. "Feeling any better?"

Duncan blinked in answer, and then said, "A little. Even if my head feels like it's about to explode."

Rising to his feet, Mehmet reached down to grasp the rucksack, and then lifted it for Duncan to see. "It is good you are back with us. We have plans to make."

"Mehmet!"

Frowning, he switched his attention to Louisa, the arm holding the rucksack lowering under her disapproving glare.

"I know what you are about to say, but we have to make plans," he glanced to Duncan, "even though he is not yet strong."

165

"He's right. We need a plan."

The haunted look that had entered Duncan's eyes when he had last passed out was there again. Aware he was now the centre of attention, he turned his head on the pillow to peer at the monitor to watch the peaks of his heartbeat cross the screen before speaking again. "Shadow is growing too strong."

When he again faced them, the flesh to his face appeared pallid and waxy and dark rings had formed beneath his eyes, all in the space of five heartbeats. Reaching out, he grasped Louisa's arm and fixed her with a gaze of such intensity that a cold shiver worked its way down her spine.

"And I have seen its strength." His grip tightened. "And felt it."

"What do you mean?"

Mehmet's words broke whatever affliction had affected Duncan. Letting go of Louisa's arm, he closed his eyes and sighed, his hand dropping to his side.

Released from his hold, Louisa rubbed at her arm and shifted on the bed, flicking Mehmet an anxious glance. This was not the Duncan they knew – dark and gloom-laden. Either the bang on the head had caused damage to his brain, as the doctor had forewarned, or the drugs had overloaded his system. For their sake, she hoped it was the drugs.

A hand suddenly gripped her arm, fingers digging into flesh, and she screamed.

Mehmet lunged forward and wrestled Duncan's hand free of its grip. At his touch, Duncan raised his head from the pillow and fixed him with a feverish gaze, eyes wide and manic. On the other side of the bed, the peaks to his heartbeat flashed rapidly across the screen.

"The bell tower. We have to find the bell tower. That is the key. Promise me you will find the bell tower."

Mehmet nodded. Although the movement was slight and hesitant, it was enough to satisfy, and Duncan lowered his head to the pillow and closed his eyes.

"You have to find the bell tower."

The reiteration was whispered, but clearly audible in the silence that settled on the room, a silence that was broken by Mehmet giving voice to the question that rose in Louisa's mind.

"What bell tower, Duncan?"

There was no response. Reaching out, Mehmet shook his arm and asked the question again, but whatever energy Duncan had summoned to make his announcement had drained him. His chest rose and fell in the pattern of sleep, his features, whilst still holding the wax-like quality, had relaxed, and the heartbeat on the screen had steadied. Despite their need, there would be no quick answer to the question.

An hour later, Louisa stood and listened as Mehmet and Adem conversed. To her frustration, she could not understand a word they were saying and Mehmet, not wanting to punctuate the conversation with translations, had told her to be patient, that he would tell her what was discussed when they had finished. Even though their discussion only lasted a couple of minutes, it felt longer. Adem had barely left the room before she pounced.

"Well? Did they find anything wrong?"

Mehmet stepped back under the verbal onslaught, hands held out in surrender. "Enough, Louisa. Slow down. Let me breathe and I will tell you."

She raised her hands and ran them through her hair in what was getting to be a habit when under stress. Breathing deeply, she forced herself to relax, and allowed Mehmet to guide her to the chair beside the bed vacated by Duncan when they had collected him for a second scan. Then, sitting on the bed's edge, he waited for her to settle before telling her what Adem had told him.

"There is no damage to Duncan's brain. Adem is sure that his madness was caused by the drugs."

"Thank the Light for that," murmured Louisa, relieved at the news.

"He has taken Duncan off them, so he should soon wake

167

up on his own. He will be weak and suffer some discomfort, but his pain will be less." He smiled. "Is that what you wanted to hear?"

Louisa nodded, and released the breath she had been holding.

"That is good, because there is something else. It may be nothing, but ..." He shrugged, as though he himself considered it inconsequential.

Even so, Louisa stiffened at his words. Her earlier relief dissipated, and she forced herself to ask the question, even though she feared the answer. "What's wrong?"

The slight curving of Mehmet's lips did nothing to ease frayed nerves. She could tell the smile was his attempt to soften the impact of what he had to say.

"There is a shadow over Duncan's skull where the rock cracked the bone."

"A shadow?" Louisa lurched to her feet and, shaking her head, covered her eyes with her hands. Mehmet's earlier explanation of how Shadow latched onto its human host during infancy sprang to the forefront of her mind, and she feared that, in his weakened state, Shadow had found a way to bypass his defences.

Her fingertips slipped down to rest on her cheeks. Eyes haunted, she gave voice to her fears. "Has he ... is he –" – she stumbled over the next word, "possessed?"

Mehmet moved away from the bed and reached out to ease her hands from her face. Keeping a light grip, he held her gaze as he lowered her arms to her sides. "If you're asking is he now Shadow, the answer is no. Adem is convinced there is a fault in the scan. He wanted to run another, to make sure, but his superiors will not allow it. Scans cost too much money, and this is a poor country."

Tears of relief sprang to her eyes, and she buried her head in Mehmet's chest. His arms rose to wrap around her, to hold her close for a moment before he eased her away. Then, raising her chin with his fingertips, he met her tear-filled gaze, smiled, and said, "Stop worrying. He is of Light."

Louisa stepped out of his embrace to turn away and dab at her eyes with the sleeve to her sweatshirt. Over her shoulder, she asked, "How can Adem be sure the shadow is a fault?"

Mehmet shrugged. "Because there is no other explanation."

The answer was no answer at all, and despite Mehmet's confidence that all was well, Louisa had a nagging suspicion all was not as well as they would want. Before she had chance to dwell on it further, the rumble of rubber-shod wheels in the corridor outside signalled the return of Duncan. With practiced ease, two orderlies wheeled the gurney into the room and lifted him onto the bed. After covering him with a blanket, they left, leaving her and Mehmet alone with him.

After a moment spent staring at the comatose form, Mehmet moved to where the rucksack lay on the floor and picked it up to deposit it on the chair. After undoing the buckle that held it closed he reached in and removed three books. Holding them out for Louisa to see, he said, "Which one do you want?"

Confused by the request, Louisa stared at the titles, and the confusion receded. She gave a wan smile. "I'll take *The Secret Gospel of Thomas*. If Thomas laid down clues as to the end of the world, I may as well read up on what he has to say."

Mehmet nodded. "Good choice. And while you read I will look through the others, to see if I can find the bell tower that Duncan says we should look for. Who knows, his madness may not be madness at all."

Taking the book, Louisa settled into the chair to read while Mehmet left to grab a chair of his own. Although she was not a big reader, usually preferring to be doing rather than reading about it, the contents of Thomas's gospel drew her in and kept her there. She had no doubt it was due to the fact they were directly involved in its prophecy of an apocalyptic future, and were a part of the plans to prevent its happening. Lost in its contents, Mehmet's return with the chair barely registered on her awareness, nor did she notice when he left again some time later to fetch them coffee.

Minutes turned to hours. Unaccustomed to long stints spent staring at written words, her focus began to drift, until they began to merge into one. At that point she flipped the book closed and laid it face-down on her lap to free her hands to rub at tired eyes.

Mehmet spotted the movement and closed the book he had been reading. After laying it on the floor he rose to his feet, closed his eyes and rolled his head before raising his arms to shoulder level to stretch.

"Ahhhh. That is better. I feel like my head is about to explode."

Louisa had to agree. Her eyes felt dry and gritty, and the muscles in her back and legs ached from sitting in one position for too long. Leaning back in the chair, she stretched to ease the aches and pains of inactivity.

"You understand better what we face?"

In all honesty, she didn't. A lot of what was prophesised to happen had been happening for centuries. The floods, the tsunamis, the riots, the wars, religious battles; you name it, whatever Thomas had foretold would come to pass had been happening for a long, long time. To her, it seemed as though the world had forever lived on the edge of insanity.

Keeping her thoughts to herself, she placed the book on Duncan's bed and then rose to walk across to the window to ease apart the blinds. Her free hand caressed the medallion through the fabric of her sweatshirt as she gazed at the world beyond. Outside, traffic was building up. A purple haze of colour-muting exhaust fumes hung heavy in the air, and the shadows were lengthening. In a matter of hours darkness would chase away sunlight for another day. After a moment's contemplation she allowed the blinds to flick closed, and turned to face Mehmet. "Why now?"

With a casual shrug of his shoulders in a gesture of not knowing the answer but having a stab at it anyway, he said, "Why not now? Like me, you have seen the news. The world is in a state of unrest. We have wars, famine, riots, and natural disasters. There have been floods, volcanoes spitting fire, tsunamis. All is madness, and getting worse every year. Just as Thomas foretold."

Louisa leaned back against the window sill, palms and backside resting on its ledge. "But we have always had these. What makes the 'now' so special?"

"I do not know the answer, but in here," he patted his chest, "I know that now is the time. Why would you and Duncan appear if now was not the time? And what about the Light? Why did the Guardian appear if now is not the time?"

Louisa sighed. He was right. Coupled with Duncan's assertion that Shadow was growing too strong, she knew that 'now' *was* the time. Even so, there was one part of Thomas's prophecy that made no sense, and she decided to ask about it, even though she doubted its happening or not happening would have any effect on what was to come. Giving Mehmet a half-smile, she said, "But the skies haven't rained blood yet, have they?"

Instead of smiling, Mehmet sighed, and moved across to lean against the window sill beside her. Turning his head to meet her gaze, he said, "Ah, but they have, in Kerala, southern India, September 2001."

Dumbstruck, Louisa was at a loss as to what to say. Her jaw dropped, and she knew she gaped like some sort of dullard.

"Scientists think it may be alien, from an exploding meteor. News reports in India said that people heard a big boom in the sky before it rained blood." He shrugged. "So it could be so."

"How …" Louisa paused to gather her composure. "How do you know all this?"

Mehmet's eyes glazed in memory. "Father Mason."

"Duncan's mentor?"

Memhet nodded. "He studied Thomas's prophecy and he found out about it. I think he was getting close to the answer as to how Shadow will fight its war. That is why he died. Even though Duncan said it happened in an accident, I know Father Mason was killed because he knew too much, and used his knowledge to help us." He looked away to gaze at the floor in abstraction. "He was a good man."

"That he was."

Duncan's whispered words snapped Louisa's attention towards the bed. Eyes, bright and free from drug-induced miasma gazed back at her. Her lips curled into a smile of relief, and she shoved herself away from the sill to move over to the bed. It creaked as she sat on its edge.

"How are you feeling?"

"Like a train ran over my head."

Duncan's eyes fixed on the book beside her, nestled on the bed cover. Sighing, he briefly closed his eyes before again fixing his attention on her. There was a hint of fear behind the gaze that worried her, but before she had chance to question it, he spoke.

"How did that get here?"

"I went back with Hiki to the village to get it." Stepping forward from the window, Mehmet grabbed the remaining two books from beside his chair and brought them over to the bed, and laid them beside the one Louisa had been reading. "I brought them back. Hiki has stayed behind to work on the farm. He will come when we need him."

Reaching out, Louisa lightly gripped Duncan's arm. "And I think he's feeling a little guilty at you being in here." She gave a half-smile.

The crinkle of skin around his eyes as he smiled dispelled the fear she had seen lurking, and she almost let the matter drop. But given his manic state before being taken for the scan, she knew she had to get him to face whatever it was that had caused his behaviour, even though he may not yet be mentally strong enough to cope.

"Duncan."

Something in her tone must have unnerved him. The fear behind his eyes returned, and she stumbled to a halt.

Mehmet, as though possessing a sixth sense, gave her a nod of encouragement before moving away from the bed to sit in the chair she had been using when reading.

In an effort to gather her courage, Louisa glanced briefly to the book cover before looking up. Bringing her free hand across to rest lightly on the hand that gripped Duncan's arm, she held his gaze and smiled, in the hope of banishing his demons.

"When you woke last time, before they took you down for a scan, you seemed to be ... well, upset." Although to describe him as upset was an understatement, she did not want to alarm him if he did not remember what had happened. "And you mentioned things that sounded like ..." she glanced to Mehmet, who again nodded encouragement, "a ... a warning, and also an instruction."

At her quietly spoken words, Duncan turned his head on the pillow to gaze towards the window.

"Can you remember?"

Silence descended on the room, as if the whole had been swaddled in cotton wool. Not a sound intruded and, not wanting to disturb the tableau, neither Louisa nor Mehmet moved a muscle. Eventually, when Louisa thought no answer would be forthcoming, the silence was broken by two softly spoken words.

"I remember."

# 24

The narrow strips of daylight between the slats of the blinds darkened as dusk began to settle outside, but Duncan hardly noticed. Both the wall and the window merged into one fuzzy image as he attempted to bury frightening memories. They refused to lie dormant, however, and demanded his attention, sucking him in to draw him back to the dark place of his dreams.

The monstrosity he had seen in the cavern appeared in his mind's-eye, floating in the space between him and the window. Suspended in the altar, its head slowly raising to fix him with a malevolent, sightless gaze. Before panic could fully set in, a warmness asserted itself in his chest, and his rapid breathing quieted.

The figure suspended in the altar emanated smug satisfaction. Even without discernible facial features to mock him, Duncan could sense it. A knot of anger formed in the pit of his stomach, anger that the being, whatever it was, could hope to control him and turn him from the Light.

As if by reflex, his right hand moved up to settle over the medallion resting beneath his gown. Still staring at the image, he said, "I am of Light."

Like ripples moving across a reflection on a still pool, the picture wavered, and then disappeared.

Duncan sighed and closed his eyes. Not a sound impinged on his awareness and, for a second or two, he imagined he was alone, safe in a world without pain and suffering, but he knew the reality to be different. Easing onto his back, he stared at the ceiling, and said, "I have seen Shadow."

Although softly spoken, he could sense both Mehmet's and Louisa's consternation.

"I have been to its lair and seen how strong it has become, how its evil is being formed. How it plans to bring about the apocalypse."

"Wh … wh … what do you mean?"

There was a nervous tremor to Louisa's voice.

"The first time I saw it I thought it was a nightmare, from the blow to the head, but the second … " He left the sentence unfinished. His mind had drifted back to the cavern with its altar and the monstrosity suspended within.

"Duncan, from the beginning. We do not understand. Please, tell us what you mean."

There was an impatience in Mehmet's voice that pulled him back. Even so, the image in his head remained, giving him focus for the story he once assumed was a figment of feverish dreams.

As he described his first visit to the cavern and the lead-up to his fleeing at the end of the second, his initial reluctance to give voice to what he suffered whilst unconscious disappeared, and he found himself wanting to share, to have them understand what they faced, for he firmly believed the cavern to be real, and that evil was gaining its own creature. Light had the Guardian, but what form would the essence of Shadow take?

By the time he had told them of his escape his throat had gone dry and he was having difficulty speaking. Almost apologetically, he asked for some water.

Rising from the seat beside the bed, Mehmet grabbed a beaker and jug from the bedside cabinet and handed the beaker to Louisa while he poured. Then, after replacing the jug, he eased his hands under Duncan's head to raise it while Louisa placed the drink to his lips.

After drinking half, Duncan felt ready to continue, and nodded his thanks.

Once again seated, Mehmet leaned forward, hands clasped, elbows resting on his knees, and said, "Tell us of the bell tower. What has it to do with the cavern?"

Duncan stared at the ceiling again and shook his head. "I'm not sure. All I know is that it blazed with Light, as though it was a beacon, and that it stood near the entrance leading down to the cavern." Turning his head, he met Mehmet's earnest gaze, "And, like I know the obscenity to be real, I know the bell tower is there to help us. How, I don't know, but we have to find it."

Mehmet held his gaze before nodding, and then settled back into the chair, fingers interlaced across his chest as he stared into space.

"What do you think we have to do?" Louisa asked.

After a moment's contemplation Duncan finally answered, "We have to find the cavern and prevent the creature from gaining life."

Louisa sighed, and grimaced, her hand reaching out to grasp his arm. "Somehow, that is what I thought you'd say."

"Duncan is right. We need to find this demon before it is too late. But first we need to find the bell tower. For then we will know where to look for the cavern. Can you describe the place you saw?"

The image of the market square was indelibly imprinted in Duncan's mind and it did not take much to describe the location, or the image of the bell tower and church. Once he had recalled all he could, Mehmet rose to his feet.

"Right, I will go and search the internet while you get your strength back. And you," – he glanced to Louisa and smiled, "take good care of him."

"But how will you know where to start?" Louisa asked. "The bell tower could be anywhere in the world."

Mehmet shook his head. "It is in Turkey. I will find it, no worries."

"But ..."

Mehmet reached out and placed a finger to her lips.

There was a sombre undercurrent to his voice as he then said, "Believe me, it is in Turkey. Why else would we all be here if it were not so?"

Giving a smile of reassurance, he then walked towards the door. Before leaving, he turned, and said, "I will get Adem to bring in a TV. That way you will not get ... how you say?" He grinned. "Bored."

Despite the solemnity of the situation, Duncan smiled as the door softly closed on his exit. "Sounds quite chirpy, doesn't he?"

"That's because he has something to focus his attention on. Something to do other than to worry about how we can hope to replicate what was done over two thousand years ago."

She moved over to the window and eased aside the slats to gaze at the world beyond. Her Light glowed brightly against the darkness of twilight, and Duncan allowed himself the luxury of revelling in her inner beauty, his thoughts drifting.

In a short space of time he had come a long way. Only a matter of weeks ago he had been safe, if unhappy, studying theology at Blackfriars, and was now thousands of miles away in a foreign country, involved in the saving of mankind.

The thought brought a smile to his face. The idea would have been laughable if he hadn't had been through the experience in the Cavern of Rebirth and subsequently seen for himself the powers at play. Even now, after the trials of the past few days, he found it hard to believe he was a direct descendant of Judas, and others who had shared the lineage, and felt unworthy to continue where they'd left off. And to think that all he'd ever wanted was to decide for himself what he wanted to do with his life.

"If we defeat the creature in the altar that will not be the end of it, will it?"

Louisa's question broke his train of thought. She had turned away from the window and now leaned back against the sill, arms folded across her chest. Dark rings had formed beneath her eyes, and Duncan could see tension lines in her face. She looked tired, and a little afraid. Much like he felt, in fact.

Giving a half-smile, he said, "No, only the beginning. I believe the creature is to Shadow what the Guardian is to Light. Mankind has created a god in its own image, and that is what I believe Shadow is attempting to do. By feeding the world's evils and wrongs into one focal point they intend to create the ultimate evil." Duncan's lips curled into a lopsided smile. "The antichrist, for want of a better description, and then we will have the apocalypse – in person. Wherever it treads, catastrophe will follow. Like Mehmet told us, Shadow has no interest in balance and harmony, it seeks total control."

"But if we kill it, doesn't that make us evil too?"

"And therein lays the paradox."

The skin around Louisa's eyes crinkled as she frowned in confusion. "I don't understand."

"And neither do I. Believe me, that is one of many similar discussions I had when I was at Blackfriars, none of which answered my questions. All I know is that in this case, the end will justify the means. How can we turn aside and show the other cheek when we know that will also be slapped?"

Louisa's lips quirked into a wry smile. "Now you've lost me."

Duncan returned it with one of his own. "I think I've lost myself as well."

The door to the room opened and an orderly appeared with a television set perched on a trolley. Without glancing at either of them, he pushed the trolley to the far corner of the room and plugged in the TV at the wall socket. After turning it on to make sure it worked, he flicked through the channels, using the remote, before turning it off again and leaving.

After his exit, Louisa looked to Duncan and said, "At least now we have some entertainment."

"For you, perhaps. I suddenly feel very tired. Sorry, but I'm worn out." A smile tugged at the corners of his mouth. "Must be all that talking."

Louisa's eyes widened. "Duncan, I'm so sorry. With all the talk about Shadow and bell towers I forgot all about you being injured. I'll go grab a coffee while you get some sleep."

Instead of moving away, however, she held his gaze. Duncan knew she saw something other than his face as she stared down. Puzzled, he frowned, and asked, "What is it?"

"The last time we left you alone, you …"

"I what?"

Cheeks puffed out, she tilted her head towards the ceiling for a moment before again turning her attention to him. "You destroyed your room."

This time it was his turn to be surprised. "I did what?"

Smiling, Louisa said, "Tomorrow, hey? You've had more than enough excitement for one day." Rising, she made to leave.

"I destroyed my room?" Other than his visions, the last thing he remembered before waking up in the hospital was being in Mehmet's shack in the mountains after his brush with Shadow on the trail. He certainly had no recollection of anything else happening. "What do you mean?"

Louisa sighed, and moved across to settle on the bed. It creaked in protest. "I think it must have been when you used your medallion to escape your dreams. You said it heated up when you faced the … the thing in the altar, and then more so when you fled from the bell tower, when you sensed you were in danger. Whatever power drew you back to your body blasted into the room." She paused a moment before continuing. "And destroyed it. When Mehmet and I ran in you were kneeling on the bed, arms outstretched, not a mark on you or the bedding. But the rest of the room … "

Duncan gazed at the ceiling, his eyes drawn to a fly that was walking near the light fitting. He had no memory of the events she described, and could not understand how he could destroy a room without having some knowledge of it.

"And your medallion, it blazed with white light."

At the mention of the medallion, Duncan lost interest in the fly and reached inside his gown to pull the disc of metal free and stare at the slots on its surface, their pattern now as familiar as the features to his face. How could something so simple imbue such power? Turning his attention to Louisa, he asked, "What are they? Why do they react to us as they do?"

"I asked Mehmet that question after we ... after we found you, but he didn't know for sure. All he said was that as far as he knew, they acted as a conduit for all that had worn it before, that some of our ancestors' life-force was stored within the metal, to help those that followed. It sort of made sense at the time, so I accepted it on face value." This time her smile was not forced. "And, like you, I have felt its help when needed."

"Even so, you're afraid to let me stay alone in case Shadow comes after me again."

Louisa nodded. "You could say that." Making light of the situation, she laughed, and added, "And I doubt whether the hospital could stand to have another room destroyed."

A snort of amusement escaped Duncan's lips. He raised the medallion, and said, "But it appears I have this to protect me."

The smile on Louisa's face faded, and her eyes narrowed in concern. "But will it be enough? You've said yourself how strong Shadow is getting. Will they ... will *we* be enough to prevent what Thomas has said will come to pass?"

"One thing at a time, hey? First I have to be strong enough to get out of this bed." Smiling, he continued, "Now go get that coffee. I'll be fine." On seeing her eyes narrow further, he added, "Really. I'll be fine."

She nodded her acceptance and rose to leave, but halted at the door to look back. "You sure?"

Duncan raised a hand to shoo her away. "I'm sure." The smile on his face remained fixed in place until after she had flicked off the light and the door had closed on her exit. Once she had gone his confidence faded and, rolling onto his side, he cushioned his head beneath his hands and stared at the wall opposite. She was right, they were so few and Shadow appeared to be so many, how could they hope to succeed? By telling both her and Mehmet of his vision he had given them all direction, but would that be enough?

A voice, female and loud, broke the silence, and flickering light illuminated the room. Too fast, he rolled over towards the direction the voice had come from, and winced as a stabbing sensation shot through his head.

He squeezed closed his eyes and fought the pain to lever himself up on to his elbows, to wait for his head to stop spinning before he dared open them. Gradually, the spinning sensation settled, the nausea passed and the stabbing pain in his head receded. However, fearful of their return, it was with some trepidation that he slowly eased open his eyelids to stare at the flickering screen in the far corner of the room. Somehow, the TV had turned itself on. The beat of his heart quieted at the realisation, and he chuckled. The orderly must have messed with the controls when he'd set the damn thing up and pressed a reminder button, which was the only explanation for its sudden burst into life.

Taking care not to move too suddenly and set off the pain in his head, he pulled back the blanket, intending to swing his legs free and turn off the racket, but the American drawl of the presenter had him pause and stare at the TV. The channel was CNN, and the caption at the bottom of the screen read: 'Istanbul, Turkey'.

But it was the figure at the centre of the picture that captured Duncan's attention. It was the Guardian. He stood in front of a bank of six large TV screens set in a curved wall behind a circular table around which sat twenty world leaders, his arms outstretched towards the cameras and the politicians seated at the table stared up at him in open-mouthed astonishment. Dressed in the black ankle-length coat, black combats and T-shirt he had been wearing when

181

Duncan had bumped into him at the airport, his appearance was unmistakable.

"Today, at the G20 summit in Istanbul to discuss mankind's descent into anarchy, the world's leaders were shaken when this man suddenly appeared in their midst."

As Duncan watched, the TV screens behind the Guardian sprang to life.

"At the same time, the in-house monitors were hacked and brought under outside control."

Images of war, famine, death, destruction and natural disasters flashed onto the screens, each image reinforcing the message of what the summit was about.

"The images displayed on the screens appear to be in support of a unilateral peace programme and a halt to all warfare, but also suggest that Mother Earth is rebelling against mankind's meddling. Is it a warning? Given the sudden, explosive ending to this encounter, we could be forgiven for thinking so."

The images on the screens flashed faster and faster. Each hideous picture ran into the next with increasing speed until it became impossible to discern one from the other. At the point when all seemed like it would spiral out of control, the screens suddenly went blank, and the Guardian smiled. Turning, he looked towards them and raised a hand. Immediately they sprang back to life, each bearing one letter, blood-red against a backdrop of a nuclear wasteland. In English, they spelled

THE END

At their appearance, tables within the auditorium were shoved aside and armed guards raced towards the Guardian, guns drawn and aimed towards him as the world leaders speedily retreated from camera shot.

Instead of running or offering himself in surrender, the Guardian continued to smile, and then clapped his hands. As though it were a command, the screens exploded, sending a shower of glass into the room. The camera taking the shot must have been affected by the explosion, as the picture shook and was briefly affected by bright flashes and wavy lines before a dust and smoke-obscured picture returned.

A knot of fear formed in the pit of Duncan's stomach and he found himself willing the TV screen to clear, to see that no harm had befallen the personification of Light. Although he could not see what was happening, he could hear cries of terror and shouts of confusion emanating from the room. In the midst of the mayhem a gunshot rang out, swiftly followed by a scream of pain.

Without realising, Duncan found himself perched on the edge of the bed, eyes glued to the television. He had no doubt its jump into life had nothing to do with the orderly, that it had everything to do with their mission, and that the Guardian was somehow responsible, doing what he could to help. But would his essence perish for the cause? Could it perish for the cause?

Eventually, the picture cleared enough to reveal the after effects of the explosion. Toppled tables lay on the floor and crouching guards, guns still drawn, inched their way through a haze of smoke, treading on broken glass, spilled drinks and spoiled table-linen as they made their way towards the spot where the Guardian had stood. But he was not there. He had disappeared as suddenly as he had at the airport.

The knot of fear in Duncan's stomach unwound and the tension in his muscles eased. He knew by the reaction of those that sought him he had not been captured or shot.

The voice of the newsreader again intruded as a picture of the Guardian filled the screen, his eyes all-knowing and his smile, like the Mona Lisa, enigmatic.

"Despite a thorough search of the government building where the summit was taking place, the location of which has been, and still is, a closely guarded secret, the intruder has not been located. Nor has his point of entry. Security staff are at this moment going through CCTV footage in an attempt to find out how he entered the building and how he managed to bypass the high levels of security that were in place. Also a mystery is how he managed to infiltrate the in-house television controls."

As though it were a signal, the TV switched off, and the door to Duncan's room crashed open. An oblong shaft of yellow light from the illuminated corridor outside slanted across the bed, a man-shaped silhouette at its centre.

"Did you see him? Did you? The Guardian?"

Mehmet stood inside the threshold, eyes wide, his hand on the door-knob.

"I was on the internet when he appeared. Phuff!" He strode into the room and snapped his fingers for emphasis. "Just like that. By magic." He shook his head and pursed his lips in a show of admiration.

Duncan smiled as he noted the excitement and wonder shining from his eyes. "Forgive me, I forgot you have never seen him before."

"Never seen who before?"

At Louisa's polite enquiry, both men looked towards the doorway. With brows drawn in puzzlement, she stared at them, a cardboard beaker of coffee held in one hand.

Duncan glanced to Mehmet before he spoke. "I think you'd better turn the television on. There's a programme we think you should watch."

"And then we go to the internet room," said Mehmet, "because there is something I have to show you." There was excitement in the gaze he flicked to each of them in turn. "Both of you." Standing, he gave a low bow and bade her enter with a sweep of a hand. "Enjoy your coffee while I go and get a chair with wheels for Duncan."

Louisa had barely walked three paces before Mehmet had moved past her and out into the corridor, calling over his shoulder as he left, "I will not be long." Then, with a wave of a hand, he disappeared from view.

Having watched him as he strode from the room, Louisa turned her attention to Duncan, the look of puzzlement still fixed to her face. "Just what has been going on since I left you?"

Gritting his teeth, Duncan levered himself back onto the bed and said, "I hope that coffee is as strong as it smells."

# 25

Mehmet leaned across Duncan, his right hand gripping the mouse as he moved the cursor to a link. When it hovered over the one he wanted he left-clicked. Within moments an image formed on the screen.

Duncan gasped. The bell tower that sprang to life was the same as the one in his vision, the church behind a mirror image to the one he remembered. Beneath were the words, 'Church of St Theodore and its bell tower'.

"Is this the bell tower you saw in your dreams?"

Dumbly, Duncan nodded. Even though the picture showed it to be made of dull, dressed stone, it was not difficult for him to imagine it blazing with Light.

Triumphant, Mehmet let go of the mouse and clapped his hands in delight. Turning to Louisa, whose hands still gripped the handles of Duncan's wheelchair, he said, "See? I told you the bell tower was in Turkey, and now I have found it."

"A-are you sure that's the one, Duncan?"

Duncan didn't need a closer inspection to know it was the bell tower of his vision. With its domed roof to the top tier of small arched windows, the two lower tiers of taller arched windows, its tall, square base with decorative buttresses between the corners and lower tier of arches, it was instantly recognisable.

"I'm sure." Although reluctant to take his eyes from the image of the beacon of Light that had drawn him from the cavern, he turned to peer up at Mehmet. "Where is it?"

"Derinkuyu."

"Where?" Duncan had never heard of the place, which was hardly surprising, his geographical knowledge of Turkey being next to nothing.

Smiling, Mehmet leaned back against the workstation, arms folded across his chest. "A small town twelve hours drive from here, in Cappadocia. And," he leaned forward, "there is also an underground city."

The icy fingers of nervous excitement mixed with dread that probed at Duncan's heart confirmed his feelings. Derinkuyu was the location of the cavern. He switched his gaze back to the monitor to stare at the tower, finding it hard to believe that a mere twelve hours drive away the ultimate evil was being formed. An evil they must face and overcome. All of a sudden, now that their destination was set, the task seemed even more daunting.

As though sensing his unease, Louisa placed her hands on his shoulders and squeezed them.

"All of the pieces fit. You said that evil is being formed in a cavern underground, and that the bell tower is nearby. Well, in Derinkuyu we have both, so now we must make plans to travel."

As though it was all settled, Mehmet pushed himself away from the workstation with a thrust of his backside.

"Whoa! Hold on a second."

The light touch of Louisa's hands left Duncan's shoulders as, folding her arms across her chest, she glared at Mehmet.

"Duncan is in no fit state to travel anywhere, let alone face whatever creature awaits us in that cavern. You've seen the strength of Shadow, so how can you expect us to go hot-footing it to this Derinkuyu place before we know *exactly* where we are going or how it is protected? Just the three of us? What would Hiki say if he knew we went racing off to face the … face the devil without letting him know about it first?"

Mehmet's eyes widened at the verbal onslaught. In a gesture of surrender, he spread his arms, but it did not prevent Louisa from adding to what she had already said.

"And what about the Guardian? What about his near suicide mission to grab the world's attention? Would he want us to go face that thing underprepared? I'm all for action, but –"

"Louisa."

Duncan's quiet interjection was enough to halt the tirade, and she faltered to a halt.

It was not just her words, but the rapid-fire way in which she'd said them that had sent a tingle of alarm down his spine. He'd sensed her unease whilst they had watched a rerun of the news report, but had incorrectly, as it now appeared, assumed it was a fear for the Guardian's essence that prompted it. Now, he was not so sure. Unlike Mehmet, who seemed to be looking forward to the confrontation, she was terrified at the thought.

Using his feet, he pushed the wheelchair back and to the side so he could see her. Fear lurked behind her eyes, and in her movement as she swept both hands through her hair to brush it back from her face.

"Mehmet's right. We need to go to Derinkuyu."

"But –"

Duncan held up a hand to forestall what she was about to say. "But you are also right. I'm not strong enough to cope with a twelve-hour car trip. Not yet." He raised a hand to rub at an eye that had begun to water. "I need time to rest or I'll be no help in what it is we have to do."

"Do? We have to kill the creature, before it kills us. That is what we have to do."

At Mehmet's words, Duncan's brows rose. "And you a man of Light?" Although what he'd said was correct, he was surprised by the vehemence in his tone.

In answer, Mehmet closed his eyes and tilted back his head, exhaling sharply through his nose before daring to exchange glances with both Duncan and Louisa.

Palms facing out, he held up his hands. "Please, let me explain." Sitting on the edge of the workstation, he glanced to each of them in turn before continuing. "Since I was a little boy I was told of the evils of Shadow by my people, and of how we were chosen by Thomas to protect the Cavern of Rebirth and its secrets. That one day it could be me, as a direct descendant, who could lead the disciples of Light in its battle. Like those who went before me, all my life I have known of this, unlike you –" he gestured to each with a hand, "who did not know until recently. You understand?

"I am trying to say that now I know it is to be in my time I want to face the enemy. Destroy that which wants to destroy us. I have had a lifetime of knowing, and now want to carry out what I was born to do, so that harmony may be restored."

A zephyr brushed Duncan's face as Louisa stepped passed him to lean in and embrace Mehmet. Hesitantly, his arms rose to encircle her.

After a moment she stepped back, letting her hands slide down his arms to lace her fingers between his. Meeting his gaze, she said, "I understand, really I do. But that is exactly why we can't rush in like fools. We have to be ready, or your lifetime of knowing will be wasted. And who is there to follow you if it all goes wrong? Who is there ready to take over from where you left off if you die for the cause?"

Mehmet sighed. "At this moment there is no one. I am the last."

Her point proven, Louisa stepped back, allowing Mehmet's fingers to slip through her own.

He ran a hand through his hair, much like the habit Louisa had fallen into when worried, and then shook his head. "Ayayay! Sometimes I can be like – how you say? A bull in a china shop." Smiling a tight-lipped smile, he looked to Duncan. "So, what do you think we should do?"

✶✶✶

Mehmet slowed the car at the end of the drive leading from the hospital, and then shot forward into the early morning traffic that clogged the main highway. He ignored the blare of horns that greeted his manoeuvre and, with barely a glance in the mirrors, cut across the lane to overtake a slow-moving truck. The car behind them jammed on its brakes, the sounding of its horn testimony to the driver's annoyance. Mehmet's only reaction was to gesticulate out of the window and curse in his native tongue. He grinned and peered at Duncan via the rear-view mirror.

"It is good to be outside again, hey?"

Duncan had to admit that it was, even if he was seated in the back of Hiki's battered old estate car being driven around the country by a madman. The last few days spent gathering his strength had weighed heavily on him, and he was not sorry to see the back of the hospital. If Shadow did not do for him, boredom would have done had he stayed there much longer. He had been relieved when Mehmet returned in the early hours of that morning, having swapped his barely roadworthy jeep for Hiki's marginally better Volvo, and eagerly asked if Duncan was well enough to travel. Even if he wasn't, Duncan would never have admitted it.

"How is your head?"

Raising a hand, Duncan probed at the now-healed wound through the hair that had begun to grow to cover it. The stitches had been taken out and the initial rawness from their removal had receded.

"Not too bad, thanks. Adem's a fine doctor."

And a fine ambassador to their cause, he thought. During his rushed convalescence, during their many hours together while Mehmet had returned to his village, Louisa had told him of her time spent in a Turkish jail after the explosion, and of how Adem had helped free both her and Mehmet. She'd told him more besides, so that Duncan had a full history of what occurred between his collapse at Mehmet's shack and his waking up in the hospital. To his disappointment, the flirtatious nature of their first encounter had been missing, and they conversed as comrades in arms rather than potential lovers.

"He is a good man. His Light is strong. With more like

190

him, we will succeed. I know this."

Mehmet's confidence was contagious, and Duncan found himself smiling despite his reservations as to how they could hope to succeed when the only plan they had was to travel to Derinkuyu and see if they could locate the cavern. But, as Mehmet had said, it was a good start. At least they knew where to look. A detailed plan of action could follow on later, once they knew what they faced.

Sitting in the front passenger seat, Louisa arched her back and stretched to ease muscles cramped from spending yet another night sleeping in the chair besides Duncan's bed. Despite him offering to swap places, she had declined, citing his need being greater than hers as the reason. She had been correct, as Duncan still felt weak in spite of sound sleep, but even so, he felt guilt over her suffering.

"How long did you say it would take us to get there?"

Mehmet shrugged at Louisa's question. "Maybe twelve hours. Maybe less if we get out of this traffic." He slammed the palm of a hand against the horn and hammered on the brakes as the car in front suddenly stopped. "Ayayay. Are all Turkish drivers stupid?"

Duncan grinned. To his mind, there was no answer to that one.

As the traffic started to move again, Mehmet asked, "Tell me what you found out about the bell tower. Anything to help?"

Duncan shook his head. "Not a lot. Nor anything about the underground city that seemed familiar from the dreams."

Despite hours spent on the internet, neither he nor Louisa had discovered anything other than a potted history of Cappadocia, Derinkuyu and the Church of St Theodore. He had hoped to discover something tangible, something he could latch onto that would help them discover where the cavern lay and what the bell tower had to do with it all, but their research yielded nothing helpful.

"No worries. All will come clear. I know this."

He floored the accelerator and gunned the car into a gap

191

that had opened up in the nearside lane, his action causing yet more horns to blare.

The speed at which they shot forward forced Duncan back into the seat. His head bounced on the headrest, causing a sharp pain to tear through his temple. He groaned, and closed his eyes. After a moment the pain receded, and he said, "Could you ease off on the gas? All this bouncing around is giving me a headache."

"We will be out of town soon and the road will clear. You had best get some sleep if you are feeling unwell. The roads we travel go through the mountains and are full of twists and turns. There is a pillow in the back."

Duncan needed no second urging. With their early start he had not yet fully woken and still felt a little woozy, Mehmet's driving doing nothing to help. After fumbling with the seatbelt housing he eventually managed to press the button to release the belt, and twisted in the seat so he could reach into the back. The pillows Mehmet mentioned were nestled on some coils of rope that had been placed in the storage area, along with three torches, some food rations, spare clothing and waterproof jackets. If nothing else, equipment-wise, it looked like they would be well prepared for their trek underground.

After grabbing the pillows he leaned forward to hand one to Louisa, who took it with a nod of thanks. Then, settling himself on the seat, he placed his pillow between his head and the door and closed his eyes. At least a few hours sleep would make the journey seem that little bit shorter.

After taking the pillow from Duncan, Louisa pressed it against the car window and leaned her head into it. Despite the interrupted sleep patterns of the past few days, she could not follow Duncan's example and fall asleep. There was too much going on in her mind for her to settle.

When first she had 'discovered' her heritage she had assumed their role would be to go out into the world and reinforce the message of Light, sort of rally the troops to promote good behaviour, for want of a better description, she thought, much like the original twelve had done after the death of Christ.

But now, after Duncan's revelation about the ultimate evil being formed, all that had changed. They were in a war; a war the rest of mankind were blissfully unaware of. A war whose first skirmish could prove pivotal.

"What we've got to do will not end it, will it?" she asked, echoing the question she'd asked Duncan, whilst staring in abstraction through the windscreen at the battered rear bumper of the car in front.

Mehmet flicked a quick glance her way before answering. "Only if we lose, Louisa. Then it will be the end for everyone."

Annoyance at his answer caused her to cast him a dark look, before snapping, "That's not what I meant, and you know it."

The knuckles of Mehmet's hands whitened as he tightened his grip on the wheel. After taking a moment to collect his thoughts, he sighed and his grip relaxed.

"You mean will it be the end of Shadow if we stop evil being formed? Then the answer is no. Like I said in Cavern of Rebirth, we need Shadow to know good from bad, love from hate, balance from control. Life is a balance, and that is what Light is for. Shadow seeks control. What we must do is to stop this happening, so that the balance is maintained."

"But, assuming we succeed, what is to stop this from happening all over again?"

"Always there will be those of Light to do what must be done. Over two thousand years ago someone appeared to carry on the fight, and before him I have no doubt there was another who faced what Christ faced. Now, it is our turn. In the future? I cannot say, but always there are those who will oppose evil. For us, we have help from the past. For others?" He shrugged. "We must do what we must do, or there will be no strength left for Light to prosper, and then we will suffer the End of Days."

And there was the nightmare scenario that plagued her

thoughts. If they failed, humanity would suffer the consequences and the Guardian would cease to exist, plunging the world into an ever increasing spiral of madness where only the most evil and debauched could hope to survive. Despite the images of death, destruction, famine and pestilence that appeared in her mind's-eye, mirror images of those shown at the G20 summit, she could not shake the feeling that what they were about to attempt was their own form of evil, no matter how they sugared it. And would doing what they proposed to do only add to the problem and create yet another evil?

"But how can we justify what we do? By destroying are we not also acting against the Light?"

Beside her, Mehmet grunted before responding. "That is the 'Life' in you that speaks, and it is normal for you to feel this way. My 'Truth' tells me that what we do is needed, and the 'Balance' that is in Duncan tells him we have to stop pure evil being formed. For if we do not, then life for everything and everyone will be very short."

The explanation did not make their proposed act any easier for her to accept. After plumping up the pillow, she again leaned it against the glass, rested her head against it and closed her eyes, in the vain hope that sleep would come easily and with it, an easing of her conscience.

***

The back end of the car drifted as Mehmet swung off the road and into the car park of the Balikcilar Hotel, the rear wheels causing a cascade of small stones to fly into the air. In the back of the car, Duncan lurched forward when it skidded to a sudden halt in a parking bay, and Louisa slammed her palms against the dashboard to prevent being thrown around.

"What the hell was all that about?" she snapped. Her eyes seemed to flash sparks as she glared at Mehmet, who gripped the wheel so hard that Duncan could see the whites of his knuckles showing through the skin.

Turning his head, Mehmet returned her glare. "Why

do we have to stop? In another three hours we could be in Derinkuyu and can start what we set out to do."

Duncan sighed. The man had been driving continuously for the past eight hours, all bar a couple of petrol stops and to grab some lunch, and would never admit he was too tired to carry on. But when the car had drifted towards the edge of a precipitous drop for the fourth time in as many minutes it had been obvious his concentration levels had dropped, and Louisa insisted they rest and carry on in the morning.

"Because I would rather get to Derinkuyu in one piece than not at all! You need a break."

Mehmet closed his eyes and tilted back his head before exhaling heavily through his nose. Then, lowering his head, his lips curved slightly to form a sheepish smile. "Forgive me. You are correct. I am tired, and my manners are not what they should be."

Louisa held his gaze for a moment, her features set firm, before the twinkle returned to her eyes. Dipping her head, she said, "You're forgiven."

Duncan leaned forward and reached out to grip his shoulder in compassion. With him being in no condition to take over the driving and Louisa never having learned, he understood the pressure Mehmet had put himself under to get them to the end of their journey.

"We all want to get on with it, but you have to rest. Louisa is right, we need to be refreshed for whatever it is we have to face. We'll be no good for anything if we carry on tonight." He squeezed his shoulder again before releasing his grip. "And it's not is if we'll be able to get into the underground city tonight, is it? It will all be locked up until morning."

Mehmet grimaced in acceptance, and then twisted in the seat so that he faced Duncan. "I know this, but ..." He shrugged and gave a wry smile.

Louisa pulled on the door handle and pushed the door open. Once outside, she turned and pressed her palms against the car's roof and leaned down to poke her head inside. "You guys coming, or what?"

The mischievous smile on her face told Duncan her previous bad humour had dissolved.

The shadows were lengthening as they made their way across the gravel parking area towards the hotel, and there was a cool, damp crispness to the air that signalled night was about to fall. Had they continued on to Derinkuyu it would have been pitch black when they arrived, and too late to find somewhere to stay.

On entering the lobby, the slap of their footsteps echoed off the tiled floor and the receptionist, a gnarled old man with more wrinkles to his face than a dried prune, looked up from his paper to grin in welcome, to reveal teeth as well-worn as his features.

"You want room, yes?"

"Two," Mehmet responded, reaching inside his jacket pocket for his wallet.

The old man glanced to Louisa and then to Duncan, fixing each of them with a watery gaze before turning his attention back to Mehmet. "You want one double and one single?"

Mehmet shook his head. "A twin and a single."

Louisa took a pace forward, and then asked, "Do you have one with three beds?"

There was a nervous tremor to her voice, and Duncan sensed fear lurking behind her words.

The old man did not seem to notice the catch in her voice, and snorted in amusement at her question. "We have family room. It has one big bed and two small ones, so all will be good, yes?"

Louisa nodded, and raised a hand to run fingers through her hair.

"Are you all right?"

She turned at Duncan's question and gave a weak smile. "Now that we're close I don't want to be alone." She briefly looked to the floor before again meeting his gaze. Her lips curled into a smile. "And I've sort of got used to your company."

Duncan chuckled. "Only this time you'll have a bed to

sleep in rather than a chair."

Interrupting, Mehmet waggled a plastic key-card in the air, and said. "I have asked for some food to be taken up for us."

Duncan winced, and raised a hand to rub at his recently healed head wound. A pain, not too dissimilar to the one that tore through his head when he was on the track near to Mehmet's village had made an unwelcome appearance. And he knew what it meant. At the periphery of vision, he sensed rather than saw a movement, and swivelled on the spot to stare at an open doorway beneath a sign that read 'Dining Room'.

At his sudden movement, Louisa reached out and gripped his arm. "What is it?"

Instead of answering immediately, he continued to stare at the doorway. There was no one there that he could see, the room beyond was cloaked in darkness, but he knew they were being watched. Keeping his voice low, he said, "They know we're here."

At Louisa's sharp intake of breath both she and Mehmet turned to stare at the darkened opening, heightened senses seeking what Duncan knew to be there. No one spoke, until the old man behind the desk cleared his throat and shattered the tableau.

As one, all three turned to stare at him. He wilted under their gaze and shrank behind the desk, the smile that formed on his face appearing fixed and hesitant. Nervously, he flicked his gaze briefly to each of them before asking, "You also want drinks?"

# 26

"Will you stop messing around with that phone and turn your lamp out!"

Father Tumbletee glanced across the room from beneath a lowered brow and pursed his lips. The Regent, propped up on his elbows, glared at him from his bed. Tumbletee sighed, pressed the save button and tossed his mobile onto the bedside cabinet before slamming his not inconsiderable weight onto the mattress and pulling the duvet up to his chin.

"Light!"

A low grumble of annoyance sounded deep in his throat as he reached out to flick the switch. The bed creaked in protest at his movement, and again as he settled for sleep. Closing his eyes, he pleaded for it to come easily. The trip was turning into a nightmare and the sooner it was over the better.

Exactly three hours later – he knew because he had set the timer – his mobile rang and woke him from a deep slumber. The glow from the display pulsed in time with each ring to send flashes of light stabbing into the pitch-blackness of the room. Sleep-befuddled, he fumbled for his phone, and smirked in satisfaction at Regent Kearson's curse of annoyance.

The room brightened as a bedside lamp was flicked on. In the sudden illumination, his hair dishevelled and eyes red-rimmed, the Regent leaned on an elbow to glare across the room.

Father Tumbletee smiled in feigned apology, and pointed to the phone with his free hand as he thumbed the answer key and raised it to an ear.

In response, the Regent's scowl deepened.

"Peter! Do you realise what time it is?" A brief pause, then; "Well, it is –" he glanced to his watch, "two in the morning over here, so this had better be good."

Father Tumbletee listened intently to the silence at the other end of the phone, and his eyes widened. "Really?" He glanced across to the Regent, who now sat upright in the bed, and stared intently across the room.

"Whoa! Slow down. I shall have to write this down. Let me get a pen and some paper."

Before he could move aside the bedclothes the Regent had whipped off his own duvet, moved to the dresser, sat himself down, grabbed the Balikcilar-embossed pen and headed notepad and turned to face Tumbletee, pen poised to scribble down whatever it was that 'Peter' was about to impart.

It took all of Father Tumbletee's self-control to prevent himself from grinning at the sight. To gain time to compose his features he raised a hand to stifle a mock yawn, not daring to lower it until he was sure there was no danger of a smile betraying him. Then, as though confirming someone else's words, he said, "You know where Connors is heading, and why he has been summoned." He frowned. "Summoned? Are you sure that is what it says?" He looked to the Regent, pleased to note the ripple of fear that showed in his eyes.

"What underground cavern? In Derinkuyu underground city, down a tunnel leading from the grave site? Peter. This makes no sense. Are you sure that is what you have found? But why would Connors be summoned to such a place?" His face paled and, mouth agape, he stared at the Regent in horror. "Duncan Connors is to be killed to provide the life-force for the devil! B-b-but why?" He kept his gaze firmly fixed on the Regent as he said, "As a direct descendant of one of the apostles, the DNA contained in his blood will give power to the beast, enable it to roam the world and bring about the End of Days. Connors is to be the sacrifice that will bring about the end of the world as we know it."

During the one-sided conversation the Regent had not written a word on the paper. He'd sat immobile, staring.

"Do we know when this sacrifice is to be carried out? Do we have a timescale? Peter? Peter? Are you still there? Peter!" Father Tumbletee held the phone in front of his face and glared at the screen for a moment before meeting the Regent's gaze. "We've been cut off."

"Well ring him back, you imbecile. We have to know what else he discovered."

The phone slipped from the priest's fingers as he made to make the call. Retrieving it from the bedclothes, he tried again. After a moment he met the Regent's gaze once more, and said, "He's not answering."

The Regent cursed, and stormed to his feet. "Get yourself dressed. We have no time to waste. We have to beat Connors to this cavern." On reaching his bed he dropped to his knees and reached under to pull out his leather bag. Once it was clear, he moved the five combination wheels to set the code and then flicked open the catch.

It was with some interest that Father Tumbletee looked on as the Regent delved inside the bag. He had long wondered what it contained and, whilst he had his suspicions, it would be nice to see them confirmed.

The first item to be removed was a bottle of holy water, a white cross clearly adorning the clear glass of the bottle. Next came four black candles, swiftly followed by a bulky canvas bag whose contents could not be determined by visual inspection. Soon after, a large silver crucifix was taken out. Each was placed reverently on the floor beside the bag, but the Regent barely registered them. His hands plunged into the bag again to remove a large tome. It was leather bound, the hide covering dark and mottled through age, and it was this that demanded his attention. He exhaled in relief as his fingers traced an embossed pattern on its surface.

From where he was sitting, Father Tumbletee could not

make out the faded, gold-coloured lettering on the spine, and leaned forward for a closer inspection. The bed creaked at his movement, and the Regent's gaze snapped to him.

"Haven't you dressed yet?" The Regent placed the book back in the bag, closely followed by the other items he had removed. He snapped the lock closed and then rose to his feet. "I want to be away from here within the hour, so get yourself moving."

It was just over the hour when finally, after rousing the ancient receptionist from his slumbers, they emerged into pre-dawn light to make their way across the car park to their hire car.

Alerted by the crunch of gravel, and hidden from sight in some bushes behind the battered red Volvo estate Connors had arrived in, the assassin watched as the two men appeared in view, and raised his Dragunov semi-automatic, gas-operated sniper's rifle. He'd had it for years and it had never let him down, and he knew it would not do so now.

Taking aim, he aligned the telescopic sight on his target's temple and, as though caressing a lover, stroked the trigger.

Before he had chance to squeeze, his target paused in his stride to stop and stare. Eyes darker than night bored into his, and he froze. The hairs on the back of his neck stood on end and an unquenchable fear gripped him. The gun lowered and, seemingly of its own volition, angled up so that its barrel pressed into the fleshy underside of his chin. It was as though an alien force commandeered his body, rendering him impotent. His head was forced up and back. Unadulterated terror gripped him, and he broke out in cold sweat. He was about to die – by his own hand!

A soft 'whump' whispered in the air, followed by the sound of something heavy crashing into the undergrowth somewhere to their left, and Father Tumbletee jumped with a start. "What was that?" he murmured, pausing to flick an anxious glance towards the bushes.

"Nothing worth worrying about." Regent Kearson pressed the key fob to unlock the car and then tossed the keys to the priest. "Now get in. You're driving."

Soon after, the soft purr of the car's engine sprang into life, to mask the low groan of pain that emanated from the bushes.

Hidden from view by vegetation, the assassin lay on the ground with a hand pressed to a mashed ear in an attempt to stem the flow of blood. The pain was insufferable and he could feel warm, wet, sticky fluid seep between his fingers. But at least he still lived. How he had managed to move his head to the side before the bullet was fired he would never know, but was not about to question it.

Cursing, he struggled to his feet, grabbed his gun with his free hand, and staggered to where he had left his car. He would get another chance to complete his mission, of that he was sure, but first he had to get his ear seen to or he would be in no fit state to do anything. And completion of this particular contract was top of his list of things to do. In fact, on a scale of importance, it was the only item on his list.

# 27

**D**uncan's summer jacket offered scant protection against the unexpected cold as, bleary-eyed, he followed his companions towards the car. The sun had barely risen and there was a chill in the air that indicated the colder months of winter were not far away, despite it promising to be fine and clear. He shivered, and ducked deeper into his coat as he walked.

On reaching the car Mehmet caught sight of his swaddled form and chuckled. "It gets very cold here in winter. It drops to minus fifteen, and there is much snow."

Duncan grimaced, and with hands buried in his pockets, stamped his feet to get warm.

Once they were in the car and seated, Mehmet turned the ignition and Hiki's battered Volvo sprang to life. Still grinning, he peered at Duncan via the rear-view mirror.

"I will put the heater on, hey?"

Their exit from the car park was more controlled than their entrance the previous day and within minutes they were leaving the small town of Konya to continue their journey to Derinkuyu. With the road ahead devoid of traffic, they set a steady pace and it did not take long for the car to warm up, and for Duncan's eyelids to grow heavy. He felt so very tired.

He had slept little the previous night, having spent most of the time fretting about what sort of welcome they would receive once they arrived at their destination. Also, there was something about events so far that troubled him, but he could not put his finger on the answer. Despite hours of deliberation he had drawn no conclusions, and had put it down to being too tired to think straight. Now, with the heat building, he felt much the same way, but knew there was something vital he had overlooked, something that could affect what they proposed to do.

He gazed out of the dust-streaked passenger window in abstraction, running through what had happened to him, to them, since he'd first heard of Steff Mason's death, in yet another attempt to fathom out what he was missing. But it was like collecting water with a sieve; as soon as his thoughts began to gather they drained away, leaving him with the sludge in the bottom that was his experience within Shadow's cavern.

Thinking back on both out-of-body experiences he realised that at no time had he been physically threatened. It was more of an implied threat that he was one of them, that he would betray Light in some way, like they were inviting him to join them before he did, that they were after something only he could give them.

Or could it be something only bearers of Light could give them? Aside from being watched and checked on, they hadn't suffered any form of physical assault or any other obstacle to stall their plans. In fact, it seemed like Shadow were more intent on knowing what they were up to rather than doing anything about actually stopping them.

Suddenly wide awake, he jerked upright in the seat and turned his head to stare out of the bug-splattered windscreen.

"They want us to find the cavern!"

At Duncan's exclamation Mehmet's eyes appeared in the rear-view mirror to fix him with a look of stunned amazement, and Louisa swivelled in her seat to stare back at him.

Duncan let his gaze rest briefly on each of them before repeating his words, only this time with less emotion. "They want us to find the cavern."

"What makes you say that?" asked Mehmet. A frown creased his brow as he switched his attention between the road and Duncan via the mirror.

"They haven't tried to stop us."

"But what about in your dreams?" Louisa interjected. "They tried to stop you then."

"Did they?" Duncan looked out of the side window again. Even at this early hour there were farmers in the fields, harvesting crops and loading horse-drawn carts with produce, ready for the winter months. "Or were they giving us a clue as to the whereabouts of their seat of power?"

"But why would they do that?" Mehmet asked. "If we know where they are, then we can stop them. Why would they want us to find them?" He shook his head. "That makes no sense."

"Unless it's a trap."

At Louisa's words, Mehmet blanched. He stared at her, dumfounded, before he eventually murmured, "I am such a fool. Why did I not see this?"

The blare of a horn dragged his attention back to the road. Cursing in Turkish, his eyes widened in alarm as he yanked on the steering wheel. With a screech of tyres, the car swerved back into its correct lane, out of the path of a tour bus travelling towards them.

The car rocked and wallowed in the slipstream as the bus sped by, missing them by millimetres, its horn still blaring. Duncan wilted, closed his eyes and slowly exhaled as the car gradually settled. That was too close for comfort. Each of them must have felt the same way as they had travelled a good mile along the road before any of them dared to speak.

Eventually, Mehmet, his voice lacking its usual confidence, said, "I am sorry for my lapse. My mind was on Shadow when it should have been on the road."

"As was mine," admitted Duncan.

"But why would they want to trap us?" Louisa asked, ignoring the apology, the hint of a tremor in her voice. "What do we have that they could possibly want?"

Duncan fumbled inside his shirt for his medallion. The disc repeatedly squirmed free of fingers that still shook from their narrow escape before he finally managed to grasp it and pull it clear.

"These, perhaps?" He gazed at the polished surface with its pattern of cupped hands and a bird flying free, so familiar and comforting, and his nerves began to settle. "The question is," he looked up to briefly lock eyes with Louisa, "do our ciphers hold a power they want, or do they want to destroy the discs to prevent others following on if we fail?"

This time when Mehmet spoke he kept his eyes on the road. "I think you are correct with the first one. It makes sense. If they kill us before we reach the cavern the discs will survive, ready to be found and handed to the next generation."

Louisa snorted in wry amusement. "What next generation?"

Mehmet frowned. "What do you mean?"

It was Duncan who answered. "What she means is that we are the last, aside from Faith. I have no kids. Do you?"

Mehmet shook his head. "None that I know of."

"Neither do I," Louisa murmured.

"Which confirms it's the discs they're after. That's why they're allowing us to find them. Or at least where they're hiding."

"Then why try and kill you?" Louisa asked.

The fear that Duncan had seen lurking behind her gaze the previous evening when she thought she would be left on her own returned, and he could tell she was looking for a reason, anything that she could latch onto to disprove the theory, even though she knew the reasoning to be sound.

In answer he said, "I don't believe they were. I think they wanted to see how powerful the discs had become over time. Had they wanted to kill us, I'm sure we would not now be travelling to confront their ultimate being. The fact that they haven't, or even tried, means they hope to use the discs for their own purpose."

"But they aren't magic," said Mehmet, his eyes narrowed in confusion. "They are merely conduits that hold feelings and auras from those who previously wore them. They hold no power to give others not of our line."

"It would seem that Shadow thinks differently," said Duncan.

Louisa closed her eyes and sagged back into her seat. "So we are walking into a trap," she said. "Just what I needed to hear."

"Maybe not. I have a feeling I saw something that Shadow did not expect me to see."

Understanding twinkled in Mehmet's eyes, and he grinned. "The bell tower."

At its mention, Louisa twisted in her seat to stare first at Mehmet and then at Duncan. "But we have no idea what it stands for, or how it can help us."

"One thing at a time, Louisa Cooke. One thing at a time." There was barely suppressed excitement in Mehmet's voice. "If Shadow seeks to use us, it can think again. Is that not right, Duncan?"

In answer, Duncan smiled. The next trick would be to work out where the bell tower came into all of this. Was it merely a talisman for their cause, or did it hold a secret they could use in the battle that lay ahead? He rather hoped it was the latter, because at that moment he was bereft of ideas and felt totally unprepared to face the ultimate evil.

As they drew nearer to Derinkuyu the scenery changed. Green fields and clusters of stone-built cottages gave way to a more barren landscape. Jagged walls of dull, ochre-coloured rock rose either side of the road. Every so often, small, dark window-like openings would randomly appear, and in places huge slabs had sheared away to reveal the outlines of previously concealed rooms, tunnels, and ladder-type indentations leading from one room to a higher level. To all intents and purposes, they looked like giant beehives that had been broken open.

The visible tunnels that connected the rooms appeared to be narrow, only large enough to accommodate one person at a time moving at a stoop, and the carved niches that were used for stairs, precipitous. Either early man was substantially shorter and more squat than modern man, or the narrowness of the tunnels was a means of protection against attack. Either way, Duncan suspected their travels in the underground city could prove to be a little restricted.

The nearer they drew to Derinkuyu the more frequent the outward sign of cave homes. More and more window openings appeared in the rock and, on occasion, a more modern dwelling had been built at the base of a 'chimney', pigeons using the upper windows as access to night-time roosts, the ground-hugging inhabitants the shack below. Also, the traffic increased, mainly tour buses heading towards where they now travelled.

"Seems popular around here," Louisa murmured as yet another bus slowed them.

Instead of cursing and looking to overtake, Mehmet shifted down a gear and settled for staying behind the bus. "It is a main tourist area. Everyone comes to see the underground city. We are nearly there now. Another ten minutes, I think."

His time-frame proved accurate. Following the tour bus off the main road and into a large car park behind an open-air market, he brought the car to a halt some eight minutes later. Once parked, no one moved. Immersed in their own thoughts, each sat in their seat, staring out at the hordes of tourists who had to force their way through the massed ranks of locals trying to sell them something, anything, in order to lure coins from their pockets.

For Duncan, this was the location of his dream. He'd recognised it the moment they drew into the car park. Nervous excitement vied with fear for dominance now they were within touching distance of their destination. He stared at the mass of humanity that milled in and around the tented village, and hoped their destiny would prove to be the one

they desired rather than the one Shadow apparently wanted.
With there only being one way to find out, he opened the
car door and stepped outside.

After the aircon coolness of the car's interior, the heat of
the day immediately assailed him and beads of sweat prickled his skin. By the time Mehmet and Louisa joined him he
had removed his jacket and slung it over a shoulder. Even
so, damp patches appeared under his arms, to soak into his
T-shirt.

The sound of air brakes had him spinning in surprise as,
behind them, a minibus came to a halt, effectively forming a
blockade. His heart skipped a beat before it began to pound
urgently against his chest, and only settled once the bus's
doors opened to disgorge its passengers. He closed his eyes
and exhaled in relief, cursing himself for a fool as he fought
to calm nerves stretched taut.

"What is the matter, Duncan?" asked Mehmet, frowning.
"Is your head still sore?"

Duncan gave a wry grin and shook his head. "I'm fine.
Still a little tired, is all." Stepping forward, he clapped him on
the shoulder, and said, "Shall we?"

Together, they joined the small group of tourists that had
disembarked from the minibus and followed them through
the sea of tents that lined the paved path leading away from
the road and car park. Once in the throng he felt strangely
calm. If anything, given his usual aversion to large crowds,
he thought the opposite would be the case, but the jostling
and noise reminded him of Oxford.

Raising his voice so that he could be heard over the
hubbub, Mehmet turned to Duncan and said, "Where do
you want to go?"

Duncan shrugged. "We go with this lot. They seem to
know the way."

He frowned, and then grinned. "Ah. You joke. That is
good. You must be feeling better."

It seemed to take an age to fight their way through to
the end of the market stalls, by which time Duncan had

changed his mind over the similarities with Oxford. There, no one ever tried to drag you into a shop to force you to buy their goods, or waved bracelets, gaudily dressed dolls or other cheap trinkets in your face as you walked passed, jabbering on in a language you had no understanding of. In the space of a hundred yards he must have been grabbed a dozen times, and had nearly become separated from his companions at least twice.

Within a couple of minutes the constant barrage of noise and jostling caused panic to set in and, when yet another trader tried to drag him away, he reached out to grab hold of one of Louisa's hands. She tightened her grip and pulled him along after her. To his relief, she appeared far more used to dealing with a large heaving mass of humanity than he, and his panic started to recede. Even so, the heat, the noise and the close proximity of hundreds of people took its toll. His head began to ache and his face felt waxy.

To their right, a cafe cum general store appeared. Louisa thumped Mehmet on the shoulder to get his attention, pointed in the cafe's direction, and shouted something Duncan could not hear.

Mehmet glanced in his direction and then nodded. Forcing a pathway through, he dragged both Louisa and Duncan after him, finding them a table close to the store rather than one near the thoroughfare.

Once seated, Duncan leaned forward and cupped his face in his hands. He felt awful, but at least the tingling sensation that had started to prick him all over was diminishing now they were out of the crowd. A hand rested lightly on his shoulder and his head snapped up. On seeing it was Louisa, he gave a weak smile.

"You okay? You look like crap."

"I've felt better." Leaning back, he closed his eyes for a moment and sighed. "Where's Mehmet?"

Louisa settled into a chair on the opposite side of the table and began to waft a placemat in front of her face. "Gone to get some drinks." She smiled. "You looked like you could do with one."

Duncan snorted. "You could say that." He looked over her shoulder at the stream of people heading away from them, moving towards a large stone arch that he instantly recognised.

Louisa paused in her wafting to stare at him, and her eyes narrowed. "What is it?"

With eyes still glued to the stonework, he murmured, "We're at the right place."

Unnoticed, Mehmet arrived beside them. Clasped in his hands were three paper cups, which he placed on the table. "Of course we are at the right place. And, if the man in shop is correct, the bell tower is over there, across the square." He waved an arm in the general direction he meant. "What do you want to see first?"

There was an excitement in his voice that was at odds with the fluttering in Duncan's stomach. Not wanting to deflate his obvious good humour by showing his anxiety, he smiled and reached out to take one of the coffees. "The bell tower sounds good. I doubt whether a trip underground would do me any favours at the moment."

"Nor me," echoed Louisa, grasping one of the cups.

Her hands shook as she raised it to her mouth, and a dribble of coffee slopped over the lip to run down the side of the cup, where it beaded at the bottom. Almost in slow motion, the droplet detached itself to drop to the table.

"The bell tower is good," Mehmet enthused, oblivious to their discomfort. "Should we go now?"

Duncan chuckled. In some ways Mehmet reminded him of a kid in a sweet shop, eager to get on to the next best thing. The man's natural enthusiasm was contagious, and he shook his head in amusement, his earlier misery pushed to the back of his mind. "Why not? We may as well finish the morning on a high."

In an attempt to avoid the main thrust of the crowd they walked alongside the shop-front and soon emerged, unscathed, at a large town square. The area was remarkably devoid of people and a stone fountain stood in the centre. Judging by the cracks to the stonework and the missing sections to its basin, it was disused and had long run dry, but it was what stood beyond the fountain that made them pause.

Louisa reached out and gripped Duncan's hand as they stood and stared.

"This is the place, yes?" asked Mehmet. He stared at the bell tower, an almost manic grin on his face.

Across the square rose the splendour that was the Church of St Theodore, its algae-covered slate roof topping the expertly crafted stonework with its cross-shaped upper windows. The bell tower, looking exactly as he had remembered it, stood apart. It was stunning in its simplicity, and its yellow-brown stone seemed to absorb the sunlight, but, to Duncan's chagrin, on seeing it the expected tingle of excitement was missing.

There was no aura of Light around its structure, no pull that would identify it as a bastion against Shadow, and no hint of the power he had witnessed in his dream. What felt like a lead pellet formed in the pit of his stomach, and he began to wonder whether, in his drug-induced coma, his mind had played tricks. Not willing to speak in case his disappointment showed, he merely nodded in affirmation at Mehmet's question. After all they'd been through he was not willing to admit that maybe he'd led them on a fool's errand.

Laughing, Mehmet clapped him on the back. "Now we go and take a look."

Striding out, he set a brisk pace across the square. Duncan made to follow but was halted by Louisa hauling him back.

"Something's not right, is it?" she asked, turning him to peer up into his eyes.

He sighed, and briefly glanced to the ground in case she saw his uncertainty, but the damage had already been done. Unlike Mehmet, who only saw what he expected to see, Louisa's insight delved deeper. She had seen through his thin veneer of confidence with apparent ease.

"I feel nothing. No spark, no pull, no … no nothing." He shrugged, at a loss as to how to explain his feelings.

"Are you saying this is the wrong place?"

With a shake of his head, Duncan said, "No, but," he exhaled heavily through his nose "it doesn't feel right. Not like in my dream. Then it was obvious it was a beacon of Light. Now? On seeing it for real?" He shrugged and shook his head again. "I'm not so sure."

The grip on his arm increased and Louisa's gaze grew intense. "What did you expect, a fanfare? The dome to be blazing Light to show us we were in the right place? Come on Duncan, get real. The bell tower is a beacon, nothing more, nothing less. Yes, there may be more to it than that, but we won't know until we need it, otherwise you wouldn't have been drawn from the cavern by its power."

"But what if –"

She yanked sharply on his arm. "Stop it right now. If that is the tower from your vision then we are in the right place and it has a part to play. What, we have yet to find out, but you moping around like someone's stolen your favourite toy is not going to help, is it?"

Duncan's eyes widened at her verbal onslaught. Although he'd always sensed an inner strength to her that she rarely showed, the intensity of her words took him by surprise.

"Do you understand where I'm coming from?"

Dumbly, he nodded.

Louisa grunted an acknowledgement. Then, smiling sweetly, she released her grip on his arm and threaded her own through his. "Good. Now we have an understanding, shall we join the rest of our army?"

Too stunned to answer, he had no option but to follow as she set the pace across the square. Mehmet had already reached the low stone wall surrounding the church and its tower and gazed back at them, arms folded across his chest, exuding impatience as he waited.

Out of the corner of her mouth, Louisa said, "And don't

you dare voice your doubts to him. Out of all of us, he is the one that holds all of this together. If he believes in you, then so should you." Looking up, she peered into his eyes, the hint of a smile playing about her lips. There was a softer, warmer edge to her voice as she said, "And so should I."

# 28

The midday heat was in stark contrast to the dawn coldness that had greeted them that morning. Sweat trickled down Duncan's back as he sat, arms wrapped loosely around drawn-up knees, on a stone slab the size of a pool table that had been set into the ground to the west of the bell tower. He stared up at the dome, seeking inspiration, or divine intervention, he was not sure which, that the tower was something more than a skilfully crafted housing for a bell. Despite them having spent the better part of an hour looking for clues as to its importance they had drawn a blank.

There were no strange markings on the stone to decode, no concealed doorways that could lead to a hidden vault long-since forgotten, nor any hint as to what role it would play in the battle to come. He had begun to suspect its implied importance was all one big con, that the image had been planted in his head by Shadow to lure them to Derinkuyu, miles away from where the altar actually lay. If, in fact, there was such an altar.

Wrapped in his melancholy, he reached down and placed the palm of a hand against the slab, and used it as a pivot to roll onto his knees. He winced as a jagged edge of stone gouged into flesh. Kneeling, he raised his hand to examine the wound. A flap of skin hung from his index finger, the grove below white and yet to weep blood. Cursing silently to himself, he placed the injured digit in his mouth to suck and spit free any algae or muck while staring at the slab to see what could have caused the damage.

His brow furrowed as he spotted a ragged hole in the surface of the stone. It was as though a thin crust had given way under his weight. His wound forgotten, he leaned forward, hands splayed either side of the hole, and lowered his head to inspect the opening more closely. The frown on his face deepened. The shape beneath where the veneer had collapsed appeared too regular to be a fault. With its chiselled edges, it looked more like it had been carved. His heart began to thump against his rib cage and a form of paralysis crept into his limbs. Incapable of movement, he knelt and stared, unblinking, at the partial reveal of a symbol he knew so well.

"Duncan, you're hurt."

Only vaguely aware that his name had been spoken, he continued to gaze at the carving.

"Duncan? Duncan, are you okay?"

The brush of a warm breeze caressed his face as Louisa dropped to her knees opposite him. Reaching out, she placed a hand under his chin and eased up his head. Meeting his gaze, her voice low and filled with concern, she said, "Are you okay? You're bleeding."

He nodded, and she let her hand fall away.

"I'm fine, really. So you can take that worried look off your face." Thrusting back off the slab, he rested his backside on his calves.

"That is good," said Mehmet, "because we are not." There was an undercurrent of anger mixed with disappointment in his tone. "Twenty minutes we spend in the church and we find nothing. Just some paintings on the walls." He raised a hand and ran fingers through dishevelled hair while tossing the church an accusatory look.

"Have you a hammer?"

His question halted anything further Mehmet may have said. Wide-eyed, with fingers still entwined in his hair, he stared at him as if he had taken leave of his senses. "Why do you want a hammer?"

"Because I have something to show you" – he reached out

to touch the collapsed crust of stone with a finger – "here."

"There is nothing there," said Mehmet, scowling.

Louisa stared at the jagged surface for a moment and then shrugged. "It's just a broken bit of rock."

Duncan shook his head, his lips compressed in annoyance at their inability to see what he saw. "No. It's more than that." Rising to his feet, he scanned the ground for a large stone to further expose the carving. Spotting one that looked the right size to break through the thin covering, he strode the ten paces to grab it before returning to kneel at the slab, to chip away at the edges of the carving he had partly revealed. The crack of contact reverberated around the enclosed grounds.

Mehmet's hand shot out to grab his arm. "Duncan, you cannot do this." He quickly scanned their surroundings. "The Jandarma will hear and we will be in big trouble."

"More trouble than if Shadow gains control?"

There was a passion within that eradicated all emotion other than the need to make them see what he saw, and he snatched his arm from Mehmet's grasp. Raising the stone, he brought it crashing down on the slab. The sound on impact was like a gunshot, and its loud retort echoed around them.

Louisa gasped, and Mehmet swore. His head snapped up and his eyes flicked anxious glances around the square.

Unmindful of potential consequences, Duncan dropped the stone on the ground beside him and then reached out to remove sharp-edged slivers from the exposed recess. Eagerness caused him to rush, and he winced as splintered stone punctured flesh. Droplets of blood oozed from the wound to join the flow from his injured finger, but he barely noticed, and continued to clear the debris.

Once cleared, he rested back on his haunches and surveyed his work, and raised an arm to wipe the sheen of sweat from his brow. Grinning, he stared at the carving that had been skilfully concealed for goodness knew how long.

"Now what do you see?"

Mehmet, whose attention was firmly fixed on their

surroundings, snapped his gaze to Duncan. His eyes blazed with anger. "Are you mad? You will get us locked away, and then what good will come of it?"

Refusing to be cowed, Duncan held his gaze. "Tell me what you see."

Louisa reached up and gripped Mehmet's arm. "I think you need to look at this."

Mehmet scowled, exhaled noisily, and then shifted his attention to the slab, muttering in his native tongue as he did so. On seeing what Louisa referred to, his muttering stopped and his eyes widened. Slowly, he stooped and reached out, his fingers tracing the pattern that had been revealed. There was a tenderness, like a lover's caress, to his touch.

"It is your cipher."

Duncan nodded, and his grin widened. He knew he must look like some form of manic Cheshire Cat, but he did not care. The cipher proved them being there was not a trick, that Shadow was expecting them and that Light would help them. How, he had no idea, but his earlier concerns dissipated, evaporating into the heat of the day.

"But what does it mean?" asked Louisa, looking first to Mehmet and then to Duncan.

"It means," said Duncan, "we have work to do." On rising, his knee joints creaked, and he winced. Ignoring the pain, he held out a hand to help her to her feet. "And that work starts with the underground city."

Once standing, Louisa bent down and brushed dirt from the knees of her jeans. Her blonde hair, pulled into its customary ponytail, gleamed in the sunlight, seeming to radiate Light with its glow, and Duncan smiled. For the first time in weeks, the invigorating warmth of confidence permeated his body.

# 29

Having tagged on to a British tour party, they remained at the rear of the sixteen-strong group as they entered the maze of tunnels and vaults. Although the glow of bulbs, linked by drooping cables, illuminated their path, the light was dim and it took a moment or two for their eyes to adjust to the gloom. The heat of the day soon faded after entering the warren and the sound of their footsteps became strangely deadened, as though the stone absorbed all echoes. Also, there was the unmistakable smell of animal in the air. Years, even centuries, of the upper level having been used for stabling had left its indelible imprint in the rock.

The deeper they walked into the stable complex the stronger the smell became, and the more Duncan's body tingled with suppressed tension. Although he could detect nothing untoward, he knew they were entering what could be the seat of evil's power, and his every sense reached out, invisible tendrils alert for the first sign of trouble.

A nudge in the back had him spin in alarm. His heart raced, but on seeing it was Louisa urging him to follow the group of tourists who headed towards a portal in the rockface ahead, he relaxed, and grimaced in apology before stepping after them.

Through the portal was a large, vaulted cave. Grottoes had been carved into the walls at regular intervals and a number of tunnels led off at various points around the perimeter. But it was the doorway through which they had entered that had Duncan gasping. Alongside it stood a large millwheel, a hole at its centre, exactly like the one in his vision.

"What is it?" Louisa asked, grabbing his arm.

"The millwheel," Duncan responded in hushed tones as he stared at the circular mass of carved stone. "It's the same as the one in my dream. It blocked the tunnel that led through to the cavern of the altar."

"I see you have spotted the millstone."

At the sound of the voice, Duncan looked up, and met the twinkling gaze of the tour guide. She was young, around twenty-five, had a smile to die for, and seemed pleased that he had noticed the circular slab of rock. "Have you any idea what it was used for?"

"It's a door," Duncan replied, switching his gaze back to the wheel, "that can only be opened and closed from one side. It's for protection." His voice was flat, devoid of emotion. The sight of the wheel had caused ominous memories to resurface.

The girl smiled, and nodded. "Very good." Turning, she called for the attention of the group and directed them towards the millstone.

"Here we have the first line of defence for those who used the underground city in times of trouble. We have passed through the area where the livestock were stabled and have now entered the start of the underground city proper. This area is a communal area where we have bedrooms, a kitchen and a meeting room." She pointed to various openings in the rock. "If an attack was imminent, one or two men would roll the millstone closed. See?"

She raised an arm to indicate the grooves in the ceiling and floor where the wheel would roll, and then to the housing in the opposite face that the wheel would lock into, effectively blocking the entrance.

"It can only be opened and closed from one side with ease. From the other, it would take many men to move it. Here –" she pointed to the hole in the centre, "is where defenders would shoot arrows or jab spears at their attackers, giving their families time to flee to the lower levels. We are at level two and as we travel down to level twelve you will see many millstones such as this."

"Is that the lowest level?" one of the tourists asked.

The girl smiled and shook her head. "It is the lowest level we can get to. The tunnels to the lowest levels are blocked and not scheduled for excavation for many years."

"Sounds like a good hiding place for Shadow," Mehmet whispered, leaning in to Duncan.

"We will stay here for a few minutes to give you a chance to examine the rooms and then we go down deeper. Is anyone scared of enclosed spaces? The tunnels get narrow and the way down to the lowest point is the same as the way up, so it can get very busy."

At the news, a middle-aged woman to Duncan's right raised a hand. She was short and overweight, but was dressed for the occasion in boots, khaki combats and a jacket. Her hand shook and her face had drained of all colour. On attracting the guide's attention, she lowered her arm and gave a hesitant smile. "If you don't mind, I think I'll pass on that one."

The guide nodded, and indicated an opening in the rock wall some ten feet away. "If you go through there and follow the blue arrows you will come to the exit." She glanced to her watch. "We will meet you back at the coach in two hours, if that is okay with you?"

The woman nodded, then grabbed hold of her male companion's hand and yanked him towards the portal the girl had indicated. Judging by the tight-lipped smile he gave the guide, he was not as relieved to be escaping the tunnels as his partner.

"Has anyone been down to the lowest levels?"

The tour guide smiled at Duncan's question. "Not for many years. In 1975, two government officials went down with an explorer to see if they could be opened up for tourism. They never came back."

Duncan frowned. "Didn't anyone go down to try and find

them? They could have just got lost."

The girl shrugged. "The tufa is softer the further down you go, and is more prone to collapse."

"Tufa?"

"Compressed ash from volcanic eruptions millions of years ago. This whole region is formed from it. It's soft and easy to carve, which is why there are so many underground rooms. Air hardens the exposed surface of the stone so that it forms a crust, but the lower levels have not been hardened in this way and can shear away. You saw the rooms and tunnels revealed in the rocks as you travelled to Derinkuyu?"

Duncan nodded.

"Further down it is like that, and too dangerous to allow tourists to enter. The men sent to find the ones missing discovered a large section of the tunnels that had recently sheared away, revealing a fast-flowing underground river below; the water source for the city. It seems likely the first group were the cause of the landslip and were swept away. No one knows for sure, but the government decided to keep the lower levels closed until they'd been properly examined and made safe, just in case. We're still waiting for that to happen." She smiled. "One day, you never know."

Something caught her attention and she shifted her gaze to peer over Duncan's shoulder. Her lips compressed into a thin line, and she shook her head. "Sorry, but someone is trying to get into a tunnel I'd rather they didn't. Please excuse me."

Moving away, she called out and waved an arm in the air. "Excuse me, Sir. Yes, you, the man with the blue jacket. Don't climb into that one unless you want a long fall; it's a well. Please come away before you get hurt."

Duncan exchanged meaningful glances with Mehmet and Louisa before stepping forward to follow the guide. By the time they reached her she had called the remainder of the group over and was in the process of leading them through another portal on the far side of the room. Like the last, this was also protected by a millwheel. Walking in single-file, they made their way along a series of twisting tunnels that sloped ever downward. Rooms carved out of the rock appeared at regular intervals on either side of the tunnel; bedrooms and storage areas, as did soot-stained niches in the walls. The air within the tunnels remained fresh, despite the enclosed nature of the environs, and the temperature an ambient fifteen degrees.

After ten minutes of walking each tunnel started to look like the last until, eventually, the guide halted at the head of a set of steps. Turning, she raised her voice and called down the line. "We are at level eight, and these steps take us down to level twelve. It's a long, steep climb that leads to a meeting area and an ancient church and, for those that want to go deeper; there is another tunnel that takes you down to an old grave. Down here, the roof of the tunnel dips in places so you may have to stoop. Also, this is the only way up as well as down, so it could get cramped. For those that do not wish to go further, you can wait in one of the side rooms for us to return. Okay?"

Without waiting for an answer she turned and made her way down the steps. Duncan followed. The way was steep, as the guide had forewarned, and he had to duck a number of times as he made his way down due to the low ceiling level. At the halfway point there was a room carved into the side of the tunnel to their right, and their party had to enter it to allow a group from below to pass. In the room was another millstone and across the passage its receptacle. There was a bedroom carved into the rock beside the wheel and it was obvious the room was some form of gatekeeper's lodge.

"This is a good protection point," said the guide, having noticed Duncan's interest in the room. "Here, only one person can attack at a time coming down the steps, so it is impossible to break down."

"But what if the attackers waited for them to starve? What good is it being trapped down here if you can't get out?"

"There are many entrances to the underground city. The

one where we came in is the only one that has been kept open, for safety reasons. Others are in houses around the village and surrounding countryside, now blocked off, and there is supposed to be one in the grounds of the Church of St Theodore." She shrugged. "But no one knows where that one is. It probably collapsed centuries ago, or in the last century when the church was built. There are many such tunnels close to the surface."

At her mention of the church, Duncan froze. A shiver ran down his spine, as though someone had stepped over his grave, and his mouth went dry. Fortunately, the guide didn't notice his reaction; she had spotted a gap in the flow of traffic and shifted her attention to the group, urging them to continue the descent. This time, Duncan hung around until only he, Mehmet and Louisa were left.

"Did you hear that?" he murmured, glancing to each of them in turn. At their nods, he said, "Are you thinking what I'm thinking, or would that be too easy?"

"Too easy," said Mehmet, eyes narrowed. Suddenly, he grinned and reached out to clap him on the back. "But easy is good. Your dreams say the bell tower is of Light and you find a slab showing your cipher by it, so –" his grin faded and he squeezed Duncan's shoulder – "I say we follow the signs." His grin returned. "Do you want to go back to the tower now?"

His good humour was infectious and Duncan found himself smiling, despite the potential significance of the discovery. He shook his head. "Later, when it gets dark. Somehow, I'm thinking we will need the car to move that slab, and the fewer people around the better. And, now that we're here, I wouldn't mind visiting that ancient church. I've never been to one under the ground before."

By the time they reached the bottom of the steps the rest of the group were mingling with others who had ventured down. In all, there must have been around forty people inspecting the thirty metre by ten metre room with its vaulted ceiling, the hushed tones of their whispered chatter eerie in the gloom. To the rear right of the man-made cavern Duncan spotted a shadowed recess where tourists appeared and disappeared at regular intervals, and assumed that was where the church had been carved into the rock. Leading the way, he stepped forward, but halted when halfway across the shoe-smoothed surface of the floor. He was being summoned.

It wasn't a voice that called to him, nor was it physical touch. It was a presence, as when the bell tower had pulled him free of the cavern, only this time there was no feeling of release. He stumbled to a halt, and Louisa bumped into his back.

"Sorry. I didn't see you stop. Duncan? What is it?"

He didn't answer, looked to his left, his eyes fixing on the dark maw of an opening in the rock wall. As he stared, the pull grew stronger and, involuntarily, he found himself walking towards it. The hairs on the back of his neck rose and the tingle of something akin to fear, but not fear, thrummed through his body.

Louisa grabbed his arm. "What's going on?"

Without saying a word, he pulled free and continued walking.

Unseen, Louisa glanced to Mehmet, palms held out in a gesture of confusion. Mehmet shrugged in reply and indicated they should follow.

The gently sloping tunnel they entered was gloomier than the ones they had previously travelled, and was also low and extremely narrow. In order to negotiate it they had to walk in a stoop. One bulb illuminated a small section halfway down, but there was an arched silhouette of dim light at the end, some thirty metres away, and it was from this light that the pull on Duncan's being emanated.

Although the hairs on the back of his neck had settled, his mouth remained dry and his body still quivered with unnatural fear. The sensation was similar to how he felt a condemned prisoner must feel on his walk to the gallows, even though he couldn't sense a direct threat to his person.

Even so, it was with some trepidation that he emerged into the partial light of the burial chamber.

There were three couples already in the small cave, effectively filling it, and what Duncan assumed must be a warden standing off to one side, next to an iron grating that sealed off another tunnel. On seeing Duncan and his companions enter, the couples moved away from the stone sarcophagus carved out of the rock in the room's centre and made their way to the exit. Duncan was barely aware of their passing as they moved past him and up the tunnel he had emerged from. His attention was firmly fixed on the coffin; the source of the pull.

As though reluctant to move closer, each halting footstep was slow and measured until, after what felt like an age, he stood beside the opening in the ground. He felt the presence of Mehmet and Louisa halt beside him. Together, the three of them stared at the carved, man-sized hole. Chisel marks scarred the surface of the rock and it had a raised section at one end where the head of the deceased would have rested. It was to this that Duncan was drawn.

Mehmet and Louisa remained silent observers, and stepped aside as he moved to the head of the coffin, whereupon he knelt and leaned forward, resting his weight on one hand as he brushed away dust and rock particles that had accumulated in the chisel marks with the other. The recently formed scabs on his fingers broke free at the contact, and droplets of blood appeared on his flesh.

The more debris that Duncan cleared away the more defined the chisel marks became. Only these marks were different to the ones that blemished the rest of the sarcophagus. These marks formed a distinct pattern, a pattern identical to the one on the slab in the churchyard in every detail. For some reason the reveal of his cipher did not surprise him. It was as though, deep inside, he'd expected to find it there. Even so, a numbness began to form within him, and with it came a sense of melancholy. He could not shake the feeling he was looking at his own grave, even though he knew it was not possible.

Leaning back, he stared at the markings, clearly visible now that his shadow no longer cloaked them, and wondered which of his ancestors they belonged to.

Into the silence a voice asked, "Anyone you know?"

There was an undercurrent of amusement in the tone. No, not amusement – mockery.

Opposite, stood the man he had assumed was a warden. He was scrawny. The khaki uniform he wore looked like it was made for someone of a more generous proportion. A large, hooked nose dominated craggy features, and dark, close-set eyes gave him an air of the criminally deranged. A sneer marred his features as, arms folded across his chest, he stared down. He began to laugh, a laugh that rapidly grew manic.

A great rage began to build, and previously leaden limbs became infused with anger. Duncan rose slowly to his feet, fists clenched by his sides, lips compressed into a narrow ribbon. A red mist of rage threatened to break free of carefully constructed defences, and he took a step forward. A hand shot out to grab his arm. He was not sure whose it was, but it did nothing to quell his anger, and he shook his arm free. This only served to feed the warden's amusement, and the laughter escalated.

In a last-ditch attempt to control his emotions, Duncan raised his hands and pressed them against his ears to block out the sound, but he need not have bothered. The laughter penetrated, smashing through his resistance. With a cry of rage he launched himself at the man, arms outstretched, claw-like fingers poised to grip him by the throat, but they closed on fresh air, and his anger turned to surprise as his foot caught on the edge of the coffin and he fell, sprawling to the ground.

Within moments, Louisa and Mehmet were at his side, reaching down to help him to his feet.

"Duncan, what *is* the matter with you?" Louisa asked, once they had pulled him up.

In answer, Duncan wrestled free. His feverish gaze darted around the cave as he searched for the warden. "Where is he?" he demanded, when he could see no sign of him.

"Who?" asked Mehmet, eyes narrowed in confusion. "There is no one here but us."

"The warden guy. The one who was standing over there," he pointed towards the grating, "when we came in."

Louisa reached out and gently took hold of his hand, easing his arm down. Holding his gaze, she said, "There was no one there, Duncan."

"B-but I saw him. And when I uncovered the ..." his voice trailed off and, closing his eyes, he breathed deeply and then sighed. After a moment spent calming frayed nerves, he fixed his attention on her, and said, "It would seem Shadow is playing tricks." His lips quirked into a wry smile.

The sound of laughter only he could hear followed his retreat as he made his way towards the exit. But, aside from a slight tensing of his shoulders and a minimal pause in his stride, he gave no indication he had heard it.

# 30

Father Tumbletee and Regent Kearson remained hidden in a darkened recess until the last of the day's tourists made their way to the exit. In preparation for their trip down the grated tunnel they had been out earlier to buy torches, and had acquired a small crowbar. They'd also taken the opportunity to grab something to eat before re-entering the underground city. Now, skulking in the shadows, appeasing hunger pangs was the least of their worries.

"Are you sure it is the correct tunnel?" asked the Regent, his voice not rising above a whisper.

"What other tunnel could it be?" Father Tumbletee countered, leaning out to see if the coast was clear. "There is no other burial chamber on the tourist route, so it has to be the right one." After one last look to make sure there were no stragglers hanging back, he stepped out of concealment and shuffled across the cavern towards the entrance. The Regent muttered something under his breath and, clutching the crowbar and his bag to his chest, swiftly followed.

The silence, broken by the soft rasp of their shoes on stone, was eerie, the short journey down the long, sloping tunnel, seemingly interminable, but they made it without mishap and began the descent to the grotto. When they were halfway down, the lights went out for the night and the tunnel plunged into darkness.

The Regent cursed, and slid to a halt to fumble with his torch. A beam of light brightened the gloom as he found the switch, and he continued the descent, sweeping the ground ahead to ensure he did not trip on an unseen rock. By the time he reached the chamber Father Tumbletee was already at the grille, his torch lying on the ground, the metal grating swinging open.

"I thought it was locked?" he asked, glancing to his crowbar.

The priest grinned and held out a hand. Nestled in the palm was a padlock, its clasp open. "Well, it had this through the bolt, but, as you can see, it wasn't secured, thanks be to God. Using the crowbar may have alerted someone to the fact we were down here."

The Regent shone his torch down the tunnel. Like the one they had used to get to the chamber, it was low and narrow. "How far do we have to travel?" he asked.

Father Tumbletee shrugged. "I really have no idea. But there's only one way to find out." He picked up his torch and headed through the opening, his wide girth only just squeezing between the walls.

Five paces behind, the Regent followed.

Without deviation, the corridor angled down. The floor was rough and uneven, showing it had not suffered the same traffic as the tunnels above, and there were no signs of it widening or giving them more headroom. Stooped over, they continued their descent, the light from their torches their only companion as they made their way ever downward.

Nothing was said as they walked, each immersed in their own thoughts, until, after twenty minutes had passed, the Regent broke the silence. "This cannot be right. We have been walking for an age and still there is no sign of this mysterious cavern. We should go back, before we get lost." His voice sounded dull in the tunnel's confines.

"Lost? How can we get lost? The only direction is down, and Peter was most specific in his instructions: 'Follow the grated tunnel that leads from the burial chamber, for that leads to the lair of the beast.' I am sure we will get there soon enough. Just try and be a little patient."

As though his words were an omen, a further five minutes of walking saw a green-tinged light assert itself on the craggy walls of the tunnel, and he halted to glance back over his shoulder. "I think your patience will not be tested any further."

Soon after, they emerged into an amphitheatre. It was immense, and they paused at the threshold to gape in astonishment.

"I never envisaged something so … so vast," muttered the Regent, stepping forward to gaze in amazement at their surroundings.

Father Tumbletee said nothing. His gaze was firmly fixed on something in the distance. After a moment's contemplation, he reached out to grab the Regent's arm to draw his attention to what he could see, and said, "I somehow get the feeling your current wonderment is about to be overshadowed, in the most dramatic of fashions."

# 31

The sun's brightness was painful after the gloom of the underground city, and Duncan found himself shading his eyes with a hand as he emerged, blinking into daylight. He had said nothing further about the visitation during their ascent and his companions, sensing his abstraction, remained silent, content to let him lead the way.

Once outside he headed back towards the church and its bell tower. Long, purposeful strides carried him quickly through the massed ranks of tourists and traders that clogged the main thoroughfare. Whether there was a madness in his gaze that drove people from his path or an aura of menace surrounding him, he would never know, but his trek through to the square was relatively unhindered and he was free of the throng before he had chance to become agitated by the mass of humanity milling around them.

The neglected fountain passed by on his left as he walked, but, immersed in his thoughts, he barely noticed. He only had eyes for the bell tower and, next to it, the slab that held his cipher. Instinctively, he knew it covered the entrance to the devil's lair, for want of a better expression, and felt sure its marker had been inscribed by the incumbent whose grave they had visited, a sign for the successor who would follow in his or her footsteps years – maybe centuries – in the future. He would never know who the ancestor was, or how death came about, but sensed that Shadow had played a major part in the demise.

Once inside the churchyard Duncan turned right and headed for the slab. The shadows were lengthening and the one cast by the bell tower stretched long and slender towards the entrance, patches of sunlight dappling the ground via the arches. In a matter of hours it would be dark and their work would begin. His features set firm and resolute at the thought. Soon, he would continue the work his ancestors had started, follow the markers that had been left to aid him, and fulfil his destiny.

Louisa and Mehmet held back as Duncan strode across the square, and waited until he reached the entrance in the low stone wall before walking across to join him. Events in the burial chamber had affected him badly, this Louisa sensed, but had no idea what had happened, other than someone neither she nor Mehmet could see had provoked him and ignited a blaze of anger. Although he tried to give the impression he had calmed, she knew he hadn't. The heat of ire shone through his skin, tinging his emanation of Light with a deep, blood-red glow.

"He is still angry," said Mehmet, confirming her thoughts as they walked through the gateway.

She snorted. "Angry? I'd say he was furious." She shook her head and fixed the distant figure with a steady, apprais-ing gaze. He stood, hands pressed straight down his sides, head bowed, standing at attention as he stared at the stone slab. "And looks ready to kill."

Mehmet paused in his stride and gripped her arm to haul her to a halt. She saw the fear in his eyes as he gazed at her.

"We have to calm him," he said. His fingers tightened their grip on her arm as he spoke. "If we confront evil with evil in mind it will undo all that Light stands for. We *must* calm him."

Louisa sighed and looked over her shoulder. Duncan's Light still glowed red with anger. It swathed his body like a second skin. "That could be easier said than done," she murmured.

A shiver ran down her spine, and she hoped it was not a premonition of things to come. She was already terrified at the prospect of facing the being that Duncan had seen in his vision and the thought that he could add to that evil did not bear thinking about. Instinctively, she grasped her medallion and felt taut nerves begin to settle.

"He is our Spear of Light, isn't he?" she asked, turning her head to peer up at Mehmet. "The one chosen to vanquish evil?"

Mehmet nodded. "It would appear so. If we are to believe what Duncan has said of Judas and his role in Christ's death, then, like his descendant, he is also the chosen one. It is our job to make sure he carries out his role for the Light and not for his own reasons, or the Light will lose and Shadow will control. All will be lost and the End of Days will be upon us. We must make him see this, for if he does not, we will lose everything."

Why did she get the impression he had handed that responsibility to her? "And what will you be doing while I make sure he stays calm?"

Mehmet grinned and let go of her arm. "I shall be our eyes and ears."

He did not elaborate further, but strode towards where Duncan stood. Louisa gazed at his back for a moment before following. Just when she'd thought their role could not get any more difficult …

Duncan did not acknowledge their presence when they arrived beside him. Instead, he continued to stare at his cipher. The glow of anger, for the moment contained, still shrouded him, but Louisa knew it would not take much for it to break through the barriers he had created. With the shadows lengthening by the minute it would not be long before night fell, leaving her little time to calm him.

Two minutes stretched to three and still Duncan stood and stared. Louisa, not having the faintest idea on how to open up a relevant conversation, glanced to Mehmet for guidance, but he merely shrugged, and gestured with a narrowing of his eyes and a flick of his head for her to say something, anything to break the deadlock.

"They killed him, you know." Although whispered, Duncan's words were clearly heard in the stillness of late afternoon.

Louisa stifled a yelp of surprise as her gaze snapped to him. He still stood, head bowed, unmoving, but, to her relief, she noted a lessening of anger in his aura.

"Who did?" she asked, her voice soft and neutral. Although she suspected the answer she sensed that he needed to say the word.

Eyes haunted, he looked up. "Shadow." His lips quirked into a cynical smile. "I wonder if he was tormented by its demons as I have been, driven to thoughts of murder."

The tinge of anger again coloured his aura, and Louisa flicked an anxious glance to Mehmet, who studiously ignored her. Panic welled and, not knowing what to say, she resorted to feminine charms and stepped forward to throw her arms around his neck and pull him into an embrace.

Initially, his body stiffened at her touch, but within moments she felt him relax and the heat of his anger fade. His head lowered until it rested on her shoulder and his arms slipped out from between them to return the embrace. Neither of them said a word, each immersed in their own thoughts until, reluctantly, she eased away.

Her hands slid down his arms to grasp his as they moved apart, and she was reassured to note his ire had almost dissipated. Almost, but not quite. It was still there, but appeared to be controlled rather than ready to explode into action. She smiled, mostly with relief, but also because she had enjoyed their moment, their brief union, and wondered what may have been had they met under different circumstances.

Duncan returned her smile with one of his own, albeit with a trace of embarrassment. "I'm sorry about before. In the cavern. I don't know what came over me. I think … I think Shadow's taunting got to me, and nearly pushed me over the edge." He held her gaze. "It won't happen again."

At his words his pupils dilated, ousting the blue of his eyes.

Involuntarily, Louisa shuddered. Her arms came out in goosebumps and she took a step back, letting go of his hands. There was no hint of a red tinge to his aura now. In fact, she could not sense his aura at all. Her eyes widened in alarm, and then concern as Duncan dropped to his knees. His face contorted in agony and he slapped the heel of a hand against the recently-healed injury to his skull.

Without pause for thought, Louisa raced forward to kneel by his side, her earlier fear vanquished, and wrapped her arms around him. His flesh was ice-cold to the touch and he quivered, as though in shock. Her hold tightened, and she found herself rocking to and fro in an attempt to ease whatever it was that afflicted him.

The shadow of Mehmet cloaked them and she glanced up, a silent entreaty for help, but Mehmet looked as stunned as she felt and offered nothing by way of support.

Without warning, Duncan pushed out with an arm and forced her away. She cried out in surprise and tumbled backwards. Within seconds Mehmet was beside her, his strong hands helping her to her feet as they both stared wide-eyed at Duncan.

With his face contorted and a hand still clamped to his head, he fumbled under his T-shirt for his medallion with his free hand. Once he had hold of it his aura of Light sprang back into being and his features relaxed. The pallid, waxy sheen that afflicted his skin began to colour, and his breathing deepened. Although his eyes remained closed they weren't screwed shut, and his posture grew more erect. As they watched, the hand pressed to the side of his head began to lower with a slowness bordering on hesitancy, and the lids to his eyes eased open.

On seeing Louisa and Mehmet standing before him, he said, "It has to be tonight. Shadow is growing too powerful. Evil is close and I am weaker than I thought. Even now it's trying to force me to choose Shadow over Light and I don't know if I'm strong enough to fight it." He pulled up his T-shirt to reveal the medallion and stared down at it resting on a palm. "Even with the help of this."

"Of course you are strong enough, so stop this stupid talk." Stepping forward, Mehmet reached down and hauled him to his feet. Once he was standing he moved in close, until their noses were merely inches apart. Pitching his voice low, he said, "You are the one that Shadow fears. That is why they play tricks with you." He jabbed an index finger into Duncan's chest for emphasis. "It is all one big trick. You fall for it and we all fall. You are of Light, and do not forget it."

Turning on his heel, he stalked away, calling over his shoulder as he went: "If you want to fight Shadow tonight then you have to eat. Come. We go to the cafe to get some food. Fighting is no good on an empty stomach. The entrance will still be there later."

Louisa folded her arms across her chest and stared at Duncan, unwilling to show the compassion she felt in case it undermined the case Mehmet had put forward so succinctly. To give him credit, Duncan did not look to her for sympathy, but simply sighed and walked past. She gazed at his back as he walked and wondered whether she would ever know the true Duncan Connors. He appeared to be a man full of contradictions. One minute he was angered and ready to fight anyone and everyone that stood in his way, the next he was unsure and fearful. Which one would be with them when they entered the cavern? Would it be the right one? She certainly hoped so, because the consequences of the wrong one turning up at the ball game did not bear thinking about.

# 32

Dust spiralled into the air as the leather bag hit the ground with a dull thud, but the Regent was oblivious. With his eyes fixed on the being suspended in the altar, he dropped to his knees and signed the cross in the air before him.

The grey, sickly flesh of the being rippled and its head, shielded by its arms, began to emerge from concealment. With slow, careful movements, the Regent rose to his feet as more of the hairless dome came into view, and gasped as eyes darker than night fluttered open. He knew that if he met that gaze he would be drawn into madness, and dropped to his knees once again to fumble with the lock to his bag.

"What are you doing?" asked Father Tumbletee, flicking his gaze between the Regent and the creature.

The Regent glanced up. "An exorcism, of a special kind, and I will require your help." The clasp that locked the bag flipped open and he delved inside to remove the crucifix. It was large, around eighteen inches long, and heavy. Once removed, he laid it on the ground beside him.

The priest's lips twisted into a sneer. "And you think that lump of metal will help you overcome such as He?" He inclined his head towards the altar.

A frown formed on the Regent's face and he paused in the act of removing the leatherbound tome. There was something about Tumbletee's manner that didn't sound right.

The priest's shadow flowed over him as he walked past,

towards the altar, where he halted to stare up at the being.

"Somehow, I am thinking it would take more than a few words and a sculpted piece of scrap iron to prevent the resurrection of the one true God."

Still on his knees, the Regent twisted his head to look on in horror as Tumbletee prostrated himself before his 'God'. In response, the creature's lips curled into a smile.

The Regent reached out to grasp hold of his crucifix and then rose to his feet. "There is only one true God." He held the crucifix before him, a protective barrier against evil. "And it is not the beast I see before me."

The smile on the antichrist's face faded and it looked to the Regent, who refused to meet its gaze. Instead, he focused on the priest, who rose to his feet to turn and face him.

"I think you will find that it is." He clasped his hands before him, and smiled. "And that your precious Mr Connors will be along anytime now to fulfil the legacy initiated by his long-dead ancestor."

A frown tugged at the Regent's brow. "What has Connors to do with all of this?"

"Don't you listen?" The priest laughed. Short, sharp, and without humour. "Like I said back at the hotel, his DNA is the blueprint that will empower our God. With his blood, God will truly walk amongst mortals, unlike the pretender you worship. You don't think Connors works for your false god, do you?" He chuckled. "Rest assured, you will be sadly mistaken." His gaze hardened. "Unlike his ancestor who betrayed us at the last, Connors will be true to the cause. *Our* cause."

The Regent took a pace forward, but a ripple of movement within the beast halted him, and Tumbletee smirked.

"Connors will never betray the Church. You said yourself that he is true to *us*."

"Did I?" His eyes widened in feigned innocence. "Or did you misinterpret? Believe me, Connors is one of us."

"*Never!*"

Echoes of the Regent's loud shout reverberated around

the cavern and set shadows scurrying. He looked up in alarm as a host of dark shapes flowed over craggy outcrops, slithered across the ground and scurried over rocks, all heading towards the altar and where he stood.

Tumbletee threw wide his arms and, head tilted back, laughed. "Behold, our servants come to greet you."

A breeze ruffled the Regent's hair. Where it had come from he had no idea, but suspected it was to do with the evil, fluid horde that congregated around him. It grew in strength, as did Tumbletee's manic laughter, and he knew he did not have long to live, and that if he died, all They had planned would come to nought. Centuries of nurturing what remained of the true line would result in abject failure, and the world would be plunged into a living hell.

He thumbed the concealed switch on the crucifix and the sheath concealing the ten-inch blade slipped free. Thanks to Tumbletee he knew the beast required Connors' blood to break free of the womb that fed it, and vowed that that would not happen whilst he still had breath in his body. He had to complete what he came here to do.

Too quick for Tumbletee to realise what he intended, the Regent lunged forward to thrust the dagger up under his ribcage, where it tore through his lungs before piercing the heart.

Blood frothed from his mouth as he stared at the Regent in surprise. Then, choking, he turned to his 'God' for help. When none was forthcoming he attempted to reach out, a silent entreaty, but life left him before he could complete his appeal, and his body slumped to the ground.

A wave of anger battered the Regent, but he refused to look towards the altar and fall prey to the warped mind-games of the beast. Instead, whilst shadows fled the scene, he walked back to his bag, his mind completely focused on what he must do, to carry out what Louvière had told him he had to do.

# 33

Hiki's battered Volvo was already in the grounds when Louisa and Duncan arrived at the entrance to the churchyard. Mehmet had driven it over the grass and was in the process of reversing it towards the slab. Duncan felt his flesh tingle with nervous energy. Although he'd given his companions the impression he'd fully calmed, in truth, he hadn't. His fury was not far away. It bubbled beneath the surface, waiting to erupt like an angry volcano, and it was taking a large part of his willpower to keep it under control.

The tailgate of the car opened and Mehmet leaned in to pull out ropes, torches and a bag of tools. He was on his knees, scrapping at the turf with what looked like a tyre lever when they arrived beside him.

"What are you doing?" Louisa hissed, casting nervous glances around the square. "Someone might see you. Shouldn't we wait until it gets fully dark?"

Mehmet paused in his work to look up. "I am making a groove for the rope to slip under so we can pull off the slab with the car. Don't worry. No one will notice. Derinkuyu is like a ghost town when night falls. It only comes alive for tourists. No one stays here but villagers, and they are all at home." He grinned. "Relax. All will be well."

"That's easy for you to say," she muttered, and continued to scan their surroundings.

Duncan rummaged in the toolbag for something to scrape at the soil and his fingers closed on a large screwdriver.

241

Dropping to his knees, he began to work at the opposite end to Mehmet and in a matter of minutes they had dug enough soil away for the rope to slip under.

Mehmet rose to his feet to grab a coil from beside the car and began to form a large lasso. Once he was satisfied with the knot he looped the rope under the end of the slab and ran the free end back to the car, where he tied it to the tow bar. Then, slapping his hands together to rub them free of grime, he looked to Duncan. Without saying a word, he gave a single nod and turned to walk to the driver's door. Once inside the car he turned the ignition and the Volvo burst grudgingly into life.

The deep, throaty roar of the exhaust sounded loud in the silence of the night, causing Duncan to mimic Louisa's earlier actions, flicking an anxious gaze into the gloom. But there was no one around to see them, the bell tower being the only witness to their desecration.

The rope went taught as the car eased forward, and began to stretch, but there was no movement of the slab. The exhaust roar grew louder as Mehmet gave the car more gas, but it refused to budge, and the tyres whined in protest and tore at the grass. For all his efforts, they were getting nowhere fast, and Duncan left Louisa to keep watch while he strode to the driver's side to rap on the window.

The car settled back as Mehmet took his foot off the accelerator. On winding down the window he shook his head. "It is no good. The rope will break before the slab moves." He slapped his hands against the steering wheel in frustration. "And we have no tools to lift it."

Stooping, Duncan lowered his head to the window. "Why not try to move it sideways?"

The frown that formed on Mehmet's face said it all. He thought Duncan had taken leave of his senses. "What do you mean?"

"The wheels are slipping on the grass. Over there" – he pointed towards the church – "is solid ground. You should get a good grip and be able to heave it sideways."

Mehmet grinned, and slammed the car into reverse. It immediately shot backwards, causing Duncan to leap to the side to prevent being dragged with it. Cursing, he watched as the car skidded round to face towards the church, leaving a furrow of torn turf in its wake. One thing was sure, they were leaving their mark. Come daylight it would be obvious what had gone on in the churchyard. Then again, if it all went wrong, their trashing of the grounds would be the least of the world's problems.

The rope went taut as the car inched forward. With better traction, the wheels gripped and the slab, ever so slowly, began to move. Inch by inch it slid to one side, and with every inch that it moved Duncan's heart beat harder against his ribs. Blood rushed through his veins, the roar of each beat loud in his ears.

Time slowed, each passing second seeming like a minute, and still the gap was not large enough to allow someone in. Impatience got the better of him and he raced to where Mehmet had dumped the torches to grab one before returning to the hole in the ground. On reaching it he flopped to his belly, shone a beam of light into the cavity and lowered his head through the gap.

Beneath the slab was a tunnel, just as he'd hoped, but, to his horror, it was vertical. To add to his dismay, the light of the torch wasn't strong enough to illuminate the bottom. He directed the beam to the walls in case there was another, more accessible route for them to travel, but the sides were sheer. There was no way but down. His eyes narrowed as something caught his eye, and he directed the torch to the rock wall to his left.

Niches, carved at regular intervals, tracked their way down to the darkness below. They appeared to form a ladder, of sorts, but not one that looked particularly safe. If the rock proved as soft as the rock in the lower levels of the underground city they could end up reaching the bottom far more quickly than they intended.

He pulled his head clear and, lips pursed, rested back on

his knees to stare into the hole, the beam of his torch still aligned on the carved steps. Beside him Louisa gasped.

"We have to go down there?"

Looking up, Duncan grimaced. "Looks like it. Just as well Mehmet brought the ropes."

On rising, he brushed dirt from his knees, but paused in his actions when he noticed that she still stared into the dark opening. A prolonged grating sound jangled frayed nerves as the slab slid clear and, despite the gloom, he saw panic in her eyes.

"What's the matter?" he asked, moving to her side and turning her to face him.

Instead of meeting his gaze, her attention remained fixed on the hole in the ground. "I ... I'm scared of heights."

Her words were spoken in a whisper and Duncan sensed her fear.

The ever present grumble of the car exhaust died and silence descended. The light breeze faded to nothing, creating the illusion that, along with Louisa, the world held its breath.

The spell was broken by the slam of a car door, closely followed by the heavy tread of booted feet on grass. When Mehmet arrived beside them he also peered down the hole, and eyed the steps thoughtfully. "Looks like we need the ropes."

Duncan felt Louisa stiffen, and said, "We may have a problem."

"Mmm?" Mehmet frowned and pulled his gaze from the tunnel. "What problem?"

"A scared of heights problem."

Mehmet's gaze slid to Louisa. Then, stepping forward, he reached out to grasp hold of her arms. At his touch, she dragged her attention away from the focus of her anxiety to meet his gaze.

"It is no problem. It will be just like going to the Cavern."

Her throat rippled as she swallowed, and Duncan sensed

244

no lessening of her terror.

"I will go and get the ropes. You will be safe." He squeezed her arms for emphasis. "No problem."

As though the matter were settled, he smiled and moved away, heading towards where he had dumped the ropes.

Duncan reached out to rest a hand on her shoulder. "I'll go first. That way you'll know where the bottom is. It can't be too far down." He grinned. "And that way I can catch you if you slip."

His words were intended as a joke, but the tightening around her eyes indicated she hadn't found it funny, and he sighed, his hand dropping to his side.

"I'm sorry. I shouldn't have said that."

Louisa tilted back her head, closed her eyes and issued a sigh of her own before meeting his gaze and giving a half-smile. "It should be me that's sorry. Mehmet's right. If I managed to get down to the Cavern of Rebirth then I should manage this one okay."

Hiki's car fired into life, diverting their attention as it reversed nearer to the tunnel mouth. Once it was within three metres Mehmet turned off the ignition, pulled the handbrake on and then stepped out. "We will use the tow bar," he said, leaning in to grab the ropes he had deposited on fetching the car. "That way, the car will help take the weight in case you fall."

His eyes widened and fixed on Louisa as he realised what he'd said.

In response, she gave a wan smile and wrapped her arms around her chest.

In an attempt to cover his poor choice of wording he handed one end of the rope to Duncan, and said, "We need to make a lasso, like with the slab. Then we wrap the rope around the tow bar to take your weight as you climb down. Clear?"

It did not take long to prepare for the descent and within minutes Duncan was perched at the edge of the drop, the rope wrapped around his waist. Mehmet held on to the other end, ready to feed the rope as Duncan descended. Duncan's torch had been tied to his belt and he thumbed it on before turning his back to the hole. Mehmet gave a thumbs-up and he took a deep breath before kneeling and backing towards the opening.

Louisa stood the on other side of the tunnel mouth, torch in hand, shining it on the steps as Duncan lowered a leg to feel for the first indentation. He found it easily enough and eased his other leg over the edge. His hands gripped clumps of grass as his feet probed the indentations. To his surprise, they were deeper than he expected and he was able to gain a secure footing. Now all he hoped was that the rock was solid enough to take his weight. He did not fancy trusting the clumps of grass to prevent his falling, or having to place his faith on the rope and Mehmet's strength, albeit aided by the tow bar.

After taking a deep breath he began the descent, carefully feeling for each foothold to ensure its integrity before moving on to the next. To aid the climber, each carved step had a slight, raised lip, which enabled his fingers to gain purchase, and he felt his admiration grow for the people who had created the maze of underground tunnels and rooms.

Without warning, one of the lips crumbled and his foot slipped. The rope went tight around his waist and, by reflex, his fingers clamped onto their handholds. The scabs from his recently injured fingers broke free and he groaned.

"Duncan! Are you okay?"

Louisa's concerned call echoed down the shaft before being absorbed by soft tufa.

With his body clamped to the wall, Duncan risked a look down. He could see the bottom in the light of the torch suspended from his belt, and breathed a sigh of relief. It was around ten metres away. Looking up, he could see a patch of darkness sprinkled with stars. He was over halfway down.

"I'm fine," he called back. "My foot slipped. I'm nearly there."

The rest of the descent was made without mishap and his

feet touched solid rock some five minutes later. The muscles of his fingers ached from being clamped to the rock for so long. The ones in his legs and arms fared not much better, but at least he had reached the bottom.

Fumbling at his side, his fingers closed on the handle of his torch and he swept it upward to study his environs. From where he had landed a tunnel led off at an angle that would take it under the church, if his sense of direction was correct. It looked to be curved, and sloped down quite steeply. Like the one leading to the old grave, it was only wide enough for one person to pass through at a time.

Satisfied that they at least had a direction in which to go, he loosened the rope around his waist and slipped the loop over his head. Then, with a hand cupping his mouth, he shouted, "You can pull the rope up now. I'm down. There's another tunnel down here that leads off under the church, so it looks like we could be on the right path."

The rope began its ascent and Duncan watched it rise. Had it not been for the fact that Louisa was the next one down he would have explored the tunnel, gone ahead to make sure it wasn't a dead end, but he daren't in case she needed him. It was one thing to overcome your fears to begin the descent, but to give in to them when halfway down could cause no end of problems.

The dark silhouette of Louisa blocked out a section of stars as she backed to the edge of the shaft, and Duncan felt his nerves begin to tingle. It was now or never. She had to commence the descent straight away or she never would.

"The indentations are really deep," he called up, offering encouragement. "Just take your time. Don't panic. Remember, you can't fall. Mehmet's got you. Just ease yourself over the edge and feel with your feet for the footholds."

The silhouette moved and the rattle of small stones falling had Duncan scamper to the side tunnel to avoid being pelted. Once the clatter of pebbles had ceased he edged out and looked up, but could see nothing outlined in the circular patch of night sky.

He snatched at his torch and angled the beam up the shaft. In the dim, furthest reaches of its light he could make out the distant figure of Louisa, clinging to the handholds as she lowered a leg in search of the next one.

"That's it. You're doing fine. Just take your time. It's not that far to the bottom. You can do it."

Louisa's progress was slow and methodical, but she eventually made it to the bottom without incident, where she collapsed into Duncan's arms. Her whole body shook. Whether it was due to the stress of the climb or the relief at beating her fears, he wasn't sure, but held her close and stroked her hair as she calmed.

There was a vibration to the rope and he looked up, easing back from the embrace to shine his torch up the shaft. Above, Mehmet was using it to abseil down in preference to the niches, and Duncan helped slip the lasso over Louisa's head before pulling her into the side tunnel to leave room for him to land.

Mehmet was nearing the bottom when he suddenly plummeted. Duncan heard the whoosh of breath escape his lips as he hit the ground. Seconds later, the rope snaked down to land on top of him, and Louisa screamed.

Rushing forward, Duncan dropped to his knees beside him. To his relief, Mehmet gave a rueful smile, and said, "That hurt."

"Didn't you tie the rope off properly?"

Mehmet winced, and pushed himself to a sitting position, where he wiped dust and debris from the sleeves to his jacket. "I thought so, but … " He shrugged and began to untie his torch from his belt, and flicked it on to make sure it still worked. A bright beam illuminated the base of the shaft, and lit up the coil of rope that lay on the ground.

Duncan pursed his lips and shook his head. "You're one lucky bastard. If that had happened when you were higher up … " He left the sentence hanging.

A grating sound from above caught their attention. As one, their eyes fixed to the top of the shaft. A straight edge appeared to one side of the circular patch of night sky. The rumble of stone against stone continued and the stars began to disappear.

Duncan surged to his feet to glare up at the rapidly shrinking opening. "We're being shut in," he murmured in disbelief.

"Wh-what's happening?" Louisa asked, emerging from the side tunnel. Her footsteps were tentative, and her eyes flicked to Mehmet, as though seeking reassurance he was fine.

Mehmet rose gingerly to his feet, the cleanly severed end of the rope held in a hand. He waggled it in the air to show her as he spoke. "It would seem Shadow not only knows we are here, but intends to make sure we stay here."

Louisa's eyes widened. "B-but why?"

The last of the stars winked out as the slab slid home, and the grating sound stopped.

Duncan sighed, and said, "To make sure we meet with their leader." He let his gaze rest briefly on each of them before adding; "Either that or we've fallen for their trap and climbed down to our grave."

At his words, Louisa gasped, and Mehmet threw the rope to the ground in disgust. "They better hope it is our grave they have sent us to."

"My thoughts exactly," said Duncan. Anger filled him and, with lips compressed, he stepped forward to shine his torch beam down the tunnel that led underneath the church. "And it would seem there is only one way to find out."

# 34

Duncan cursed as he paused to wipe yet another net of cobwebs from his face. The place was festooned with the stuff, and it was obvious the tunnel had not been used in a very long time. But, with a macabre sense of déjà-vu, he knew he had been there before. The gentle, spiralling curve of the passageway was exactly how he remembered from his dreams, but in reality it was a lot more oppressive. Air movement was nil and the tang of dust and stale air clung to the palate, to dry the throat and leave an unpleasant taste in the mouth. There were no side-rooms carved into the rock or niches that could be stepped into whilst others passed, and he could almost feel the weight of the millions of tons of rock that pressed down from above. Even so, the similarity to the one in his vision convinced him they were on the right path rather than being led to a slow death by attrition.

His conviction was both a relief and a worry. Relief because it meant they were not trapped under the ground wandering aimlessly until they died of starvation, but worry because he knew they were expected. That was the most galling thing to accept; the fact they had been shepherded to this place at this time when all along they had thought it was they who had made the choice. The one thing that gave him some perverse pleasure was the fact that Shadow thought it could use the medallions for its own ends, but it would soon find out differently.

Another cobweb wrapped itself around his face and he

yanked it clear without breaking stride. And the sooner Shadow knew of its error of judgement the better.

Unexpectedly, the tunnel opened into a small grotto before continuing on its way. Duncan halted in the centre of the small room and shone his torch to the vaulted ceiling. It arched some three metres above their heads and a chain of faded red crosses decorated it at its junction with the walls. To the left were three arched openings, separated by columns that had been carved out of the rock. The area of chisel-smoothed stone above the arches had also been decorated, but with a band of red and rock-coloured squares rather than crosses, and looked much like a long chequerboard.

"What is this place?" asked Mehmet, as he and Louisa added their light to the gloom.

"Some sort of ancient church," Louisa suggested. "Look." She shone her torch on the wall to the right, to where a large, primitive cross had been painted. Again, the paint was faded through time.

"You could be right," said Duncan, from where he had walked between the arches, his voice sounding hollow and muffled. "It certainly looks like it was used for some form of religious practice."

"Are you ready?" asked Mehmet. "We should be going."

"In a minute. I think I've found something."

Mehmet scowled and walked to where he stood. "What is it?"

"Another tunnel."

Behind the arches, two seats had been carved to the rear wall, separated by a soot-stained niche, while a small tunnel ran off at right angles to where Duncan had entered. Crouching, he examined the rock around the tunnel mouth and then shone his torch through the opening. Although the mouth of the tunnel was only large enough to crawl through, it opened out after a couple of feet and looked to be as large as the one they had been travelling through.

"Why are you interested in that tunnel," asked Mehmet, standing behind him, "when we already follow one?"

Duncan grinned, and looked up to peer at him. "Because this is the tunnel we're going to take."

Mehmet opened his mouth to protest, but the appearance of Louisa in the central archway halted him.

"What are you two up to?"

Mehmet shook his head. "He says we should take that tunnel, but it is not big enough. How will we stand up and walk? And why that one?" He tapped a finger at his temple. "He is mad."

"No, not mad," Duncan retorted, rising to his feet. "Just following the trail left by my ancestor." He shone his torch to a set of marks on the wall above the opening. Clearly carved was an image of a bird flying from cupped hands. "And don't worry, it opens up after you crawl through." Not wanting to hang around and encourage further argument, he dropped to his knees and made his way through.

Like he'd anticipated, the tunnel opened up after four or five feet and he was able to stand. It was slightly wider than the previous one, and was just as low, but, at this early stage, had fewer cobwebs, which was a relief. Stooping, he called through to his companions: "Next!"

The grotto proved to be the first of three they encountered, and each time they searched for the concealed tunnel marked with a cipher instead of heading down the obvious one. On leaving the third Duncan glanced at his watch. They had been navigating the maze for nearly an hour and still seemed no nearer to their objective, and he hoped his gut feeling that they followed the correct route proved to be accurate. At the previous stop Mehmet had given voice to his concerns they were being played for fools and suggested they turn back and take another route, but Duncan had resisted, saying that the trail left by his ancestor had got them this far so they should trust it to take them the rest of the way. Despite his growing suspicion the trail was false, Mehmet followed his lead, but Duncan knew if they did not come across the cavern soon, there would be division in the ranks.

They had travelled less than one hundred paces along

the new tunnel when they came upon an obstruction that blocked the passage. It was a millstone. Inwardly, Duncan groaned, and shone the beam of his torch over the circular slab of rock. A tingle ran down his spine as he did so, and his frustration lifted. It was the exact same one as in his vision.

 "Why do we stop?" asked Mehmet, from somewhere behind.

There was irritation in his voice, and Duncan sensed he was not far from turning around and going back.

"We have a slight problem."

Pushing forward, Mehmet peered over his shoulder and groaned. "I told you we followed a false trail and now I am proved right. Why do you not listen? We have to try the other tunnels. This one is no good."

In response, Duncan shone his torch to the left to reveal a small room that had been carved into the rock, and then to his right to where the millstone rested in its recess. "I wouldn't be too hasty, if I were you. This one can be opened from this side." He moved to the recess and leaned in to examine the wheel housing. "If we can get the damn thing to move."

"Let me see," Mehmet urged, easing his way passed. Stooping, he also examined the housing.

"Er, guys?"

At Louisa's call they paused in their inspection.

"Millstones were used to prevent attackers from following folk down into the city and killing them, weren't they?"

Duncan glanced to Mehmet, eyes narrowed in confusion, before nodding in agreement.

"And they could only be opened from the side the defenders were secure behind?"

Again Duncan nodded.

"Then why can this door be opened from this side? The uphill side, where invaders would be coming from?"

"What do you mean?"

"She means," said Duncan, "that this door was used to stop those within from coming up rather than being a barrier

253

against attackers getting down."

Mehmet shrugged and returned to his inspection. "That is good. It means you are right and we are on the correct path." Straightening, he said, "The wheel will move." He laid his torch on the ground and eased between the millstone and the wall to wedge himself into position.

"Aren't you the least bit concerned that the danger down there warranted a stone barrier being used to stop it escaping?" Louisa clutched her torch to her chest, her face distorted by the harshness of its light and shadows cast by her features.

"The danger is no greater than we already suspected," said Duncan. "We can't turn back now."

Hesitantly, she nodded, and Duncan gave her a smile of encouragement before joining Mehmet at the millstone. Unlike in his vision, where it had refused to budge until abject terror had given him the strength to move it, the one in the tunnel began to shift almost immediately. Dust and gravelly stones rattled down from above as it slowly rolled in its groove. Between them, they managed to roll it halfway into its housing the other side of the corridor before it came to an abrupt halt.

On inspection, it was apparent it would roll no further. A section of the ceiling had dropped and obstructed the groove in which the millstone rolled, but it mattered not. There was enough space for them to squeeze through.

As he prepared to lead the way, Duncan halted beside the millstone, the beam of his torch shining down the arced passage, and his nose twitched. Looking to Mehmet, he said, "You smell that?"

Head raised, he sniffed at the air, and then said, "It is smoke, like the smell from a candle."

Lips pursed, Duncan nodded. "That's what I thought. They're waiting for us." Looking to Louisa, he said, "You can wait here if you don't fancy going any further. Hell," he snorted in wry amusement "*I* don't feel like going any further. No one will think the worse of you if you decide to stay here until it's all over."

Mehmet nodded his agreement. "Duncan is right. They know we come. It will be –"

"Dangerous?" Louisa stepped towards them, arms folded across her chest. Her lips were compressed into a narrow ribbon and her eyes seemed to flash sparks in the gloom as she glared at each of them in turn. "In case you've forgotten, I didn't sign on for this to back out at the first hint of trouble. I am of Light, like you, and have no intention of sitting on the sidelines like some dumb-ass cheerleader while the 'boys' make the score. You got it?"

So saying, she strode forward and shouldered Duncan aside to make room for her to step through the opening. Once on the other side she turned and smiled sweetly. "You boys coming, or would you like to wait there where it's nice and safe?"

Brows raised, Duncan looked to Mehmet, who shrugged, before he followed her into the passageway beyond. She set a fast pace, too fast for prudence, and he hissed at her to slow down. With the smell of smoke getting stronger it was apparent they were nearing the cavern and, even though he knew they were expected, a semblance of caution was still required. To his relief, she heeded his advice and the pace slowed.

As with the previous tunnels, this one curved its way downwards so that the end could not be seen. Fortunately, after five minutes of walking, a brightening in the density of light gave them warning they were nearing the end. Duncan increased his pace to tap Louisa on the shoulder. She stopped and looked back, and he raised his torch to switch off its beam. She nodded, and did likewise, and the tunnel darkened perceptibly. It darkened further still as Mehmet followed suit.

Duncan placed a finger to his lips to reinforce the need for both caution and silence, and then patted his chest before pointing down the tunnel. A momentary tightening around the eyes was Louisa's only attempt at defiance before she pressed her back against the wall to give him space to squeeze past. Grateful she had acquiesced so readily, he gave a small smile of thanks.

Even with her back wedged against the wall there was not much of a gap for him to slip through and he found himself pressed tight against her. The warm closeness of her body and the sweet scent of her perspiration, on any other occasion, would have stirred longings he had long given up on, but with Shadow being within touching distance he was away before such thoughts could enter his head.

Stooped over, he padded silently along the final leg of their journey. Adrenaline coursed through his body and every nerve seemed on edge. His earlier anger had dissipated, replaced by a nervous need to confront the enemy, to destroy that which would destroy them. How, he had no idea, but hoped that divine inspiration would show them the way when needed.

Further thoughts on the matter were pushed to the back of his mind when the cavern, like a sun emerging from an eclipse, came into view. Their pace slowed even more, and they hugged the wall as they eased their way forward.

Like in his vision, the cavern was huge, easily the size of a national sports stadium. The ground between them and the far side was littered with boulders, large and small, and stalactites hung down from the rocky canopy above. A sickly green light emanated from the rock and, whether it was his imagination or a trick of the light, shadows seemed to scurry like ants over the rocks.

"Is this the place of your dreams?" Mehmet whispered, sidling up to Duncan as he paused at the threshold.

Duncan nodded, and then jerked his head towards the far side of the cavern. "The altar should be over there."

Unconsciously, his hand rose to grasp at his medallion. Then, with a grim smile, he delved inside his T-shirt and pulled it free. To his mind, it glowed more brightly as he held it and gazed at his cipher one more time. "For the Light," he murmured, then raised it to his lips to kiss its copper-coloured surface before holding it aloft to gaze on the pattern that had become so familiar.

From nowhere, a light wind tousled his hair. The disc in his hand glowed more brightly and began to vibrate. It was only slight, but enough to send a tingle through his fingers. Whether it was his imagination or not he could not be sure, but it seemed as though the very air around the disc also vibrated, to create a low humming sound, and the hairs on the back of his neck stood on end.

Within the cavern, something else heard the vibrations, and eyes darker than night flicked open to gaze in undisguised malice at the man standing before it.

"For the Light," Duncan repeated, lowering the now quiescent disc to gaze at its dulled surface. The hairs on his neck had also settled, but he could not shake off the feeling that something had occurred that would not be laid to rest so easily. With an increased sense of foreboding, he forced his mind to the task at hand and turned to lead the way across the cavern floor, before his companions could notice his distraction.

He had been there before, albeit in a dream state, and could remember which boulders and rocks he had previously used to navigate the cluttered interior. Ducking low, it did not take him long to reach the one he knew the altar lay beyond, and gestured for the others to stop behind him. Around them, the shadows ceased their scampering, and settled for fidgeting observance.

Duncan's heart beat loud and painful against his ribs and his breathing sounded loud in the quiet, but even so, he could make out the low murmur of a voice beyond the boulder they hid behind. He could not make out the words, but, by its depth and cadence, could tell the voice was male, and was raised in prayer. After glancing to his companions, he eased out from hiding – and stopped dead.

His vision did not do the edifice justice, could not do it justice. It was immense. They had emerged some ten metres from where it stood, but he still felt dwarfed by its size.

Colossal, it demanded attention and filled his vision, the man standing before it, arms outstretched, seeming insignificant. Whereas in his dream the albumen had been red-tinged, it was now a deeper shade, with the being suspended in its yolk sac a fully formed humanoid. The dark pits of its eyes were fixed on the man.

"By the Light." The words were out of Duncan's mouth before he realised.

At the interruption, the figure before the altar spun, arms still outstretched, grey hair dishevelled, his face a mask of surprise. An open book and two black candles lay on the ground between him and the altar, nestled between arcane markings that had been scratched on the rocky surface.

"Kearson!"

A surge of anger engulfed him, and Duncan stepped forward. Seeing the Regent praying before the false God, with the open book and candles as in his first vision, confirmed what he'd suspected all along; he was of Shadow, and that ultimately, he was responsible for the death of his friend and mentor. As he continued to walk towards him, he spotted a crumpled figure lying before the altar. Blood stained the ground beneath it and eyes glazed over in death watched, unseeing, as he approached. Despite the features being contorted with the agony of violent death he recognised who it was immediately, and his anger deepened.

The Regent flicked a glance between Duncan and Tumbletee before again imploring Duncan to leave. "Connors! This is not what it seems. You have to trust me. You have to leave. Now!"

Duncan ignored the words and continued walking. A hand grabbed his arm, and a voice said, "Duncan. You have to listen to him."

It was Mehmet, but what did he know? He snatched free of his grip, his focus remaining firmly fixed on the Regent, who backed towards the altar.

"Duncan! He is carrying out an exorcism. Can't you see the candles, the Bible, the pentagram? He is one of us!

*Stop!"*

At Mehmet's loud shout, the being within the altar moved and, unable to help himself, Duncan looked over and above the Regent. He paused in his march, mouth agape. Instead of the beast he expected to see, his eyes lit upon features he remembered so well, features that had melted away in the heat of a fiery death many years ago.

"Avenge me, my son. Avenge me. They murdered me to get at you. They deserve to die. Kill them all!"

His father's words ended in a shriek of pain as flames engulfed him. Like heated wax, the flesh to his face began to melt, and Duncan's anger exploded. Hands outstretched, he raced for the one person he could hold accountable for the world's evil, and for the untimely death of his family.

Around him, dark shadows flowed over every rocky surface to converge on the altar.

The red flare of anger blossomed into existence the moment Duncan looked upon the face of the monster suspended in the altar. Like a shroud, it swathed him. The shield that had prevented his controlled rage from breaking free had been smashed, and Louisa knew he was seconds away from doing something that could jeopardise their whole reason for being there.

*"Duncan!"*

She lunged at him, intending to grab him and make him stop what he was about to do, but was too late; he had already surged forward. She stumbled and almost fell, but caught her balance and continued to race after him. She cried out his name and begged him to put a halt to his madness, but he took no notice. An all-consuming rage had him in its grip. By the time she reached him he had Kearson bent backwards, hands gripping his throat, his intent obvious.

In an attempt to drag him off she hauled at his arms, Mehmet's warning about carrying out their task for the right reasons foremost in her mind, but it was like trying to move the immovable, and she began to panic.

*"Duncan! Duncan!* You have to stop. This is not the way.

259

Duncan!"

Despite her entreaties and continued yanking at his arms he refused to let go. If anything, his grip tightened.

The flesh of Kearson's face turned a weird shade of puce under the pressure, and he clawed at Duncan's hands in a desperate attempt to free his windpipe, but his efforts were in vain. He was weakening and Louisa realised that, before her eyes, a man was being throttled to death. An anger of her own spread through her, and she heaved back on an arm, desperate for Duncan to realise what he was doing was wrong. In retaliation, he lashed out.

The power of the blow sent her staggering back. Her vision blurred, bright specks danced before her eyes, and the sound of rushing blood filled her ears.

A foot caught the body on the ground and she stumbled. She knew she was falling, but it all seemed surreal. The impact of her head hitting the hard, jagged edge of a solid surface brought back reality, and she cried out in pain. Wetness pooled at the nape of her neck. She tried to rise to move free of the water or whatever it was she had fallen into, but her limbs felt as though they were encased in lead. It took all her effort just to move her head a fraction.

To her annoyance, the movement caused the pool of wetness to spread further down her back. She would just have to lie there for a while, until her strength returned, and then she would roll free and give Duncan a piece of her mind.

From her prone position, she saw Mehmet rush forward through the fog that blurred her vision. His black hair bounced around his shoulders, and his mouth was open as though he cried her name. But she could not hear him. She smiled. He looked so handsome. Why had she not seen it before? She wanted to tell him she would be fine in a moment or two, but the words refused to come. Instead, her vision faded and the cavern turned black.

# 35

**N**o!" The cry of distress reverberated around the cavern. Like a landslide, each echo gathered momentum until it merged with the next. Within seconds they had coalesced into one howling, primordial scream that sent the cavorting shadows into paroxysms. But it was not the scream that alerted Duncan to the fact something was wrong, it was the anguish behind it. It burned into his chest, above his heart, and drove away the heat of anger, replacing it with a sense of loss he could not understand. Gradually, awareness filtered through. He stared at his hands, and the mottled features he despised so much that were grasped between them. Instead of satisfaction he felt revulsion, and released the Regent from his grip to thrust him away.

Kearson slumped to the ground and sucked in rasping gulps of air, while Duncan stared at his hands in horror, unable to believe what he had just tried to do.

A low keening dragged at his conscious. It came from close by. He looked round, and cried out in despair.

"Do you see what you have done? Do you?" Mehmet's words were ground out between clenched teeth and filled with venom. "Like Judas, you have betrayed the Light, as Hiki said you would, and have brought about the End of Days."

He was sitting beneath the altar, Louisa's head cradled in his lap. Her eyes were closed and she looked at peace, as though she was sleeping. But the large pool of blood that stained the base of the altar and dripped to the ground before it gave lie to the scene.

Duncan took a step forward, but Mehmet's glare halted him.

"You are not one of us, Duncan Connors. You stay away or I will kill you."

"Wh-what do you mean? What happened?"

"You do not know what you did?" Mehmet appeared incredulous. Even so, there was no lessening of the antipathy that shone from his eyes. "You killed her, that is what you did. And she was only trying to stop you from committing murder in the name of the Light, and for that you killed her."

Duncan was lost for words. Slack-jawed, he stood and stared, unable to recall the events leading to what Mehmet said he had done. "I-I don't remember."

A glint to Louisa's chest caught his eye and his gaze fixed on it. It was her medallion. It had begun to glow. Its soft radiance shone out in the gloom, like a beacon in a storm. Could it be that she still lived? As he stared, the glow intensified and her skin tone deepened to the golden brown that had first attracted her to him. His heart skipped a beat. She was alive.

Ignoring Mehmet's roar of anger, he ran across the short expanse of ground and slid to his knees beside her. He felt the warm brush of her breath on his cheek before his head was roughly yanked up by the hair.

"What are you doing?"

Flecks of spittle splattered his face as he stared at Mehmet's snarling features. Holding his former friend's gaze, he said, "She's alive." He winced in pain as Mehmet tugged at the handful of hair he held in a clenched fist.

"Do not play games with me, Duncan Connors. She is dead. By your hand!" The last was underscored by a savage twisting of his hair for emphasis.

Tears sprang to Duncan's eyes, and not through grief. "She's not dead. Look for yourself, if you don't believe me."

In response, Mehmet glanced down. The grip eased and, taking advantage, Duncan pulled clear. Strands of brown locks dangled from clenched fingers as, with a snarl, Mehmet fixed him with an icy glare.

"She's alive," Duncan murmured, resting back on his knees and holding his gaze. His head hurt like hell where his hair had been wrenched out, but his only thought was to get Mehmet to see what he had seen.

The silence between them stretched on, Mehmet's indecision obvious as mistrust warred with the need to know. After some deliberation, he eventually looked down, laid a hand on Louisa's chest and lowered his head so that it hovered above hers. He remained in that position for what seemed like an age before looking up, the fire having faded from his eyes.

"How is this possible? I saw for myself she no longer breathed. How can this be?"

A movement at the periphery of vision diverted Duncan's attention, and he gasped in alarm. The creature within the altar had begun to move. Its muscles rippled beneath grey flesh as it tore at the sac, and Duncan could feel its frustration rise with each testing of its prison.

"You have to get her out of here," he snapped, rising to his feet and casting nervous glances towards the being. "Now!"

On seeing where Duncan looked, Mehmet's eyes widened in alarm, but the look he then gave Duncan was wary.

"Look. I know you don't like me very much at the moment, but you have to do as I ask. If you value Louisa you have to get her out of here. Before that thing, whatever it is, manages to get free."

There was a tearing sound as the beast sought once again to release itself. Around them, shadows covered every rock and craggy outcrop with their dark, flowing, malevolent presence. The air within the cavern took on a menacing charge, and Duncan knew it would not be long before the beast walked. He also realised that it was he who had to prevent that from happening. All the clues pointed to him being the one destined to carry out the deed, and he could better figure out how if he knew his companions were safely away.

"But how can we get out?" Mehmet asked. "The shaft is blocked."

On the ground, the Regent groaned and struggled to his knees, a hand massaging his bruised throat. "I know a way." His voice was hoarse and raspy.

"Why should we trust you?" snapped Duncan, fixing him with a piercing gaze. "Priest killer!"

"He was one of them," the Regent responded. "He tried to stop me."

"Leave him alone," said Mehmet. He laid Louisa's head on the ground and then moved to his knees beside her. "He is of the Church. If you had not been consumed by a need to kill you would have seen he had placed wards to contain the devil we face. Wards that have now been broken by your actions."

Having said his piece, he worked his hands under Louisa's body before rising to his feet with her clamped firmly to his chest. The flow of blood from the wound to her head had ceased, but there was a matted, red thatch of hair above and slightly behind her left ear to indicate where the skin had split. On the ground, a dark stain marked where she had lain.

"Can you walk?" he asked the Regent.

Kearson nodded. "I think so."

Somewhat gingerly, he worked his way to his feet, where he stood for a moment, swaying on legs that looked like they were made of rubber.

The sac tore and an arm snaked out to push aside the seam. Within seconds another arm reached through. It would not be long before it broke free, and still Mehmet had not made a move to flee the cavern. It was at that point Duncan realised it was he who was not trusted.

"Look. I know you don't have faith in me, and I don't

264

blame you. But you have to believe I am of Light, despite what you saw. I can't defend what I did, because I can't remember, but I intend to finish what we set out to do. You *have* to trust me."

The being in the altar roared, deep and primal, and Mehmet made his decision. He began to hurry away, Louisa cradled in his arms. Regent Kearson stooped to pick up a leatherbound book from the ground before stumbling after him, but had gone no more than twenty paces when he stopped to look back.

"Be true, Duncan Connors," he called.

"I am of Light." Softly spoken, the words were more self-confirmation than a bold statement of fact.

Not waiting to see if they left, Duncan spun around to face the altar, but stepped back in fear as the devil within stepped free to stand on the plinth. Without warning, its legs buckled and it roared in surprise. Previously quiescent shadows scattered as it toppled forward to crash to the ground. A cloud of dust blossomed on impact and, for a moment, all was still. Then, as the dust began to settle, there was movement. It attempted to rise, but only succeeded in rolling onto its side.

From within the haze, twin vortexes of darkness stared out to transfix Duncan with their hypnotic gaze. Unblinking, he succumbed to their pull, and staggered forward a pace before finding the willpower to resist. The pull intensified and excruciating pain coursed through his body. It felt as though his very essence was being torn away. In panic, he attempted to grasp his medallion, but his arm felt as though it rose through thick treacle. With back arched, teeth clenched and eyes screwed shut, he fought to retain a grasp on his soul, and willed his hand to move more quickly as it reached out for the perceived safety at his chest. At the point were he thought he could take no more his fingers brushed against the surface of the disc. A shock, like an electrical charge, arced between the metal and his skin, and the attack faltered.

Given respite, he snatched hold of the disc and the pain vanished, as did what little strength remained in his body. His legs gave way and he crumpled to the ground, where he lay for a moment to gather his senses before attempting to rise. But he did not have the energy, and called on resources he thought depleted to work his way to his hands and knees. Each movement was laboured and caused him pain, but he was determined to face that which would kill him. Beads of sweat formed on his forehead and the taste of vomit clung to the back of his throat, but, somehow, he succeeded. With head lowered, his breath coming in ragged gasps, he succumbed to the nausea and threw up.

"You have done well, Duncan."

The sound of a melodious voice speaking to him caused him to flinch. Still gasping for breath, vomit dribbling down his chin, he looked up to meet the gaze of androgynous beauty.

"Far better than my previous attendant."

The body of Father Tumbletee lay a couple of metres away and, automatically, Duncan found himself looking at it.

"Where are your friends?" The being raised its head and winced, as though movement caused it pain. "Ahhh. They flee." Its head flopped to the ground. "But that is of no consequence. Thanks to you they have played their part and Light's blood has been shed to complete the cycle."

A smirk marred the being's perfect features, and Duncan realised they had been wrong all along. It was not the medallions they were after but their blood. All its trickery, its manipulation, its shepherding had been for one thing only; the death of one of the pure to bring about the birth of their god. But Louisa had not died. Light had saved her, so the cycle was not yet complete. Although fully formed, Shadow's god did not have the strength it needed to walk the world, and it wanted him.

"And now you must conclude your task." This time the smile that quirked its lips was predatory. "Come to me, Duncan, so that, together, we can bring unity to a world torn apart by war and greed. That is what you want, isn't it? A world without division?"

The realisation of what Shadow was after gave Duncan the strength to rise to his feet, drive back the nausea and face that which would have his soul. The shadows that clung to every available rocky surface began to quiver with excitement, and the being's smile deepened.

"I knew you were the one, Duncan."

In response, Duncan staggered back a step and shook his head. "I will not fall for your lies. I am of Light."

The smile faded and the twin pools of impenetrable blackness began to whirl, but Duncan was prepared. He grasped his medallion and continued to back away. The metal disc was warm to the touch and invigorated leaden limbs.

"You are of Light?" It snorted in disgust. "You have no concept of what you speak. Without Shadow there would have been no Light. We were a part of this world at its inception, at one with the barren, roiling cesspool of molten rock and poisonous gases, and watched as mankind took its first steps. We sought friendship, and for a while lived in harmony, mankind's natural greed and urge to destroy feeding our hunger. Gradually, it changed. Victors grew fat and indolent, and forgot we existed. But we did not forget."

Muscles rippled beneath flesh and the being rolled onto its hands and knees. Its movements were awkward and stilted, but it seemed to have gathered a strength it previously lacked.

"And now it is time for us to claim back that which was taken. Mankind created gods in its image, and now Shadow has created one in *its* own."

Duncan continued to back away, his eyes darting from one shadowed cleft to another, seeking a clue as to how to fight that which he faced. He had worked his way behind the altar but had seen nothing that could help him in his cause.

The self-proclaimed God of Shadow sneered and began to crawl after him. "There is no use in running away, Duncan.

There is nowhere to go, and I will catch you. My strength is growing; I can feel it. My followers feed me by their actions and their thoughts, and I will soon be strong enough to escape this prison, even without your spirit." It paused, fixed its dark, malevolent gaze on Duncan and smiled the smile of the hunter. "But the taste of your blood on my tongue will make my completeness so much the sweeter."

Duncan ran. He had no idea where he was running to or what he was looking for, but knew he had little time in which to find it. Above and around him, dark shapes flowed over rock. He thought they were following him, but realised they were flowing over and past him, towards the rock wall some forty metres behind the altar. Acting on impulse, he changed course and headed towards where they were congregating. They had to be protecting something, or else why would they bypass him and head to some obscure corner of the cavern?

"Come to me, Duncan. You cannot escape."

Was it his imagination or was there a hint of anxiety in the tone? He glanced over his shoulder as he ran, and tripped. Dust spiralled into the air as he crashed to the ground. On impact, a sharp pain tore through his right kneecap as it connected with something sharp and solid, but he did not pause to look to see what damage had been done and rose to continue his run. But his injured knee screamed at every step, and he knew his injury was bad. With his run reduced to a slow, awkward limp, he doubted whether he could continue for much longer before his knee gave out altogether.

Up ahead, the shadows swarmed around what appeared to be a recess within the rock, and he headed for it. He hoped they gathered for the reason he believed they did, or he was lost. His leg was about to give out and would have no strength to defend himself against Shadow's ultimate being, and the End of Days would begin.

As he reached the recess he glanced back, and gasped. It was closer than he expected. A mere twenty-five metres separated them, and it was closing. It scuttled across the ground like some large, malformed spider, and a shiver of fear ran through Duncan's body. The warm, sticky wetness of blood oozed between his fingers as, teeth clenched, he leaned down to grip his knee with both hands and limp inside, snatching quick looks over his shoulder as he hobbled forward.

To add to his terror, the light from the cavern disappeared as soon as he entered, as though the slithering mass of shadows absorbed it, preventing him from seeing what he needed to see, but he refused to succumb. Instead, he gritted his teeth and urged leaden limbs to function.

The recess seemed to go on forever, and he realised he was in a tunnel, even though he could not see a thing. The darkness was absolute, and yet fluid, like it had substance, and he could almost feel an enmity in its presence as it flowed around him, through him, over him. It was like walking through thick, gooey mud, and his pace slowed even more.

Behind, he heard movement, the scrape of stone on rocky ground, and knew the creature had entered the tunnel. It would not be long before it caught up with him and all would be lost. A ripple of pleasure thrummed through the blackness, and the red mist of anger descended. Gripping his leg more firmly, Duncan lumbered forward and yelled his defiance. The volume of his shout sent ripples through the gloom, and it lifted. Not enough so he could see where he headed, but enough for him to see the ground at his feet. But that one small achievement was enough. Shouting like a madman, he hurled abuse at those that sought to entrap him and forged his way forward. The medallion at his chest began to glow.

With every pain-filled step the medallion glowed more brightly, and the tunnel began to lighten. Like a panic-stricken mob, shadows flowed over rock and ground in all directions, and he could sense their fear and uncertainty. The realisation that there was something they did not want him to get to fired his determination even more and, from somewhere, he drew on hidden reserves to increase his pace. From behind, he heard a roar of anger, and laughed.

Unexpectedly, the tunnel ended and he found himself in a grotto not too dissimilar to the ones they had encountered on the journey down to the cavern, and knew what he must look for. As with the first one there were three arches to his left, and he headed for them. As before, two seats had been carved into the wall behind and, as previously, there was a tunnel to the right, only this one was blocked with a stone slab. His cipher had been carved into its face and beside it there was a corroded metal lever that protruded at a sixty-degree angle from the wall. He had no idea what would happen when he pulled it, but knew that was the task he was down there to carry out.

A cry of anger had him halt when two paces away. The so-called 'God' of Shadow had crawled into the grotto and was heading for the recess. The dark pools of its eyes swirled as it crawled inexorably forward.

Duncan stepped to the lever, and grinned when a ripple of fear showed on the being's features. "Not so high and bloody mighty now, are you?" he muttered, reaching out to grasp it.

It halted and raised its head to stare at him. "Do not pull that lever, Duncan. You know not what you do."

"You're right: I know not what I do. But I'm sure as hell going to find out."

Muscles bulged and he pulled down on the metal rod. At first, it refused to move, and a twisted grin formed on the being's face, which disappeared as the lever slammed down. To Duncan's dismay, nothing happened. He stared at it in horror, wondering if he should have pushed up instead of forcing it down. He attempted to move it back up, but it refused to budge, and remained firmly stuck in place.

"It would appear that centuries of neglect have played their part. And now, Duncan, it is time for you to play yours."

There was a smugness about the voice that made the hairs on his neck stand on end. He let go of the lever and turned to face death head-on. Although his medallion still glowed, it could not help him now. Nothing could. He had failed, and the world would suffer for that failure. The only solace was that he would not be around to witness the chaos that followed.

A low rumble caused the ground to tremble. Duncan staggered, and cried out in pain as he shifted his weight onto his injured leg. He reached down to grasp at his knee, and a jet of ice-cold liquid struck him in the face. He looked towards the stone slab, and frowned. It was leaking water. His tongue probed at a dribble that ran down his face. It was spring water, pure and unpolluted. Could this be what evil feared? A substance uncorrupted by its touch?

Ignoring the throbbing in his leg, he stooped to look closer, and was blasted from his feet by an icy gush as the slab suddenly lifted. He did not have time to react, and the torrent smashed him into the wall at the opposite end of the recess. The breath whooshed from his body and he cried out in agony, certain he'd fractured ribs on impact.

Through pain-dulled senses he heard a shriek of terror as the beast was swept away. Its loud cry echoed down the tunnel through which they had entered, and Duncan realised he would have to go that way too or drown. It was the only way out. He thrust himself sideways through one of the arches, crying out again as injured ribs protested, and allowed the water to take him wherever it was going. In truth, he had no other option.

The ice-coldness numbed the pain to his knee and his ribs, but did nothing to dampen the injuries he received when being buffeted down the tunnel. He bounced off craggy walls and tumbled into outcrops and when he finally emerged in a rush of water, he was bleeding from countless cuts and abrasions. The power of the flow was much reduced once in the cavern, but was still too strong for him to fight against. And it was deep. He could not touch the ground and, being too weak and in too much pain from his injuries, could not swim against the current.

Unable to change his course, he was carried towards the

271

altar, where he spotted the being clinging to the plinth. The blackness of deep, baleful eyes filled with hatred glared at him as he was swept by. After a moment spent staring at him it snarled in rage and, using its anger as leverage, thrust itself up and out of the water. Immobile, it rested on its hands and knees as water lapped at the base of the platform. Flesh hung off its frame in tattered strips, to reveal muscle and bone beneath.

*"This is not over, Duncan Connors!"*

Its voice echoed around the cavern, and scattered the cluster of shadows that had congregated on the rock surrounding the altar.

*"This is only the beginning!"*

An outcrop of rock caught Duncan on the head and snagged the cord holding his medallion. Bright specks danced before his eyes and he knew that if he blacked out he would drown. In an attempt to remain conscious he fixed his gaze on the altar and looked on in astonishment as his adversary's body collapsed. As he watched, a dark shadow emerged from the prostrate form to float above the plinth, where it pulsed and eddied as though it were caught in a breeze. Then, to his horror, it began to expand.

No, he realised. It wasn't growing bigger, it was hurtling towards him. Fear gripped him and he grasped for his medallion, but it wasn't there. The shadow was almost upon him and he was helpless. Stranded. Alone.

# 36

Louisa came round to find the Guardian bent over her. On seeing his smiling face, her heart skipped a beat before hammering a tattoo against her rib cage.

"Am I dreaming?" she murmured.

The Guardian did not answer. Instead, he moved out of vision. She panicked, and tried to raise her head to see where he had gone, but cried out as bright lights shot through her skull.

"Easy, Louisa. You have been hurt. You must lie still. Keep your eyes closed and do not move suddenly."

It was Mehmet.

"Hurt?"

She realised she was lying down, and raised a hand to probe at her head. It had been swathed in bandages.

"Wh-what happened? Is Duncan –"

She tried to rise, but was pressed back onto the ground. She knew it was ground as she could feel rough stone digging into her back through the thin covering that had been laid beneath her. A light breeze caressed her face and she could smell lemons, which seemed strange.

"Hiki and some of my people have gone down into the underground city to get him. I am sure they will be back soon."

She remembered her vision, and asked, "The Guardian? Is he here too?"

She could hear the reverence in his voice as he answered.

"Yes. He is here."

Her lips curved into a smile and she relaxed. "Then everything is okay and we beat Shadow. I knew Duncan would do it."

A babble of voices in Turkish brought anxiety to the fore and had her asking what was going on, but Mehmet did not know, and bade her lie still while he went to investigate. The wait for him to return seemed interminable, and she was eager to find out what had caused so much excitement. She guessed it must be something serious if it could outdo the Guardian being amongst them.

Eventually, the presence of Mehmet settled beside her and she turned her head towards him. "Did you find out what was happening?"

"They have found Duncan."

There was an unsaid 'but' in his tone that she immediately picked up on.

"And?"

"It is not good, Louisa."

"Is he – is he – dead?"

Lips pursed, Mehmet shook his head. "No, not dead, but he may as well be."

"Wh – wh – what do you mean?"

The sound of a heavy sigh warned her that what she was about to hear would not be to her liking.

"He is now of Shadow. He has been possessed by the spirit of the beast he stayed behind to fight. It would seem he lost his medallion during the struggle and, being too weak from his injury, could not defend himself. The Guardian is down there now with Hiki, placing wards over the grating to prevent his escape. The water is rising and it will soon flood the burial chamber, and anyone left in the lower tunnels ..." He shrugged and did not elaborate.

A lone tear tracked down Louisa's cheek, and she choked back a sob as she said, "Can't we save him?"

The lack of comment from Mehmet told her all she needed to know, and she wept.

The Guardian backed towards the exit as the water rose. Already it covered the base of the grating and it would not be long before it flooded the chamber he stood in. But he would have left before then, as Hiki had done moments ago.

From behind the metal bars, eyes darker than night glared at him and he felt a brief twinge of regret. Not for the beast within, but for the man who once was. The feeling surprised him, and he frowned. During his centuries of existence that was one emotion he rarely experienced.

A smirk formed on the bruised, blood-smeared face of the thing that was now Duncan. "What's the matter? Suddenly got a dose of remorse? You could always release me to ease your conscience."

Instead of answering, the Guardian raised a brow, and then turned on his heel, hands clasped behind his back, to make his way up the tunnel to the exit. Manic laughter followed him, taunting him, but he took no heed. For now, balance was restored, and that was all that mattered.

The beast that was Duncan stared at the Guardian's back with undisguised malice, and continued to stare at the dark opening of the tunnel long after he had disappeared from view. The water had risen to his chest and it would not be long before it covered him, but he was unperturbed by its rise.

A smile formed on his face as he heard the distant scrape of footsteps on rock, and he stepped back from the grating. A figure emerged from the tunnel mouth and his smile deepened.

"And there was me thinking you had forgotten all about me."

Hiki grimaced, and waded through the water towards the bars, the key to the lock clutched in a hand. "He took long time to go. I think he suspects something is not right, so we have to be quick. He may come back."

"By then we shall be long gone." He held out his hands

to inspect them, and flexed the fingers. "It would seem the line of Iscariot has remained strong. Both Light and Shadow exist in perfect harmony." His lips twisted into a half-sneer. "Correction. *Used* to exist in perfect harmony."

The rattle of a key in the lock caught his attention and he fixed Hiki with his gaze. "You have done well, despite doing your best to eliminate my intended vessel."

Hiki grunted, and then pulled open the grating. "How was I to know he have weak head?"

"Indeed!" He turned his attention to the gateway, and then said, "Are you sure the wards are ineffectual?"

Hiki nodded.

"Then let us go forth." He stepped through the portal, and shuddered as a tingle of pins and needles prickled his flesh. "We have a world at our disposal, and who are we to disappoint?"

# 37

An icy wind made a mockery of her many layers as Sarah stepped outside. She shivered, and hugged Faith closer to her chest. It was freezing. She glanced down at the sleeping child and smiled. Swathed against the coldness of winter in a fluffy white blanket and woollen bonnet, only thick eyelashes and rosy cheeks visible, she seemed snug and warm. Sarah shivered again. Which was more than could be said for her.

Hunched over, she made her way down the stone flag steps, taking care where she placed her feet in case she slipped. Stone crunched beneath her boots as she reached the bottom and began the short walk along the gravel-lined path to the crooked gateposts that marked the entrance to the old church. Her car was parked just outside and she longed to be in it and heading for home, where she could relax and enjoy the rest of the day in front of a roaring fire, sipping coffee and reading her book, until Faith woke and demanded to be fed.

The service had been simple, as she had wanted, and over and done with in twenty minutes. The new priest for the parish, Father Kearson, had gone through the motions, despite there only being an old tramp with a missing ear, no doubt sheltering from the cold, as witness to her child receiving the blessing of the Church. She could still see the look of surprise on the priest's face when she had turned up alone and informed him there were would be no guests or godparents, and thought he would refuse to carry out the service. But he hadn't, and had performed as though there had been a full congregation.

On reaching the gateposts she fumbled in her pocket for the key to her car and pressed the remote. In a wink of indicators, the door locks popped and she moved to a rear passenger door to open it. Leaning in, she placed Faith in the baby seat and snapped the safety straps into pace. Faith burbled at the movement, but did not waken, and Sarah eased herself out.

A shadow fell across her as she softly closed the car door and she spun, expecting it to be the priest come to see her away. But it wasn't, and she stepped back in surprise.

Facing her was a man she was sure she'd never met, but who seemed strangely familiar. He was encapsulated in a long black overcoat whose hem almost dragged on the ground, buttoned to the neck to keep out the cold, and white, tightly curled hair and goatee framed ebony features. His lips were curved into a smile, and he clasped a small, gift-wrapped box in hands that were held towards her.

Her eyes flicked between his exquisite smile and the box. She was completely at a loss as to what to do or say. Before the silence between them became embarrassing the man spoke, and raised the box.

"For Faith."

Without thinking, she reached out to claim that which he offered, and murmured, "Thank you."

The man's smile broadened, and she remembered where she'd seen him before. It was the doctor who had delivered her child, the one who left before his colleagues arrived.

She glanced to the box in her hand, and wondered why he would bring her child a gift. A more concerning thought was how he knew Faith's christening was that day. She had told no one, but then again, it was a small community and nothing ever went unnoticed. Smiling, she looked up, but the man had gone. Suddenly fearful, she scanned the surroundings, thinking he had walked through the gates and into the churchyard, but he was not there.

The doors to the church opened and Father Kearson stepped outside. He peered into slate-grey skies for a moment and then clasped the high collar to his quilted overcoat more tightly against his neck before making his way towards the road where Sarah stood. In passing, he nodded and smiled, and she opened her mouth, wanting to ask him if he had seen anyone, but closed it again when he showed no inclination to pass the time of day.

The doors to the church opened again and the tramp emerged. He paused on the threshold to gaze at Sarah for a moment, and then switched his attention to Father Kearson before ducking deeper into his shabby overcoat and shuffling out of sight behind the church.

Overcome by a sudden need to be away, Sarah yanked open the driver's door and threw herself inside, locking the doors behind her. In her haste to start the engine, the box the doctor had given her dropped to the floor, and the key refused to slide into the ignition. Eventually, she seized control of her emotions and the engine purred into life. She dipped the clutch and shoved the gearstick into first, but a grinding of gears told her she'd failed. She pressed the clutch again, but it refused to fully dip. Something was stopping it.

Leaning forward, she reached into the footwell, and questing fingers closed on the obstruction. She made to toss it to the passenger seat, but something – a feeling, a sixth sense, she did not know what – stopped her, and she peered at the brightly packaged parcel. An overwhelming desire to see what lay inside gripped her.

The paper wrapping tore easily beneath her fingers to reveal a plain, unadorned wooden box. It was hinged on one edge and a brass clasp locked the lid in position on the other. A flick of a finger released the catch and she eased open the lid. Inside was a pendant in the shape of disc. It lay on a bed of tissue paper and had a series of slots in its face, set in a distinctive pattern. She reached in and lifted it clear by its leather thong, to hold it to the light to better see them.

279

At that moment the sun escaped its shroud of clouds and weak, winter sunlight flooded into the car. The pendant glowed brightly under its touch, seeming to blaze with inner energy. To Sarah, the slots, allowing shafts of light to dance around the interior of the car, appeared to form the shape of a full moon with a crescent moon floating above. The design's attraction was hypnotic, and she found herself staring, unblinking, at it.

Behind her, Faith chortled. The sound broke the spell, and Sarah rubbed at her eyes with her free hand before twisting in the seat to peer at her child, the pendant still clutched in her other.

Faith stared at the metal disc and bounced in her seat in excitement, while hands that were tucked inside her blanket worked themselves free to reach out. A soft snort of amusement escaped Sarah's lips, and she held it out for her to grasp.

Once in Faith's hands it started to glow, and her eyes widened as she stared at the disc. She went quiet; too quiet for Sarah's liking.

In panic, she shouted her name and leaned across to snatch back the medallion, convinced it had harmed her child, but the back of the seat dug into her side, restricting her movement, and she missed it. She cursed, and Faith giggled.

The sound was therapy to nerves stretched taut, and she sagged on the padded headrest, to gaze in relief at the happy, smiling face of her child.

Faith giggled again, and stared, bright-eyed, back at her mother. With the pendant clutched in a chubby hand, she waggled it in the air, and said, "Da da."